FIREBRAND

AN *ELEMENTAL* NOVEL

BY ANTONY JOHN

DIAL BOOKS

an imprint of Penguin Group (USA) Inc.

DIAL BOOKS

An imprint of Penguin Group (USA) Inc.

Published by the Penguin Group

Penguin Group (USA) Inc., 375 Hudson Street, New York, New York 10014, USA

USA/Canada/UK/Ireland/Australia/New Zealand/India/South Africa/China

Penguin Books Ltd, Registered Offices: 80 Strand, London WC2R 0RL, England

For more information about the Penguin Group visit penguin.com

Library of Congress Cataloging-in-Publication Data

John, Antony.

Firebrand : an Elemental novel / by Antony John.

pages   cm

Sequel to: Elemental.

Summary: In a dystopian United States, the colonists of Roanoke Island must find safety at the
mysterious Fort Sumter, but as they get farther from their home, their elemental powers begin to fade.

ISBN 978-0-8037-3683-2 (hardcover)

[1. Fantasy. 2. United States—Fiction.] I. Title.

PZ7.J6216Fi 2013

[Fic]—dc23

2012049122

Printed in the United States of America

1 3 5 7 9 10 8 6 4 2

Book design by Jasmin Rubero

Text set in Electra LT Std

To Rose

Esplanade

Casemates

The Battery

Parade Grounds

Barracks

Peninsula

Jetty

Fort Sumter

Charleston

Castle Pinckney

Charleston Harbor

James Island

Fort Moultrie

Fort Sumter

Spider Island

Atlantic
Ocean

Morris Island

N

0   2 miles

0   2 klm.

CHAPTER 1

I t was hard not to feel as though the world was ending. I stared at my tattered clothes, touched my bloodied lip, and winced from the pain of opening my mouth. I'd been able to block everything out as long as we were fighting for survival. I'd even relaxed for a moment at the thought that we had won. Now I wasn't sure what winning meant.

Below me, the ship, still at anchor, tilted gently from side to side. Light filtered through the bank of windows that ran along one side of the cabin. After the night's hurricane, everything seemed still. But the sense of foreboding that had consumed us for three long days was very much alive.

We. Go, signed my deaf younger brother, Griffin. He looked as ragged as I felt, with disheveled hair and cuts across his face and arms. Beneath the grime, though, he seemed more alive than ever. *They. Find. Us*, he added.

I understood him well enough. This was no ordinary cabin. It belonged to Dare, the pirate captain who'd kidnapped our families and destroyed our remote Hatteras Island colony a few days earlier. And we'd just discovered that he was our uncle. His cabin had been locked all night, but now it was mysteriously open. Until we could explain everything, Griffin was right: We couldn't afford for our colony's Guardians to find us here.

But what about the logbooks arranged in chronological order above the desk, and the machinery bolted onto the shelves? There were answers in this cabin, explanations about who we were and where we came from.

Just. Little. Time, I signed.

Griffin's eyes shifted to the door and back to me again, reminding me of the stakes if we got caught. But what he signed was, *All. Right.*

As always, we were a team. And neither Dare and his pirates nor the Guardians' lies about our past had done anything to break that bond. If anything, we were stronger than before.

I ran my hands across the machines and watched them spark to life at my touch. My element, whatever it was, still felt new. Power pulsed from me instead of flowing. I picked up a thin metal cylinder and focused my energy on controlling the light that instantly shone from one end. The beam seared through the dusty air and cast a yellow circle on the ceiling. It grew dimmer as my concentration waned.

I put it back carefully on the shelf.

Griffin turned his attention to a large map hanging beside the desk. Meanwhile, I touched each machine in turn, watching in wonder as they responded with lights and sounds and dials swinging wildly. Dare wouldn't have kept them all these years unless they were important, but I had no idea what they were for. It was exhilarating and frustrating. I was glimpsing something extraordinary here, but the picture made no sense.

I moved along to the final machine: a black metal box with two protruding knobs. I placed my fingers on it and channeled energy as before, wondering whether I'd be rewarded with lights or something else.

I leaped back as a man's voice filled the room. Heart pounding, I looked around for whoever had spoken, but the room was empty. Silent too. I studied the machine more closely. It couldn't have come from there. What machine could possibly trap a human voice?

Griffin had turned to face me. He must have felt the floor move as I jumped. Now he waited for an explanation.

He wasn't the only one.

With a deep breath I placed my fingers on the machine again. The voice returned instantly: "Fort Sumter, Charleston, South Carolina. This is a recorded message. All Plague refugees are advised to join the self-sufficient colony at Fort Sumter, Charleston, South Carolina. This is a recorded message. All Plague refugees are advised—"

I pulled away. I recognized the name *Carolina*—I'd seen it on a map of the mainland—but I had no idea what the other words meant. I knew what Plague refugees meant, though. Unless we could recapture Roanoke Island from the pirates, that's exactly what we were.

I wanted to tell Griffin what I'd heard, but we didn't have

3

signs for the new words. I still couldn't believe I'd made the machine work at all.

Griffin was back to studying the map again. He swept his fingers across it, committing the details to memory in case he never saw it again. It wasn't an ordinary map, either. Hatteras and Roanoke Islands were just ghostly outlines, whereas the areas of water that surrounded them were filled with indecipherable details. At the top was a large inland waterway marked *Chesapeake Bay*. Farther down was the sliver of Hatteras Island, our former home. Toward the bottom was a place called Charleston. And at the mouth of Charleston harbor, someone—presumably Dare—had added four words: *Fort Sumter refugee colony*.

Griffin raised a hand. I assumed he was going to sign again, but instead he was completely still. As a panicked expression darkened his face, he pressed his other hand flat against the wall, closed his eyes, and felt for vibrations.

I didn't ask him if he'd picked up on something. I could hear the footsteps.

Go, he signed. But he must have known it was too late for that. We'd be seen leaving, and forced to answer questions about things we barely understood.

"Thomas!" Kyte's voice rattled along the corridor. He was self-appointed chief of the Guardians and my greatest critic.

Who? demanded Griffin, unable to recognize anything but the vibrations of the footsteps against the ship's worn planks.

Kyte, I returned.

For a moment, I considered calling Kyte to join us. I imagined his surprise as he realized what I'd been able to accomplish with my element—the one he'd kept secret from me my entire life. But then reality kicked in. It was more likely that he'd turn against us. He'd link us to Dare, our uncle, and hold us responsible for what had happened to the colony. He'd always hated me, after all.

I closed the cabin door noiselessly and leaned my weight against it.

Kyte was trying each door, so I grasped the handle as he reached ours. He twisted it sharply, but I held it fast. His breathing was heavy on the other side of the wooden door.

"Thomas?" he said quietly.

I held my breath and waited.

"Thomas?"

I closed my eyes.

A few moments later, he turned on his heel and walked away. His footsteps grew quieter. I breathed again.

Griffin leaned against the wall as though he was tired—of running, and fighting, and hiding. And lying. I knew how he felt. Over the past few days, we'd dragged the truth from a lifetime of lies. But already the deception was starting up again.

The difference was that this time, we were the ones with the secrets. And I didn't feel bad about that at all.

CHAPTER 2

We had to leave immediately. Kyte would have suspected that something was wrong when he couldn't find us. Other Guardians would be joining the search soon.

Griffin's eyes were fixed on the door handle that had mysteriously come unlocked during the night. I knew without asking that he was thinking the same thing as me—that someone had wanted us to see this cabin, with its mysterious machines and logbooks that chronicled the history of our world. Had that same person wanted us to learn the truth about Dare being our uncle? And that our Guardians, every last one of them, had always known it?

We left together and latched the door behind us. Toward the end of the corridor, the trapdoor to the ship's hold was closed. The stench from below still lingered, though, a reminder of the days our families had spent locked up in the belly of the ship.

Unfortunately, there was still one prisoner on board.

I covered my mouth with my tunic and checked on our

father. He was imprisoned in a metal mesh cage in a room beneath the stairs. We wouldn't have discovered him at all except for the trail of blood that led to a hidden door. The lock on his cage was too strong to break.

Father hadn't moved. Aside from the shallow rise and fall of his chest, he looked like a corpse, battered and bruised.

Griffin touched my sleeve lightly. Until we could find a way to get Father out, it was best to let him rest.

Up on the deck, we filled our lungs with the fresh salt breeze. The last of the heavy dark clouds had flown away to the north, and the late-summer sun was searing through the wisps that remained. In the bright light, the events of the past three days seemed like a nightmare from which we'd finally awoken. But it had been real, all right.

Four days before, a storm had caught the Guardians by surprise. They'd sent us to the hurricane shelter on Roanoke Island. When we'd emerged the following day, we'd discovered that our colony was on fire. Pirates had kidnapped our families too. Only five of us were left: me and Griffin, my friends Alice and Rose, and Rose's younger brother, Dennis. Finally, the pirates had come after us, which enabled us to slip aboard their abandoned ship.

Somehow we'd survived. It should've been something to celebrate. But as I looked around me now, I felt nothing but panic.

The four Guardians were sprawled across the deck like a school of dead fish washed ashore at high tide. Having been cooped up for days, they should have been stretching. But only Kyte was well enough to move. The others lay still, heads turned toward the sun. Their faces were gaunt, lips chapped.

Rose bustled around the deck, handing out water canisters. She pointed to the stern, where we'd tethered our sailboats the night before. "I got the bags from the sailboat holds," she said breathlessly. "The boats were ruined, so I cut them free. But the bags are fine."

Her clothes hung slick against her. Her long blond braid flopped against her back. Of all of us, she'd been most desperate to rescue her parents—not just for herself, but also for Dennis. Now that they were reunited, she looked tired and relieved. Watching them, I wondered how things would change from now on. Rose and I had felt closer than ever on Roanoke, but it was no secret that her parents disliked me.

I rummaged through the bags and removed the remaining water canisters. Along with a little medicine, it was all we'd been able to bring with us from Roanoke Island. There'd been clothes and fruit and metal implements too, but we hadn't been able to carry it all. That would have to wait until the Guardians were strong enough to return. *If* they got strong enough.

Alice sidled up. She was the same age as Rose, but taller, with unkempt black hair and a perpetually suspicious expression. "It could be worse," she muttered, looking around the deck at the motionless Guardians.

"How?" I asked.

"Well, we didn't find any dead bodies," she said with typi-

8

cal directness. "Your father, my parents, Rose's parents . . . they're all here. Ananias and Eleanor too."

As if he'd heard his name, my older brother staggered toward us. Ananias rubbed his legs, trying to get the muscles moving again. Apart from his soiled clothes and bruises on his arms, he looked mostly unharmed. The look on his face showed that he was as relieved to see us as we were to see him.

"What's wrong with everyone?" I asked him quietly.

He looked around as if he wasn't entirely sure. "They're dehydrated. The pirates wouldn't give them food or water."

"*Them?*"

He lowered his voice to a whisper. "They kept us separate from the Guardians at first—me and Eleanor. Locked us in one of the cabins with blankets and water and food."

He tilted his head to the left, where Alice's sister, Eleanor, sat alone a few yards away. Ananias and Eleanor were usually inseparable, so it was alarming to see them apart. Not as alarming as the bruises that ran along both her arms, though. They were yellow-brown, not purple or red, which meant that she'd been beaten a few days before, when everything started.

"What happened, Ananias?" I asked gently.

"The pirates kept asking us questions," he said. "Stuff about a seer and a solution. Maybe they figured we'd give in quicker than the Guardians, but we didn't know what they were talking about. So they hurt her. In the end, they threw us in the hold as well."

It was killing him that they'd hurt Eleanor instead of him, and that he'd been unable to stop it. He'd feel even worse once he discovered that it was Dare who had made sure he wasn't harmed. An unwanted gift from the uncle he didn't even know he had.

Ananias stared at his hands. "I wanted to use my element to escape. I thought . . . maybe if I created fire, I could burn a hole through the side of the ship, and escape through it. But we were below the waterline. I'd have flooded the hold and drowned us. Either that, or suffocated everyone with smoke." The words came out fast, as if he was protesting his innocence.

"What exactly did they say about a solution?" I asked.

Nearby, Kyte coughed loudly. "What does it matter? The *solution* is make-believe."

"You've heard of it?" murmured Ananias, incredulous.

"People have talked about a cure for the Plague ever since it started. Doesn't mean there is one."

"Dare believed it," I reminded him.

"Dare was a delusional tyrant. Anyway, Rose tells me he's dead. Drowned, she says." Kyte pointed to Roanoke Island, only two hundred yards to the east, and choked out a single laugh. "With him gone, none of the pirates will be stupid enough to believe in this folly anymore."

Alice, who was inspecting the massive sails for damage, spoke up: "We can't take that chance." She waved her arm across the deck. "You all need time to recover. And while you do, we need to stay away from this place. They still have guns. Remember?"

"No! If we leave this place, our elements will fade."

10

Everyone fell silent. Even Kyte must have realized the enormity of what he was saying, because his hands shook as he swigged from his canister.

"What do you mean, *fade*?" I asked.

"Don't pretend you didn't notice what happened to you on Roanoke. How everyone's elements are more powerful there." He wiped his mouth with a dirty sleeve. "You leave this place, you risk losing your element completely."

"What element would that be? The one you've kept from me my whole life?"

Rose raised her hand. "Please! Can we all calm down?"

"Calm down?" repeated Alice. "We're next to an island that's crawling with pirates. The same pirates who kidnapped our families and tried to kill us. How can we be calm?"

"I'm just saying . . . let's talk it through. Be reasonable."

"Reasonable like your father, you mean?" Alice sneered. "What do you think of that, Thomas? Your dear Rose thinks her father is reasonable."

I wished she hadn't said that. She was just trying to get a rise out of Kyte, but at our expense, not hers. Sure enough, Kyte's eyes flashed from Rose to me, simmering with anger.

Alice flashed a triumphant smile. "You should be happy, Kyte. You've done everything in your power to get Thomas and Rose together."

His eyes came to rest on me. "I've done nothing of the sort," he growled.

"Please, Father," began Rose, "try to understand—"

"Stay out of this! You have nothing to say."

11

"Leave her alone!" I shouted. "Without her, you'd be dead. You call yourself a Guardian, but what have you been *guarding* the past two days? Apart from the locked hold of a pirate ship."

"We tried to resist the pirates, but we were outnumbered."

"We still are now. And nothing we have is a match for those weapons. But then, you know that already, don't you? Just as you know that Roanoke Island is perfectly safe for us. All those years you told us to stay away from it, and it turns out you used to live there."

I threw a quick glance at Ananias and Eleanor to make sure they were listening. They'd been lied to as well. Now they deserved to know the truth.

Kyte gritted his teeth. "Yes, there was a time we lived on Roanoke Island. Most of us were born there. Eighteen years ago, when everyone else evacuated during the Exodus, we decided to stay. When we heard about the Plague decimating the country, we knew we'd done the right thing. But sixteen years ago, the pirates paid us a visit and destroyed everything. After that, the colony was unsustainable, so we moved to Hatteras."

"Why not rebuild?" I asked.

"We had neither the materials nor the means to repair anything—buildings, windows, roads, bridges. A town that can't be kept alive is dead—a Skeleton Town, nothing more."

"What about the water tower? The boats? The clothes?"

"What about them?" Kyte sounded bored, as though my questions were irrelevant, instead of getting to the very heart of who we were. "They were just reminders of what used to

12

be. Historical artifacts. Why would we show you things you couldn't build or repair? It would've been cruelty to tease you with seemingly magical objects that would never work again."

"So hiding everything . . . spreading lies . . . it was all for us, then?"

"Open your eyes, Thomas. The only people you've ever seen are clan folk trapped on floating cities, or pirates who pillage other colonies to survive. We alone built a sustainable colony."

"It was built on a lie," I shouted.

Alice's mother, Tarn, raised a hand. She was tall like her daughter, and normally as defiant. Now she stooped forward, hugging her knees. "Come on, Kyte," she said. "After everything they've been through, they deserve to know the truth."

Kyte turned on her. "The *truth*? The whole truth, Tarn? Every little detail?"

Tarn reddened. As Kyte stared her down, she lowered her hand, bullied into submission.

Kyte grasped the ship's wheel and pulled himself upright. He wanted to be eye-to-eye with me, never mind the pain. "Our colony was a place to live and grow. A place where we could nurture and protect you."

"*Protect?*" I wanted to laugh, but I was too angry. "The pirates burned it to the ground. Look around you, Kyte. Is this your idea of protection?"

"We did our best. We counted on our elements to help us survive."

I let him recognize the hypocrisy for himself before spelling it out. "Except mine, you mean."

Kyte flinched, but recovered with a deep breath. He took a faltering step toward me, fists clenched at his sides. "Your element is a mistake. An anomaly. So is Griffin's ability to see the future. A generation ago you'd have been banished, sent far away where you'd be spared from knowing your true nature."

I stepped forward to meet him. "How do you get to decide what's an element and what's not?"

"It's been that way ever since the beginning of the New World." His voice was fading, but the hollow words still erupted from him. Spittle flew out of his mouth. "Earth, water, wind, and fire. Four boys. Four elements. One lost—"

He stopped speaking at the same moment that I heard a faint popping sound. Immediately, his fierce expression turned to one of surprise. His eyes grew wide. And then, quite suddenly, he dropped to his knees.

Rose jumped forward, but she couldn't catch him before his legs buckled and he hit the deck. Eyes blank, he clasped his hand against his chest.

Blood glistened vivid red against his filthy tunic.

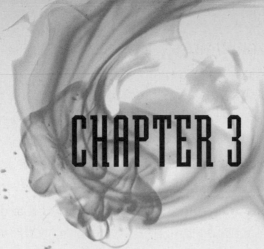

CHAPTER 3

Down!" screamed Alice.

I threw myself onto the deck. Blood had already pooled around Kyte's left side. Rose cupped his head in her hands, pleading with him to stay alive.

"What happened?" cried Eleanor, sliding over. She looked around the deck as though the culprit might be one of us.

"It must be the pirates," I said. "But how can their guns reach so far?"

I rolled to the edge of the ship and peered over the lowest rail. In the distance, a group of men were launching a cutter—a rowboat. This time they wouldn't have to fight wind and waves to get to us.

"They're coming," I shouted.

There was another group behind them. I tried to count the pirates, to know what we were up against, but they ran along the shore, paths crisscrossing. I still didn't understand how they had been able to hit Kyte from so far away. As I raised my head to get a better look, I saw something that reflected the sun. Instinctively I dropped down. A moment later, the wood beside my hand splintered.

"Pirates on the shore! Two hundred yards. They have guns."

Alice appeared beside me. She grabbed a piece of my tunic and tugged it so that I'd face her. "I saw how close that was," she whispered fiercely. "You could've gotten yourself killed!"

I couldn't think about that. Rose and Eleanor were dragging Kyte's body toward the stairs, trying to get him below deck. Dennis struggled to support their mother as she followed the trail of blood. Everything was chaos.

"We have to get out of here," I yelled.

Ananias crawled toward us. "What about our elements? You heard what Kyte said: They'll fade away if we leave."

"Can you stop those weapons with your element?"

He still seemed unsure. He clung to his precious element as though it was all he had to offer.

"Listen," I snapped. "Unless you can take on a cutter full of pirates, as well as shooters, we better move."

Finally he gave a sharp nod, and signaled for Griffin to join him at the stern anchor.

Alice was already heading for the bow so that she could raise the anchor there. I was right behind her. Side by side we pushed the anchor winch.

"We need to lower the foresail," she said.

"How? If you stand up, they'll fire at you."

"What other choice do we have? We need to start moving."

Once the anchor was up and secured, we worked the sail winch. Little by little, the sail began to show.

Straightaway, there was another popping sound—the telltale sound of gunfire. I scanned the deck, heart in my mouth, but all of us were keeping low. "What are they firing at?" I yelled.

Before anyone could reply, the sail caught the wind and billowed, pushing the canvas taut. But then there was more popping and a new sound filled the air: tearing cloth. They were firing at the sail.

Alice raised her head just enough to see the shore. "They're a hundred and sixty yards away. And still firing."

While Griffin took up position beside the wheel, Ananias joined us. "We can't afford to lose the sails," he shouted. "But how are we going to get out of here otherwise?"

"Wait!" cried Alice. "The tide is going out. Maybe the current will carry us."

"Not fast enough. We have to lower the mainsails."

"What if we lose them?"

I glanced over the rail. The pirates in the cutter were gaining on us, but the shooting had stopped. "Maybe we're too far away for the guns to reach us," I said.

Alice stared up at the torn foresail. "Then let's lower the mainsail and take our chances."

We moved along the deck and pushed the winch handle to lower one of the mainsails. I'd seen the massive canvas sheets on the clan ships that passed our colony from time to time, but hadn't realized how truly gigantic they were until now. As soon as the wind caught it, the ship jarred into motion, gobbling up water. The pirates in the cutter fell back so quickly, it was like they'd stopped moving.

While I caught my breath, Alice stared at the giant water-way before us. "I'm worried," she said. "I don't know how deep the sound is, but we need to get out of here before low tide. The currents are fierce. If we run aground, the Guardians will drown."

Usually that would have sounded crazy. Every one of us was a strong swimmer. But a quick look at her parents assured me that she was correct. Her mother, Tarn, couldn't stand up. Her father, Joven, was crawling down the staircase, presumably to check on Kyte. Neither of them had the strength to fight strong currents.

Waves crashed against the bow, powerful but oddly comforting. What lay beneath the surface was a mystery, though. Rose had once told me about the remains of ships that rested on the waters around Hatteras. She saw them when she was diving.

"Let's head for the ocean," I said.

"And go where?" Alice asked.

I didn't want to tell her about the message I'd heard in Dare's cabin, not like this. I wasn't even sure she'd believe me. "Griffin found a map in one of the cabins. There's a refugee colony to the southwest."

I waited for her to ask which cabin, but she didn't. She didn't ask for more information about the refugee camp either. Maybe she didn't want to press me for details while Ananias and her mother were around to overhear. "How do we know it's safe, Thom?"

"It can't be any more dangerous than Roanoke Island, right?" A weak answer, but she let it slide.

We were fast approaching the southern tip of the island. We'd need to make a decision soon.

"What if Kyte's telling the truth and our elements fade as we leave Roanoke?" she asked.

I shrugged. "Kyte also said there were only four elements, remember? Earth, water, wind, and fire. If he was wrong about that, he might be wrong about this. Anyway, wasn't it you who told me we're more than the sum of our elements?"

She smiled at that. "Yes. I guess I did." She stared into the distance and narrowed her eyes, engaging her element, or whatever it was that heightened her senses. Like me, her main power didn't fit the Guardians' tidy definitions of what an element ought to be. Because of that, she'd kept it hidden from us her whole life. Even though I'd discovered her secret a couple of days before, it was still hard to believe what she was able to do.

"The Oregon Inlet is about six miles away," she announced. "At the speed we're going, that won't take long. This ship is amazing."

She was right. Now that we were on open water, the wind freshened and the ship sliced through the water like a knife.

With her hair flapping about, Alice seemed to become part of nature itself. She didn't even blink as she focused on the inlet, too far away for me to make out. She didn't press me for information on the map either, or where we'd found it. Or how far away the refugee colony was, or how I could be sure it was still there. What if we sailed for days, only to discover another ruined, deserted colony? What if we didn't have enough food to make it that far? It was a miracle that Alice hadn't demanded answers.

That's when I realized that Alice had been looking for an excuse to leave all along. She'd always told me she would do anything to escape our Hatteras Island colony. At last she'd have that chance.

The Oregon Inlet was a mile-wide channel dividing the southern tip of Hatteras Island from the island to the south. Massive stone columns rose from the water, the remains of a collapsed bridge. I didn't dare to imagine how close to the surface the rest of the bridge was.

"How's the water level?" I asked.

Alice's eyes flickered left and right as she steered the ship between the columns. "All right, I think. But we lost speed when we changed course."

Sure enough, the mainsail shifted against the mast as though sniffing out the wind.

In the distance, hidden among grassy dunes, were the shells of a few wooden cabins—a tiny settlement I'd never seen from Hatteras.

"What's that?" I called to her.

Alice turned to her right but didn't answer at first. "I don't know. I didn't realize it was there."

Ananias and Griffin had noticed it too now. They stood beside the rail and stared at the mysterious settlement.

"It was a colony," explained Tarn. I'd almost forgotten that she was on deck with us, let alone listening. She ran her fingers through her hair, short like her daughter's, but matted and coarse. "Not so different from ours on Hatteras."

"What happened to it?" asked Alice. "Where is everyone?"

"Dead. Died years ago." Tarn stared into the distance, gasping shallow breaths. Her voice was hoarse. "No one believed the rats could make it out this far. The island settlements are so irregular—entire regions uninhabited. Rats need food and human waste to survive, and there's so little of it here. But then one of the clan ships weighed anchor to trade. No one knew they had rats on board. Or that a couple would get into the bags they brought with them on the cutter." She made it sound simple, almost inevitable.

"You saw it happen?" I asked.

"No. But we used to trade with the colony too. We'd row to the middle of the inlet . . . exchange news and goods and food. Then, one day, they didn't come when we signaled."

Ananias wiped sweat from his brow. "Why didn't they cross the inlet? Try to escape."

"The colony was small. The people were old too. You wouldn't understand, but sometimes it's better to die with a loved one than to live alone."

We'd passed the columns now, and the settlement had disappeared from view so completely, I would have sworn I'd imagined it. Half a mile farther and we'd be able to look back at Hatteras Island. We might catch a glimpse of Bodie Lighthouse, and imagine the place farther up the coast where our colony used to be. I wondered if we'd ever see it again.

"What's Croatoan?" asked Ananias.

21

I followed his gaze to the left-most column, where the word was written in giant letters.

Tarn hesitated. "Croatoan is a myth—a story of a colony that mysteriously disappeared from this area hundreds of years ago. Legend has it they left nothing but the word *croatoan* carved into a tree. Our neighbors would've known about the legend. They probably wrote that when they knew the end was near. Their own farewell, in a way."

There was something familiar about the word, but it took me a moment to realize why. Alice and I had seen the letters *CRO* daubed on a cabin on the mainland across the sound from Roanoke Island. More mysterious letters from an extinct civilization.

Alice beckoned me over. "Grab your binoculars," she whispered as I drew near.

"I don't know where they are. Why?"

"There are *two* words on that column."

Sure enough, when I squinted, I could see two sides. On the east-facing side, the word *CROATOAN* was large and clear. But on the south-facing side was another word, too small and faint for me to read. "What does it say?"

Alice hesitated. "It says . . . *murder*."

Before I could respond, footsteps sounded on the staircase. Eleanor paused before us, long brown hair flowing in the breeze, looking for all the world like an apparition. Only her bruises looked real.

"Kyte, Guardian of the Wind, has passed on," she said. Her voice was quiet and emotionless. "Kyte is gone."

CHAPTER 4

I hated Kyte. The feeling was mutual too. Only a few days before, he'd insisted that I had no element. When my father had argued that I was nothing without an element, Kyte had picked up on the word with almost sadistic pleasure: *nothing*.

I still wanted him to live, though. Rose loved her father. I didn't want to think of how losing him would change her.

"Kyte's dead," Eleanor repeated in monotone, as though we might not have heard.

"Are you all right, Eleanor?" Alice asked.

Eleanor seemed distracted. Confused. She wouldn't even look at her sister. "We should prepare to release his body to the water, and offer a blessing for safe passage."

The sail hung limp against the mast now, and the ship's progress stalled. We were past the columns, but we had more water to cover before we could turn south and take advantage of the ocean breeze.

Alice stared at the sail, then at her sister. We needed Eleanor's help to fill the mainsail, but something kept Alice from asking—probably the way Eleanor hadn't even looked at her yet.

I pointed to the sail. "Please, Eleanor. We need wind."

In the past, I never would've doubted that she'd come through for us. Eleanor was calm and cautious—Alice's opposite in every way—but always reliable. Her element was strong too. Now the expression on her face was distant and desolate.

She closed her eyes. High above us, the sail snapped suddenly back into place. Eleanor's hair, which had been blown backward, snapped forward, obscuring her face. I couldn't even tell that she was engaging her element, but the ship was moving again.

Job done, Eleanor walked to the bow and faced the oncoming ocean.

The Oregon Inlet receded. Islands to the north and south became smaller as we pulled away. We were charting a new and uncertain course, but it wasn't just our home we were leaving behind.

"I need to see Rose," I said. "Pay my respects."

Alice studied the sails, and the position of the sun. "Let's get the ship turned around first. I don't know how long it'll take to get to your refugee colony, but we can't waste time. We need to find food, check our water supply." She turned the wheel and the ship began to shift course.

Ananias and I worked the winches that lowered the last of the sails, and the ship kicked in response. It was an amazing vessel. If Dare had access to a ship like this, then surely the other Guardians had as well in the past. It was yet another thing they'd kept from us.

Once we'd come about and were heading due south, Griffin took over at the wheel. He seemed to relish the opportunity.

I joined Alice below deck. Kyte's trail of blood was terrifyingly easy to follow, and with each step I grew more anxious. Kyte's body had been dragged to the same cabin where I'd left my grandmother Tessa. The mysterious seer had been exiled from our colony years before but had reemerged a few days ago to help us escape the pirates.

I raised my hand but couldn't knock.

"We'll deal with it," said Alice reassuringly. "Whatever the history is with Tessa, we'll deal with it."

She was wrong about that. Tessa wasn't just connected to our colony but also to the pirates who had killed Kyte. How would Kyte have reacted to her in his final moments? Would he have told everyone that Tessa was Dare's mother?

"What am I going to say?" I whispered.

"That you're sorry."

"That's all?"

She tapped the door lightly. "Sometimes that's all there is."

In the moments before Rose opened the door, my mind raced through everything that was wrong about this scene: Her father was dead because of pirates led by *my* uncle; I wouldn't be able to hold her and console her, because my element hurt anyone I touched. Suddenly I felt like the last person who should be standing before her door, telling her that I was sorry her father had to die.

25

There was a click and the door opened. Rose stood in the doorway, eyes red, face streaked with tears. Her hair was a mess, clothes disheveled, but she was still beautiful. Everything about the situation left me tongue-tied.

She watched me without blinking, arms straight at her sides. She didn't speak, either, didn't make it easier on me.

"I'm . . . I'm so sorry, Rose," I said finally. "Kyte was—"

Her eyebrow twitched, such a small movement, but it felt significant. Perhaps she wanted to hear what I had to say about her father, the man who'd tormented me my entire life. Wanted to hear me say how much I'd miss him, when we both knew the opposite was true.

"I'm sorry," I said again.

She opened her mouth but still said nothing.

The door opened wide and Dennis moved alongside her. Behind them, their mother was kneeling beside Kyte. His body lay on the floor on the very same blankets that Tessa had been using. They were soaked in his blood. I could see it everywhere, could smell it even.

What I *couldn't* see was Tessa.

"I'm sorry, Dennis." That word again, *sorry*. It felt less meaningful each time I said it.

Dennis took his big sister's hand and pulled her back — not roughly, but with determination. Then he raised his free hand. From behind me, air rushed past, filling the room. With his eyes still fixed on me, Dennis turned his fingers. A breeze began to circle around them, making their clothes flutter. Faster and faster the air moved, kicking up dust in swirling clouds. The blankets rose too, so that droplets of blood spattered across the walls.

I couldn't take my eyes off Dennis. Not even when Alice grabbed my sleeve protectively. Or when, with the slightest flick of his wrist, Dennis slammed the door shut so hard, it crashed against the already splintered frame.

Rose was only a yard away, but the distance between us had never felt greater. A day earlier, we'd held hands, and I'd dared to believe that we were meant to be together. Now, without a word, Dennis had made it clear how his family felt about me.

"Give them time," said Alice.

I stifled an angry laugh. "Kyte's dead and Tessa's gone missing, Alice. I don't think time's going to help at all."

She swallowed the urge to snap back at me. "Tessa will be on the ship somewhere."

Yes, I thought. *And I know exactly where.*

I marched to the end of the corridor. Dare's cabin door was closed, exactly as Griffin and I had left it. I half expected to find it locked now, to discover that I'd dreamed being inside the room.

It opened just fine. The desk, shelves, and bed were exactly as we'd left them. The logbooks looked untouched. But something was different.

One of the windows was wide open.

"What's going on, Thom?" demanded Alice. "That door was locked last night."

"It was unlocked when Griffin tried it this morning."

"And you didn't say anything?" She turned her back to me and studied the map hanging beside the desk. She placed a finger beside the words *Fort Sumter refugee colony.* "Please don't tell me that's where we're heading."

"You know it is."

She smacked the desk. "So we're trusting our future to a map from Dare's own cabin?"

Instead of arguing, I walked over to the machine I'd touched earlier. When I placed my hand on it the message returned, but quieter than before.

Alice didn't move as the voice instructed us to gather at Fort Sumter, Charleston, South Carolina. I let the message play twice before I pulled my hand away.

"Why didn't you tell me about this stuff, Thom? It changes everything." She returned to the map and used her fingers to make measurements against it. She was planning, just like always. "Even with a small crew, we can just about sail this ship. If there's enough food and water, we'll be all right."

"What about the Guardians? They're sick."

"Tessa can help them."

I leaned out of the open window. "I don't think Tessa's here anymore."

Alice turned to face me. "What?"

I closed my eyes and pictured the Roanoke sound as it had looked earlier: relatively calm, a gentle breeze. "I think she's the one who unlocked the door during the night. I'm certain she opened this window, because it was closed when Griffin and I left earlier."

Alice chuckled, but it sounded forced. "Let me get this straight: You think she knew where to find a secret key. And even though she had an injured shoulder, you reckon she jumped out the window. So how did she swim?"

"She didn't need to swim. She just needed to stay afloat until the cutter picked her up."

"The *pirate* cutter? Why would they rescue her?"

I couldn't meet her eyes anymore. "Because Dare is Tessa's son. The pirate captain is my uncle."

CHAPTER 5

I mpossible," murmured Alice. She placed both hands flat on the table beside her. "Dare destroyed our colony. He killed your mother—"

"You think I don't know that?" I stomped over to the desk and prodded the logbooks. "It's all right here."

She ran a finger along the spines. "If Dare's your uncle, then the Guardians have known all along. Maybe they know this ship too." She narrowed her eyes as she ran through the meaning of it all. "We need to get out of this cabin, Thom. And we need to lock the door."

"Why?"

"The Guardians have been lying to us about Dare our entire lives. My guess is they don't want us to know what's in those logbooks. If they get in here, they'll destroy them."

"And how are we going to lock the room?"

Alice pointed to the door. A ring of keys dangled from the lock.

"That wasn't there earlier."

"Well then, I guess it's another thing Tessa wanted us to see."

Once we'd locked the door, I headed straight to my father. The metal mesh of his cage had been too strong for me to break or bend, but I wouldn't need to do either if I could open the lock.

I stepped into the tiny room beneath the stairs and gagged at the rancid smell of vomit and soiled clothes. Once my eyes adjusted to the low light, I saw the outline of his body lying horizontal against the far wall. I hated that Alice was seeing him like this. My father was a proud, strong man, but Dare's men had savaged him.

I fumbled the first key against the lock at the center of the cage. It wouldn't work.

"Don't bother." My father's voice sounded empty. "Won't work."

Hearing him speak made me work even quicker. I was desperate to get him out, but angry too. "You sure about that? We found them in Dare's cabin."

He opened his mouth. Closed it again.

"Why didn't you say that he was our uncle? Why would you keep that from us?"

Father didn't respond at first, just breathed in and out slowly. "The morning after Griffin was born, thirteen years ago, Dare killed your mother. How could I explain that she died by her own brother's hand?" He swallowed hard. "We couldn't even avenge her death because he was gone . . . and we had no way to follow."

31

My hands were shaking. Alice slid the keys from my fingers and continued trying them, one by one. None of them worked.

"He won't have left the key," said Father softly. "I'm sorry."

I'd been sure it would work. Sure that we'd be able to release him, get him out so that we could tend to him. Now I was certain that he'd be dead before we reached Fort Sumter.

"Water," he whispered, voice growing faint. "Griffin left a canister."

I felt around on the floor and found it. It was too big to pass through the tight metal mesh, so I poured it slowly through the top. Father turned his head slightly and opened his mouth, tried to catch the drops as they fell. After a moment, he grew tired and rested his head against the floor again.

I took the keys from Alice and tried them all one more time. She didn't stop me either. Just stayed beside me as I cycled through them.

"Go find Ananias and Eleanor," Father said finally. "If they combine their elements, they might be able to bend the lock."

I didn't understand what he meant by *combining* elements. I wasn't sure the lock would bend, either; the metal was the strongest I'd seen. But with no other way to get him out, I knew we had to try. The alternative was too grim to imagine.

As we left the room, Alice removed a key from the ring. "This is the one to Dare's cabin. We'll open all the cabins we can, but not that one. If anyone asks where we found the ring, we say it was hanging beside your father's cage. Understood?"

I gave a nod and went to get Ananias. We needed to explore

the ship, and fast. We needed food and a place for everyone to sleep. And Ananias and Eleanor had a job to do.

One strike later, we'd opened most of the cabins and removed whatever we could use: blankets scattered haphazardly across the floors, utensils that had slid beneath rickety furniture. Even though there wasn't much food on board, there was enough dried fruit, peanuts, and herbs to last a few days, which was more than we could have hoped for. More importantly, the hurricane had filled the ship's water harvester. Once Rose emerged from her cabin, she'd be able to tell us if it was safe to drink.

Ananias and I entered the final cabin together. "Father wants you and Eleanor to combine elements," I said, tossing him another dirty, moth-eaten blanket. "He says it's the only way to break the cage."

"I know. Fire and wind. He already asked me."

"What did you tell him?"

He moved beside a porthole and stared at the sliver of barrier island to the west. The sun was low in the sky, bathing his face in orange glow. "I only found out about combining elements by accident, believe it or not," he said, avoiding the question. "It was a few years ago. Eleanor and I were holding hands. She told me to make a flame. She wanted to see if she could move the air around it—make it *dance*, she said." He closed his eyes, savoring the memory—not of the flame, I suspected, but of holding hands. His mouth slipped into an easy smile. "Turns out, our elements combined. She blew

33

that flame three yards. Set light to a bush. I must've dumped a beach's worth of sand on it before the fire went out."

Story over, he seemed to become aware of me again. The smile faded.

"What did you say to Father, Ananias?"

He shrugged. "I said I couldn't help him. Not yet."

"Why?"

"Because Eleanor won't hold my hand anymore. She won't speak to me, or look at me. She won't talk to Alice, either. Or her parents. Something is really wrong, and I don't know what to do. I'll give her space if that's what she needs, but it's like she's slipping away from me. From all of us."

"What happened to her?"

"I don't know. Honestly, I don't."

I still wanted him to ask for Eleanor's help. Kyte, Guardian of the Wind, was dead. Dennis had the element too, but he was in shock. Only Eleanor could do this, and if Kyte was correct, our elements were growing weaker all the time. And yet, as I looked at my brother's face, I knew I had to let it go for now. It was the first time I could remember seeing him cry.

Shortly before sunset, we assembled on deck. The three Guardians, too weak to stand, sat in a semi-circle around Kyte's dead body. Dennis hugged his mother tightly, crying into her hair, while she stared ahead, unblinking. Rose stood beside her father's head, staring down at the man she'd spent her life trying to please.

No one spoke. Someone should have been offering thanks

34

for his life and blessings for his safe passage to whatever lay beyond. But what thanks could be offered for a life cut short? How could we hope for safe passage while his rust-red clothes reminded us how sudden and violent his death had been?

Rose knelt beside her father and whispered something to him. I couldn't hear what she was saying. When she was done, Dennis spoke, and their mother, Marin. Finally, Rose and Dennis took Kyte's hands and tried to lift him. His torso shifted a little, but that was all. Rose gritted her teeth and pulled harder. The body barely moved. In the moment before she let go, Rose let out a guttural cry that split the air.

It was Ananias who eased her away. It should've been me, but I didn't know what I was supposed to say or do anymore. When Ananias told me to take Kyte's other shoulder, I did it without thinking. Alice and Griffin took his feet, and together the four of us lifted Kyte from the deck.

I was dripping sweat, but also shaking despite the warm wind. When we heaved him onto the rail, I felt the full weight of him, the enormity of a life.

Kyte hit the water hard and disappeared beneath the waves. When he reemerged, he was already several yards away. I kept my eyes trained on the body, shocked at how quickly it disappeared from view.

"We should return to Roanoke," croaked Marin. "You all heard what Kyte said: We'll lose our elements if we continue on this course."

I didn't want to cross her, especially now that she'd lost her husband, but no one else seemed willing to speak either.

"Other Plague survivors have managed without elements," I reminded her. "We will too."

She pressed her fingertips against her temples. "We're not like other survivors, Thomas."

"Until a week ago, I was *exactly* like them." I signed so that Griffin would understand too. "We can't take on the pirates. There are too many of them, and they have weapons. If they were willing to risk everything to get to the solution before, they'll risk everything again now."

"The solution isn't real—"

"But the pirates think it is," interrupted Alice. "Look, there's a refugee colony near Charleston. We can get there in a couple days. It'll give us a chance to rest. Maybe it'll be better than what we left behind."

I expected Alice's father, Joven, to have something to say about that. The fact that Alice had suggested it would normally have been reason enough for him to forbid the plan. Now he was silent. He wasn't even looking at her, but at Eleanor, several steps removed from the rest of us.

Alice's mother, Tarn, gave a long sigh. "What if it's deserted?" she asked.

Alice shrugged. "Then we'll settle it ourselves. If it worked once, it can work again. Just like Skeleton Town."

"And if there are rats?"

"Then we have the solution," replied Alice, without hesitation. "Dare risked everything to get to Griffin. It has to mean something."

I stopped mid-sign and glanced at Griffin. I wasn't the only

36

one either. As he looked from one to another of us, I was sure he was connecting our odd behavior to that word: *solution*. But either he'd already worked out that he was the solution, or he still didn't understand. I hoped the latter.

I shot Alice an accusing look. She had no business revealing that Griffin was the solution. What if the Guardians didn't already know, and turned on him? We'd risked everything to keep him safe. All I cared about now was finding somewhere that my brother could live normally. But as Alice stared right back, it hit me: She truly believed that Griffin might be a solution to the Plague. Even more surprising, I wasn't certain that she was wrong. After all, we were the only people who could control the elements. Was it so difficult to imagine that we might do even more?

Marin interrupted my thoughts. "So how long do we stay in this new colony of yours, Thomas? A week? A month? Forever?"

"I don't know."

"Of course you don't. How could you? You're not even an Apprentice."

I told myself it was her grief talking, but in truth, she meant every word of it. "Where we're going, there won't be Apprentices," I reminded her. "Or Guardians."

"Hmm." She stared ahead, as if I didn't really exist. "And that's what this is really all about, isn't it? It's not about the solution, or finding a new colony. You just want us to know what it's like to live without elements." She reached for her children's hands, but only Dennis was by her side. "It'd feel good, wouldn't it, to take that away from us? To give us a taste of how life has been for you."

"Stop," cried Rose. She faced the Guardians. "Look at you. You're so weak, you can't even stand. And now you say we're ready to face the pirates again." She wiped spittle from her lips with a bloodstained sleeve. "But I've seen what they can do, and I'll be happy if we never go home again."

She didn't wait for her mother to reply. With ten quick strides she reached the staircase. A moment later, she disappeared below deck, leaving an eerie silence behind her. Everyone kept quiet out of respect for her family's loss. But as I looked around, I had no doubt that our recently reunited colony was divided yet again.

CHAPTER 6

We ate sparingly, pretending that we weren't as hungry as we obviously were. Back on Roanoke, Rose had caught fish for us to eat. But now she didn't eat at all, and no one dared to ask her to catch any. Alice handed out blankets and told everyone which cabins to use. I figured that her parents would argue with her, but they didn't. It showed how weak they were. We'd be sailing the ship with a skeleton crew until they regained their strength.

Daylight streamed through the window when I woke the next morning. I'd put in a long shift at the wheel during the night, eyes fixed on the stars so that I'd be able to follow Alice's southwesterly course. I rubbed my eyes, reached for the water canister across the tiny cabin, and drained it quickly. I was replacing the cap when I heard someone cry out.

I leaped up and ran from the cabin. Just along the corridor, Ananias and Eleanor were crammed around my father's cage, combining their elements. With one hand they held each other, and with the other they shaped and concentrated Ananias's flame into a white-hot glow aimed at the cage's lock.

But something wasn't right. The flame wouldn't stay still. It didn't look very strong, either, and yet they were both sweating profusely. Maybe their elements were waning just like Kyte had warned, but something told me it had more to do with the way Eleanor leaned away from Ananias, their fingertips barely touching.

The metal lock was bending, but the flame was weakening. I wanted to help, but I'd only distract them. I was sure that if their flame went out for even a moment, it might never come back.

My father had his back to them. I didn't know whether he was asleep or if he was just protecting himself from the heat. But as the flame slipped closer to being extinguished, he stirred. He rolled over and forced a couple fingers from each hand through the metal mesh.

It took Ananias and Eleanor a moment to touch him—he looked as awful now as he had the day before—but when they did, he curled his fingers tightly around theirs. He gritted his teeth as the three of them joined. The flame grew suddenly larger and fiercer.

It was clearly Father's element at work. He and I shared the same power. But if it was surging into Ananias and Eleanor, why did they look *less* uncomfortable now than before? At the briefest touch, Alice and Rose had pulled away from me. But no one was pulling away from Father now.

The metal lock, already red hot and bending slightly, seemed to liquefy. Ananias eyed it closely, ready to snap it at the precise moment. Eleanor leaned farther back again, but now it was the heat that made her recoil.

Father's lips were pulled back, teeth chattering from the exertion. His whole body began to shake, slowly at first and then faster, so that he convulsed uncontrollably.

Ananias struck the lock with the side of his hand. The flame disappeared but the lock didn't break completely. So he struck it again, even harder, screaming from the intensity of it all.

The lock cracked and dropped to the floor, where it sizzled against the wooden planks. Eleanor fell back against the wall to avoid getting burned. Ananias collapsed, gasping for breath. And my father stopped shaking.

I slid inside the room and yanked the cage top upward. I wrapped an arm around my father and tried to drag him over the side of the cage, but he was too heavy.

"Take his legs." Alice stood beside me, legs spread wide to avoid treading on her sister. "I'll help you."

His tunic and pants were stiff from dried urine. I gagged on the stench.

"Now," she said.

We heaved him onto the edge of the cage, but couldn't stop him from slipping over and onto the floor. He didn't make a sound, not even when we pulled him into the corridor by his armpits.

"He must be unconscious," said Alice.

I placed my fingers against his neck and checked for a pulse. His heartbeat was slow. Faint too, and growing weaker every moment.

"What's happening, Thom?"

Ananias and Eleanor still hadn't moved. Using their elements had left them completely exhausted. "He combined his element with them," I said. "But I don't think he had the energy—"

I broke off as my father's pulse stopped. I kept my fingers in place, waiting for the heartbeat to return. But it didn't.

The world seemed to close in around me. Father's face and body were relaxed, as if he was welcoming death. I couldn't let that happen.

The thin thread of an element began to pass between us then. My hands were shaking, but I was conscious of channeling the flow, pouring every fiber of my being into him and emptying my mind of every thought but one: Make him live.

There were voices around me, but they couldn't break through the bubble I'd created. One after another my senses shut down as I focused more, pushed harder. Whatever was left of my element was his now.

The voices around me were shouting. I recognized the tone but not the words. It wasn't just one voice either, but several. I drew strength from that too.

My eyes were open but I was blind. I didn't even bother to breathe anymore.

I was at peace.

And then I wasn't.

"You're lucky to be alive."

I tried to raise my head. Gave up. Tilted it instead.

Rose knelt beside me. There was a candle on the floor, which meant that it was night. "How long have I been asleep?" My voice sounded strange—not really mine.

"Not long enough." She dipped a piece of cloth into a bowl, wrung it out, and draped it across my forehead. "How do you feel?"

"Terrible. What happened?"

"Alice kicked you in the head. And the arms. Body too." I must have looked puzzled, because she continued, "She saved your life, Thomas. You brought your father back, but you wouldn't stop. Everyone was shouting at you, but it was like you couldn't hear us. So she made you stop."

I closed my eyes to shut out the pain. "I can feel that, yes."

My senses had returned with a vengeance now. I felt the humidity of the night, the smell of salt water on the cloth. What I couldn't see was my father. "Where is he?"

"He's in the next cabin. Griffin cleaned his wounds. Ananias found new clothes for him." Rose reached for the wooden bangle she always wore and twisted it around her wrist nervously. "Your father's alive, but he's really weak."

"And what about you? How are you doing?"

She let go of the bangle and touched the pendant I'd given

her instead. She lifted it up and admired it in the candlelight. "I don't know how I'm supposed to feel right now. My mother seems lost. Dennis is crushed. The only thing that kept him going was rescuing my parents—"

"That's what kept us all going."

She let the pendant fall. "No, it wasn't. Not just that. I did what it took to keep *us* together too, Thomas." She removed the cloth from my forehead and dipped it in water again. "I loved my father. Trusted him, even when I thought he was wrong. But he lied to us—all of us. And at the end, when he was dying . . ." She raised the cloth and watched it drip into the bowl. "He spent his last breath making me promise I'd stay away from you."

I swallowed hard. "Why?"

"Because he was frightened of you and your family. Even though you couldn't have known about Dare being your uncle, he still wanted to punish you. And me."

I couldn't look at her anymore. The name Dare made me sick. "Who told you about that?"

"My father. So did Alice and Griffin. There's no use keeping secrets anymore, Thomas. There aren't enough of us left to take sides."

Rose squeezed the cloth and ran it across my forehead, past my left temple and over my cheek to my lips. The thin material was all that separated her fingers from my skin.

We moved at the same time, sleeves brushing lightly, then hands touching. I tried to rein in my energy, but it wasn't necessary. The hint of a smile on her lips told me she was just fine. Either my element was weakening like everyone else's, or I was too exhausted to pass any energy at all.

Our fingers intertwined, skin gliding over skin, like a warm breeze. Rose dropped the cloth and ran her free hand up my arm, kept moving until it rested on my shoulder. A finger glanced my chin, then another touched my cheek. I closed my eyes and tilted my head toward it. Here was hope. Here was proof that life would be better without an element.

Rose uncurled her legs. "You should rest." She picked up the bowl and the candle, and stood.

"Wait," I called out. "What made you break the promise to your father?"

She rested her head against the door. The braid had come undone now, and her hair hung lank across her face. She looked tired, but still beautiful. "I didn't promise him any-thing."

I couldn't hide my surprise. "What?"

"He was dying, and of all the things he could've said . . ." She bit her lip. "No. Of all the things he *should've* said, he made Dennis and me promise to stay away from you." She fixed me with her hazel eyes. "I keep thinking that if he'd lived a moment longer, he'd have told us he loved us too. But I guess we'll never know. Maybe it doesn't matter. He cared more about hurting you and your family than reassuring his own." Her eyes were full of tears now, but she didn't blink and they didn't fall. "And so I said nothing."

CHAPTER 7

I slept poorly again, plagued by nightmares of pirates and dead Guardians. A few times I woke up hungry. Once, Griffin was beside me. The next time, it was Ananias. I needed to take a turn at the wheel too, but I was so tired. So *empty*.

I woke with a start. The first light of morning filtered through the porthole. Ananias lay on his back beside me, hands raised, sparks spitting from his fingertips. Sometimes there were tiny flames too, but they flickered, like fire starved of oxygen. "There's a cup beside you," he said. "Your daily ration."

"Daily?"

"Well, Alice might give you extra. Because you skipped yesterday's meal, I mean."

I almost laughed at that. It seemed funny somehow, which I guessed meant I felt better. But Ananias didn't smile at all. He just stared at his hands, transfixed.

The cup was half-full of almost-rotten fruit and stale grains. The water canister beside it was full, though.

"Is it good?" I asked, holding the canister.

"Rose thinks so," said Ananias.

"*Thinks?*"

He shrugged. "Strange things are happening, Thomas. Our elements still work, just not the same as before."

I was parched, so I drained it anyway. "How's Father?"

"Alive. We've been checking on him, but he hasn't eaten yet. Getting him to drink was hard enough."

The words were spoken in monotone, as though he was holding something back. "What's the matter, Ananias?"

He closed one hand and made a fist. "It's my element. The echo's fading little by little, but I have a headache. It gets worse every time I make a flame."

"So stop," I said, groaning. "You should be pleased to get rid of the echo. Everyone complains about it, how much it hurts. You and Eleanor always used to say it's the price of having an element. Now you won't have to worry about it anymore."

"But what if I never make fire again? What if this is the end of my element?"

"You're more than just your element."

"Am I?" He opened the fist and channeled his frustration into a single large flame. It grew outward and then extinguished. He grimaced, either from exertion or because he wasn't able to keep the flame alive. "A week ago, I thought I knew everything. Now our colony has gone, my element is disappearing, and Eleanor won't speak to me."

"You can't blame yourself for whatever happened to her."

47

I waited for a flicker of recognition that I had a point, but he just bowed his head. "How's she doing now?"

"No one knows." Another spark from his fingertip. Another frown. "When they threw us in that hold . . . the stench and the darkness . . . it was a living nightmare. No one spoke down there. I couldn't tell who was alive or dead." He looked at me for the first time. "But you rescued us. You saved us, and I thought that maybe everything would be all right. But it's like she hasn't woken up from the nightmare yet. She's still sleepwalking."

"She combined elements with you yesterday," I pointed out between mouthfuls of fruit. "That's a good sign, right?"

Ananias pulled himself from the floor and leaned against the wall. Planks creaked underfoot. "She didn't want to do it. Alice dragged her there. I think she figured it'd give Eleanor a jolt . . . make her realize she's still part of this colony."

He didn't need to tell me that it hadn't worked. It was obvious from the way his shoulders slumped, eyes half-open as he stared through the porthole. It wasn't hard to imagine that he was picturing Hatteras Island, two days' sail away but still so fresh in his mind.

"What did they do to her, Ananias?"

He tugged at the neckline of his tunic. It was clean, but damp from sweat. I was sure he hadn't slept well.

"The second day, before the pirates threw us in the hold, Dare took her away from me. When she came back, she'd changed."

"He hurt her—"

"No. The pirates did that to her when Dare wasn't around. He was furious about it, but . . ." He shook his head and turned away from the porthole. "I should check on Alice."

By the time he reached the door, I was standing too. I pressed my foot against the door, keeping it closed. "But *what*?"

Ananias didn't try to force the door open. "I don't think Dare laid a finger on her. She was gone such a short time. He even treated her cuts and wrapped a bandage around her arm. No, I think he *told* her something and it changed her world."

"Dare is our uncle, Ananias."

He gave a wry smile. "Yes. Alice told me that too."

"Don't you see how that would've changed things for Eleanor?"

"No, I don't. I see why it would've changed how she felt about *me*. But what about everyone else? Eleanor hasn't spoken to anyone in days."

"Maybe she doesn't know who to trust anymore."

"Neither do I. But I'm still eating. Still talking." He stared at my foot until I eased it away from the door. "It must've been something else, and I need to know what. Her father trails after her all day, but she won't talk to him. He told me straight up to stay away from her, but I won't. I can't."

He left the cabin and I lumbered after him. After a full day on my back, every muscle was stiff. My head hurt too. All the same, it felt wonderful to emerge on deck. The wind was fresh. For a moment, I just stood there, drawing deep breaths, reminding myself that we were still alive.

While Ananias took over the wheel, Alice led me to the starboard rail. To the north, a long gray band ran along the horizon, hinting at land. Alice pointed toward it. "See anything interesting?" she asked.

"Land. Also, your element is weakening. You wouldn't have needed to squint on Hatteras."

She rolled her eyes. "Everyone's element is weakening, Thom. Are you having second thoughts about this voyage?"

"Are you?"

"No." She pulled a piece of paper from her pocket and unfolded it. It was the map from Dare's cabin. "We're going to reach Sumter, and we're going to make a better life there." She lowered her voice. "And in the meantime, you and Rose can start exploring life without an echo."

"What's that supposed to mean?"

Alice raised an eyebrow. "Come on, Thom. Let's not pretend. Back on Hatteras, I felt close to you. We needed each other. But things are going to be different from now on. Anyway, we both know how you feel about her."

"A couple days ago I almost killed her, just by touching."

"Yes. And last night, you didn't hurt her at all when you touched. Or was there another reason she looked flushed when she left your cabin?"

I was too embarrassed to answer that.

"I'm just saying, our elements are weakening. You know as well as I do what that means for you both."

I was still bright red, but Alice wasn't watching. She was poring over the map again. "The sun is rising directly behind

50

us, so that land is due north," she explained, running a finger across it. "There are buildings, some of them big, so I'm guessing we're just below this row of barrier islands here."

I stared at the dull gray land. "I'll take your word for it."

She measured the remaining distance to Charleston. "We could be there tomorrow, Thom. Just one more day, that's all we need."

She was about to refold the map when I stopped her. "Wait. What are those?" I pointed to a row of markings heading north from Hatteras.

Alice smiled. "Oh, that's right—you don't know yet, do you."

"Know what?"

She wandered off, knowing that I'd follow. "You need to see something. Your younger brother has been a very busy boy."

Alice pulled the key from her pocket and, checking the corridor was still empty, unlocked the door to Dare's cabin. "I'll say this for Griffin," she whispered. "I go missing for a moment, everyone wants to know where I am. Griffin disappears for a couple strikes and no one notices." She eased the door open. "Which is pretty useful."

Griffin was seated on a crate at Dare's desk. He smiled when he saw me, but didn't get up. He looked tired. Sunlight poured through the window, but there was a melted candle beside him too.

"How long has he been here?" I asked.

"Most of the night."

"But the door was locked. What if he needed to get out?"

"Lower your voice." She grabbed my arm—no pain, except for her fingers digging into my skin—and pulled me over to the desk. "What do you see?" she demanded.

I was tired of playing along with her questions. "My brother. Imprisoned. By you."

She flared her nostrils, but then her lips pursed, and she snorted with laughter. "A little dramatic, don't you think?" She placed a hand on his shoulder. He didn't even seem to notice, he was so engrossed. "I see someone who's trying to discover why he's the solution, and what it means. I see someone who has just about finished plotting Dare's course for the past two weeks. And who has discovered the startling fact that, until a month ago, Dare hadn't thought about the solution in two years."

She leaned against the edge of the desk and folded her arms, giving the words time to sink in.

"Two *years*?" I repeated.

"Yes. It's like Dare forgot the solution even existed."

"Or maybe he realized it *didn't* exist."

"Maybe," she allowed. Her eyes were narrowed again, a determined look that said she wasn't close to done. "But then, what made him change his mind? Why'd he remember suddenly? Landing on Hatteras wasn't an accident. He knew what he was after, and never doubted for a moment that it was Griffin."

As if responding to his name, Griffin slid the last of the

logbooks over to me and opened it to the most recent entry. I wanted to ask him how he felt about being the solution, and if he blamed me for not telling him the truth about that. But he was focused on the task before him. While Alice reattached the map to the wall, he rested a finger beside the mysterious row of numbers at the top of the page: *35°54'N 75°35'W Y:18 D:36.*

We had already worked out that the last two numbers were a date, but the others were a mystery.

Griffin lifted the logbook and compared the numbers on it to those on the right-hand side of the map: 35°53' and 35°54'. There were numbers running along the top of the map too: 75°35' and 75°36'. Finally, he handed me the logbook and ran his fingers down and across the map in imaginary lines. They intersected at a point I recognized all too well.

"It's our colony on Hatteras," I said, struggling to keep my voice low. "The numbers mark a location."

"They're coordinates," said Alice. "I overheard my father talking about them once. I'd never seen a map like this one, though, so it didn't make much sense."

I tapped the map. Griffin had marked several places on it. *What. This?* I asked him.

Dare. Journey. He flipped back through the logbook, tapping each row of numbers, giving me time to make the connection for myself.

I could hardly believe it. He'd mapped Dare's journey to Hatteras. *Why. Stop. Here?* I asked, pointing to the last of the markings.

Griffin flicked through the logbook. Six days of log entries were missing.

"Pages have been torn out," I said, running a finger along the rough edges left behind.

"Yes," agreed Alice. "Someone didn't want us knowing what led Dare to Hatteras."

"Someone?"

"Dare wasn't the only one of your family who had access to this room before us, remember?"

Tessa. My head spun with possibilities. I didn't want to feel responsible for the bad things that had happened to our colony, but it was impossible not to notice that my relatives were involved in all of it.

"There's something else," said Alice. "Remember a couple days ago, when we were on the beach at Hatteras, spying on the pirates?"

"Of course."

"Well, Dare said he knew there was a plot to kill him. Said he'd known ever since the pirates had thought it up twelve days earlier." She stabbed one of the markings. "That would've been this day here. Notice anything?"

I looked closer. "It's a long way from Roanoke Island."

"Exactly. More than two hundred miles." She patted the desk. "But somehow he read their minds. In other words, his element still worked."

"So do ours. Just not as well as before."

"Actually, it's not that simple."

I leaned against the desk and took a deep breath.

"Watch the Guardians today, Thom. Kyte wasn't lying about our elements fading, but it wasn't really *us* he was worried about. It was our parents."

"I don't understand."

"We still have *something*. I can see the shore from miles away. If he concentrates, Ananias can make a flame. But the last time one of the Guardians' elements worked was when your father touched Ananias and Eleanor yesterday morning. And it very nearly killed him."

CHAPTER 8

Alice spent the afternoon measuring our progress while Griffin and Ananias pushed and pulled the winches, adjusting the large sails according to her orders. Her parents ventured on deck at last. Dennis said that Marin would be well enough to help soon, but he said it to Rose, not to me. Rose may have ignored Kyte's dying wish to shun me, but it had taken root with Dennis.

After dinner, it was my turn to take the wheel. Everyone but me went to the cabins to sleep.

Clouds had been gathering throughout the afternoon and evening, smothering the sky in gray. I hadn't paid much attention really, but now it was dark and I couldn't see the stars. In less than one strike, the wind grew stronger too. I wished that I wasn't at the wheel by myself. Such a big ship. Such a precious cargo. I couldn't even be sure I was holding a steady course.

I heard footsteps on the stairs but didn't see who was there until Rose was only a few yards away. She stared up at the sails and gave an anxious smile. "Wind's picking up."

"Yes."

"Need a break?" She placed a hand on the wheel and sidled in front of me. Her hair blew back, brushing against my face.

No, I didn't need a break. I just needed her to stay in front of me, tunic fluttering, so close that I imagined I could feel her heartbeat.

She seemed to want the same thing.

It felt strange to be on the ocean together at night—just the two of us under the immense sky. Not that we could see the stars behind the thickening clouds. The wind was gusting too.

Rose took the wheel as well to hold it steady. "Thomas, I—"

A large wave crashed against the bow and the ship tilted up. The wheel torqued, spun wildly. We grasped it and regained control, but the ship had changed course slightly now. I reversed course, hoping to get us back on track, only I wasn't sure where we should be.

"I distracted you," murmured Rose.

"No. It's . . ." The wheel felt heavier than before, obstinate, like I was fighting the weight of the ship. The vessel creaked, straining against the wind. "We need to raise the sails. This isn't good."

"I'll get help."

She disappeared below deck as another wave jolted the vessel. I thought of the sails tearing, of being cast adrift on the ocean with no way to control our course. I wondered why no one had foreseen the changing weather, but it was me who'd suggested we could live without elements.

Ananias and Griffin were first to appear. Alice was right behind them. Powerful gusts rocked the ship, so they ran to the mainsail winch. Eleanor and Dennis followed, looking lost and confused.

"Eleanor!" Alice screamed her sister's name. "The handle's not moving. You've got to take the strain off the sails. Use your element."

Eleanor stared up into the darkness, utterly still. I couldn't tell if she'd even heard. Only Dennis raised his hands. He gritted his teeth, lips curled back as he struggled to get control.

"Why isn't anything happening?" shouted Alice.

"Dennis is trying," I yelled back.

The Guardians were stumbling onto the deck now as well, but they could barely stand in the face of the wind.

"Please, Eleanor." Alice sounded desperate. "We can't do this without you."

Reluctantly, Eleanor reached for Dennis's hand. Bodies connected, they set about controlling the wind. I couldn't see what was happening, but a moment later I heard the winch spinning.

Alice leaped up. "Now the foresail."

Dennis followed her, but Eleanor remained rooted to the spot, eyes fixed on the mast rising high above us.

Rose took Eleanor's hand. "Come on. They need you." She tried to pull the older girl toward the bow, but Eleanor wouldn't move.

There was a lever to lock the wheel in place, so I activated it. I didn't know if we were on the right course anymore, but we needed all hands on deck. So I grabbed Eleanor's arm and forced her to move, even made it a few yards before her father, Joven, held me back.

"Leave her alone!" he yelled.

"We need her."

"Look around you. What have you done to us?"

I pushed his hand away. "Given you a chance to live."

"Does she look alive to you?" He cupped Eleanor's chin in his hand. "You know you can trust *me*, don't you?" he asked her coaxingly. "Just me."

Eleanor shrugged all of us off and staggered toward the bow. Together once more, she and Dennis combined their elements, easing the pressure on the sail. For a moment, her face relaxed, as if she was remembering what she was capable of. *Who* she was.

It didn't last. Before Ananias and Griffin could spin the winch handle, the sail filled with a sudden gust. The ship lurched and we lost our footing. Above us, the ropes whipped against the mast.

When the wind eased again, the winch wouldn't budge. "Rope must've caught," shouted Ananias.

Before the words were out of his mouth, Eleanor had begun to climb the rope ladder. It swung from side to side, but she moved swiftly.

On deck, Rose spread her legs wide for balance and closed her eyes. Channeling her element, she tried to calm the water

59

around us, to make it easier for Eleanor to climb. But it wasn't working. The ship continued to rock as funnels of water rose high on either side. Her element was as unpredictable as the storm itself.

Eleanor was nearing the top now. I could just make out her white tunic against the dark mast. "Be ready to move that winch," said Ananias. "I'm going up to help."

He grabbed the ladder and climbed, grunting with every step. He hadn't even reached the top when the tangled rope eased.

"Eleanor's done it," said Alice. "Turn the winch."

The handle was heavy, but we got it moving. We were working so hard that I didn't even hear Ananias yelling. It was only when Rose screamed that we stopped.

I followed her eyes to the top of the mast. Ananias held the ladder with one hand while he produced a flame with the other. In the glow we had a clear look at Eleanor as she hung precariously from the rope. She was at least a yard from the ladder.

"What happened?" Dennis's voice was small. "Why isn't she on the ladder?"

Alice was already running toward the mast. She flew up the ladder as Ananias leaned farther and farther out, trying to reach Eleanor. Finally he extinguished the flame so that he could make a grab at her. The ladder stopped shaking as Alice reached the top too. Then there was silence.

"What happened?" repeated Dennis helplessly.

"I don't know," I said.

"Please," murmured Rose. She took my hand and held tight. "Please, please, please . . . pl—"

Something crashed onto the deck in front of us. The planks splintered under the shock. Screams filled the air, but they came from above us.

I took a tentative step forward. Eleanor's white tunic looked the same as it had only a moment before. But everything else about her was all wrong: twisted, mangled limbs and bludgeoned head. I knelt beside her and placed my fingers against her neck, but I knew I wouldn't feel anything. My element wouldn't bring her back from the dead, either.

Everything passed in a blur. Tarn collapsed beside her daughter. Ananias appeared beside me, sparks erupting from his shaking hands. Alice shook her sister as if she might somehow wake up. There were screams, so many that my skull vibrated from the noise. So many hands working feverishly, believing they might still help her, this battered girl bleeding out on the deck.

The only person who wasn't crying was her father, Joven. He simply turned his head and directed a shaking finger at Alice. "It should've been you," he muttered. "*You!*"

He thrust a hand around Alice's neck. She tried to fend him off but couldn't.

Using both my arms, I pulled his hand away. "It was an accident."

His fist flew up and caught me across the face. I crashed against the deck. My already swollen cheek flared with a pain like liquid heat.

"This is your fault," he yelled. "You and Alice—always plotting." With each word, spittle landed on my face. His breathing was heavy and uneven. "You brought us here and you killed her."

"It was an *accident*," growled Ananias.

"Just like Kyte, I suppose. An accident that you drew him into the open, where your uncle's snipers could take aim." He turned on Alice again, but before he could unleash a blow, Ananias pounced. My brother gripped Joven's fist in one hand and produced fire with the other. Tears streamed down his face.

Joven seemed amused. "Got plans for those flames, Ananias? Think you can hurt me?"

Ananias was shaking. "I don't want to hurt anyone."

"Then get out of my way."

"Stop!" cried Tarn. She was kneeling, hands pressed together. "What are you doing, Joven?"

"What I should've done years ago." He lunged at Alice again, one strong hand wrapped around her neck. I saw it all in the light from Ananias's flames. Saw Joven strangling her. Saw Alice's eyes growing big. And then flames erupting from Ananias's hands as I grabbed my brother and poured all my energy through him and into the fire.

Ananias pushed me away and the connection was broken. For a moment, I couldn't understand why the fire was still burning, moving across the deck. But then a horrific figure emerged—a man engulfed in flames.

Ananias ran to him, tried to tackle him so that he could

extinguish the flames, but Joven swung his fists, keeping him away. Rose ran to the side of the ship and engaged her element, searching in vain for the funnels of water she'd accidentally summoned only moments before. Now they wouldn't come. All the while, Joven staggered backward, gasping staccato cries that were more animal than man.

In the moment before he hit the rail, he stopped moving. It was only an instant, but through the flames I saw his eyes drift once more to Eleanor's body. And when he tipped backward and fell overboard, I would've sworn it was deliberate.

I don't think I was the only one who thought so, either. Only Rose stood beside that rail and scanned the ocean for his body.

She said he never resurfaced.

CHAPTER 9

id-morning, and the entrance to Charleston Harbor opened up before us, just a gap between low-lying islands. The clouds were gone now. The wind had passed. Only the bloodstains on the deck remained.

The storm had died out as suddenly as it had arisen, and a night of drifting hadn't knocked us badly off course. Tarn had taken the wheel at sunrise and we'd lowered the sails. Alice had given instructions, we'd followed them, and if I hadn't known better, I'd have said that they were both all right. But then mother and daughter left us, and no one dared to follow. Alice wasn't the kind of girl to grieve with an audience.

Now Rose and Griffin sat beside me at the prow of the ship. From its position near the mouth of the harbor, I spotted the imposing outline of Fort Sumter.

"We need to release Eleanor's body." Rose spoke and signed—hushed tones and hesitant gestures. We were in unfamiliar territory. "If we wait until we're in the harbor, it'll probably wash up on shore."

She breathed in and out slowly, trying to stay in control. I was doing the same thing. I didn't want to tell Alice and Tarn that it was time to say good-bye. Or Ananias.

Griffin raised his hands, but a moment passed before he signed. *What. Happen. Last. Night?*

I knew what he was talking about, but I didn't have an answer. Ananias had warned me that Joven was behaving strangely, but I never would've believed he hated Alice enough to blame her for Eleanor's death. It was crazy.

When I shrugged, Griffin coiled his arms around the deck rails and stared at the harbor ahead of us. He was constantly searching for answers, but some things couldn't be explained.

"Was it an accident, Thomas?" Rose whispered. "When you touched Ananias and combined to make the flames."

She was giving me a lifeline. To everyone else I must have seemed like a child playing with a dangerous new weapon. But I'd wanted to hurt him, I knew that much. "I wasn't trying to kill him, Rose. I didn't want anyone to die."

She gave a small, sad nod. "Me neither."

I looked at my hands. There was no sign of the energy that had coursed through them ever since I was born. No scars from the pain I'd brought to others. "I hope our elements disappear completely. I hope whatever's left can fade away. I don't want this anymore."

Rose didn't answer, but when she leaned into me and rested her head against my shoulder, I knew she was wishing for the very same thing.

»«

We formed a circle around Eleanor's body, just as we had for Kyte two days earlier. We were fewer now. With my father below deck, still too weak to move, only eight of us stood there.

I'd promised to bring everyone to safety. I'd convinced them that a better future lay ahead. But who was better off now?

All eyes turned to Tarn to offer blessings for safe passage. She couldn't seem to find the words, though. So Rose began to speak, words of comfort and, above all, love.

Across from me, Ananias kept his eyes closed, fists clenched at his sides. When Rose was done, he stepped forward and crouched beside Eleanor. He rested his elbows on his knees, head swaying slowly from side to side. From the way he stared at her, I imagined that he was committing her face to memory, already dreading the day when he'd forget how she looked.

Alice took a seat across from him. She held her sister's hand, turned it over and twined fingers. They'd never been as close as my brothers and me—too different from each other—but Eleanor had been patient with Alice. She'd tried to understand her sister's quirks, and she'd been there when Joven's temper threatened to boil over. Now a lifetime together was suddenly over.

Tarn knelt beside Alice. She placed one reassuring hand on her daughter's back, and the other on Eleanor's chest, right above her heart. "All of us pay for our sins eventually," she said, though I was certain the remark was directed at us, not her daughter. Then, looking at the sky, she added, "Pity those that pay for the sins of others. Good-bye, my love. Good-bye, my Eleanor."

A few steps away, Rose's mother gave a series of gentle nods. She didn't speak, or comfort Tarn, though. The two widows who had known each other for years behaved like total strangers.

Choking on her tears, Tarn wrapped an arm around Alice and eased her away. With a single nod, she gave us the signal to lift Eleanor's body.

No one had said a word for Joven.

Rose and Griffin held Eleanor's legs. Ananias and I held her shoulders. My older brother shook as if the load was the heaviest he'd ever had to bear. In a way, I suppose it was.

We shuffled over to the rail. Griffin and Rose placed Eleanor's legs on it, leaving it to me and Ananias to push her over. But he couldn't do it. And so with no other choice, I took both of Eleanor's arms. When she left us for the final time, it was me who pushed her over.

Eleanor's body crashed into the water and disappeared beneath the waves. A moment later, she emerged again, settling on the swell. Her tunic, rust red only moments before, appeared bright white in the morning sun. It billowed around her. With her long hair trailing behind her, she looked as beautiful as she had appeared in life, and for that I was grateful. It was how I wanted us all to remember her.

The harbor appeared desolate. Gulls gave warning cries as we approached, but there were no boats on the water, or people on land. To the southwest, Fort Sumter rose fortress-like from the water. Its great brick walls pressed against the harbor swell, as if there were no island at all. A tall ship's mast peeked above the battlements on the far side.

With a turn of the winches, the ropes and pulleys lifted the sails and tucked them safely away. The ship continued to drift forward, but it was slowing. When we were a hundred yards from the island, Griffin and I lowered the stern anchor. The massive chain links clinked as the anchor splashed through the surface and continued dropping to the harbor bed. A moment later, the ship stopped moving and swayed gently in place.

I ran to the bow to lower the anchor there too, but Alice told me to wait. At first, I was confused, but as the tide pulled the ship's prow gently around, I understood. Always thinking ahead, Alice wanted us to face the harbor mouth, in case we needed to leave quickly.

The fort had the look of a place with history, and an unpleasant one at that. Even its location at the harbor mouth seemed threatening rather than welcoming. As the ship swung languidly around, the view shifted somewhat, but I still couldn't see anyone on the island. Instinctively, I scanned the ground for rats instead. There were no signs of life at all.

We lowered the second anchor and the ship sat idly in the calm harbor water. I joined Rose, who was leaning against the deck rail, hand shading her eyes from the sun. In the near distance, a door opened slowly in the fort's perimeter wall. A line of men snaked out. They strode toward the edge of the island, where a jetty protruded several yards into the water.

I was so focused on their progress that it took me a moment to notice the other faces gradually appearing above the walls: men and women, and even some children. Only their eyes and noses peeked out, as though they were curious but also afraid.

"I guess they haven't had many new arrivals recently," said Rose, echoing my thoughts. "They're going to have a lot of questions."

"I'm not sure what to tell them."

"We could try the truth for a change."

"That we have elements?" I glanced at my hands and thought of what they'd done. "I don't think they're going to trust us if they're afraid we might burn down their colony."

The welcoming party stepped onto the jetty and arranged themselves in a line facing us, hands tucked neatly behind their backs. One of them, a man in his late twenties, I guessed, raised a hand and shouted something to us. I couldn't hear him, though. Again the man shouted, but we were a hundred yards away and the breeze, though gentle, smothered his words. I tried to shout something back, but he couldn't hear me, either. Beside him, the men shifted from foot to foot, growing restless.

"They're waiting for us to lower our cutter and row ashore," said Rose.

"You can hear them?"

She gripped the rail. "No. But they're getting nervous. We need to let them know we're friendly."

"How? We don't have a cutter."

The men on the jetty muttered impatiently to one another. Their leader kept his eyes trained on us. Meanwhile, parents were pulling their children away from the walls, as though they didn't want them witnessing what was about to unfold.

We'd only just arrived and yet I could already feel the threat of what might happen if we didn't act fast.

I climbed over the rail and dived into the murky water. I sank low, then kicked to the surface and began to swim. My tunic weighed me down, but I concentrated on one stroke and then another.

Finally, I reached the jetty. I grasped one of the wooden stilts and caught my breath. Then I raised my hand in greeting.

In response, I heard a series of clicks. When I looked up, five slender metal barrels were trained on me.

So Dare wasn't the only one with guns.

CHAPTER 10

ho are you?" The man standing over me sounded scared rather than angry. He wasn't as old as the Guardians, but had the weathered face and wrinkles of someone who spent every waking hour outdoors. "What are you doing here?"

The guns were only a yard or so from my face. "We heard your message," I said quickly. "The one telling refugees to come to Fort Sumter."

He exchanged glances with his companions. They seemed intrigued, surprised even, but didn't move their guns. "And so you came," he said. "Lucky for you the message was broadcasting that day. Sometimes we need the solar generators for other things." He ran both hands over his bald head, then pulled them down, stretching the sun-damaged skin around his mouth.

"Put your guns down *now!*" An older man, maybe sixty, strode across the grass and onto the jetty. "What are you doing, Kell?" he shouted.

"We have guests," responded the younger man flatly.

"And what kind of host are you?" He pushed Kell aside. "I'm Chief," he told me. "It's what everyone's always called me, so you may as well do the same."

"Thomas," I answered.

Chief crouched down. He flicked his head at the ship behind me. "Where's the rest of your crew, Thomas?"

I looked over my shoulder. From here, it looked almost like a ghost ship. "There aren't many of us. Some of the adults are weak."

Chief's expression shifted. The guns edged closer.

"It's not Plague," I added hastily. "Just injuries. Hunger."

"What about the body you threw overboard this morning? We saw it, you know."

Everything came rushing back: Eleanor crashing onto the deck, her broken body, the blood. I shivered. "There was a storm last night. She fell from the top of the mast."

He sat back on his haunches. "I'm sorry. How old was she?"

"Eighteen." The word caught in my throat.

"And you, Thomas?"

"Sixteen."

"Sixteen," he repeated. "You've never known another world than this, you poor thing." He offered me his hand. "Come on. I may look frail, but I can still pull you out. Especially as my men seem to have forgotten their manners."

True to his word, he was surprisingly strong. His biceps bulged as he strong-armed me out of the water and onto the jetty. "So you've come as refugees, I assume."

I nodded. "We need your help."

He cast an eye over me. I was taller than him and some of the other men, but I must have cut a pathetic and bedraggled figure, dripping onto the sun-bleached wooden jetty. "I can see that," he said.

He flicked his wrist and the men who had continued to point their weapons retreated. "Listen, son. We have almost fifty men, women, and children here on Sumter. We are Plague-free and self-sufficient. And the truth is, the state of your crew has me nervous."

"It's not Pla—"

He raised a hand to stop me. "I heard you the first time. I believe you too. You've got an honest face, and I've seen plenty of men over the years that don't. But I need to protect these people, Thomas. They were refugees too, once. So I'm going to need to inspect your ship." He let the words sink in. "Would that be all right with you?"

The answer was no. My father's injuries weren't the kind you got from an onboard accident. And locked inside Dare's cabin were books and maps we couldn't explain. But I knew what I had to say. "Yes. Of course."

Chief clapped his hands and waved his men toward a cutter on the other side of the jetty. Now that the situation was resolved, faces reappeared over the battlements — not just eyes and noses, but heads and shoulders.

"Coming, Thomas?" asked Chief, motioning toward the cutter.

"Yes." But my eyes remained locked on two faces in particular: a boy about my age, and a girl who was a few years younger. They regarded me with serious expressions, their dark skin standing out against the collection of white faces. One eye closed, the boy raised a finger and then pointed it at me as if he was taking aim. When he jerked it upward suddenly, I realized what it meant. He was pretending to shoot me, as though I was as good as dead.

The cutter slipped through the water. I sat at the stern and watched Kell watching me. He hadn't dared to cross Chief, which emphasized how powerful the older man was. It didn't mean he trusted me, though.

Everyone except my father had gathered beside the ship's starboard rail. It wasn't exactly a welcoming party; more like a sign of how desperate they were to get off the ship. Griffin lowered a rope for us, and Chief removed a rope ladder from the cutter's hold. He tied it to Griffin's rope and shouted for Griffin to raise it. Griffin couldn't hear, though, so I signed that he was supposed to pull it up. Chief watched the interaction with interest. I figured he'd never met a deaf person before.

Once the rope ladder was tied to the rail, I climbed aboard. Kell and Chief followed me and explained to everyone what was happening. Finally, three other men boarded the ship. Watching them standing there, I began to worry. If they decided to take control of the vessel, we wouldn't be able to stop them.

Or was I just being paranoid? After all, if that was their plan, they would have brought their weapons.

They inspected the deck quickly but thoroughly and went below. Splitting up, they made their way along the corridor, stopping in every cabin.

"My father is in this one," I said.

Chief nudged the door open but didn't enter straightaway. I could tell he was anxious from the way he peered around the door before pushing it open completely. I waited for the inevitable questions about what had happened to my father, but Chief just bowed his head. "I'm sorry for his injuries," he said. "Voyages take a toll on all of us."

He closed the door behind him and leaned in close. "Is he the worst off, Thomas?"

"Yes," I said. "Everyone else is just exhausted."

As Kell caught up to us, he shifted his weight from foot to foot like a tethered animal straining against a rope. With a single nod, Chief unleashed him, and he continued his inspection of the rooms to either side of the corridor.

Finally, we reached Dare's cabin. The door was locked, of course, and Kell didn't force it. "What's in here?" asked Chief.

I didn't want to jeopardize our situation, but if I let him in, the others would know what I'd been hiding from them. How would Rose respond? Ananias?

"We don't know," I answered.

Both men responded with quizzical, doubting looks. "It's at the stern," said Chief patiently. "It's likely to be the captain's cabin. But you've never seen it?"

"We don't have a key." I tried to stay calm as a lie took

shape in my mind. "Our captain, Kyte, fell overboard a week ago. We were never allowed in, and the key seems to have been lost with him."

Kell obviously had more questions, but Rose had joined us now. "Thomas is telling the truth," she said. "My father is lost to the sea, and that door has always been locked."

There was a long silence. Chief faced the corridor, no doubt mulling over everything we'd said and deciding how much to trust us. Finally, he turned to me and gave a tired smile. "Tell everyone they're free to disembark. We can offer a little food, and water is plentiful. We'll also administer aid to you as we are able."

He strode away, Kell in his wake.

"Thank you," I said. Then louder: "Thank you so much."

Chief acknowledged me with a raised hand, but didn't say a word. It seemed impossible, but the few of us that remained were going to be all right. As if to emphasize how perfect everything was, Rose twined her fingers with mine. My pulse was slow and my body was relaxed, and she didn't pull away.

CHAPTER 11

Rescuing my father from the cage had been difficult; getting him ashore was almost as hard. Kell strapped a harness to him and with Ananias's help, they lowered him into a waiting cutter. People on the battlements watched it all unfold. They must have realized that we'd be a burden on their colony until everyone returned to full health.

If that ever happened.

With everyone ashore, Griffin and I tethered the cutter to the jetty and approached the main gate. Even though we were on solid ground, I imagined I could still feel the earth undulating beneath my feet, as if I carried the ocean with me.

I kept Griffin close by. I figured that most of the Sumter colonists wouldn't have met a deaf person before. He kept his head low, eyes peering through matted hair. The canvas bag he carried on his back looked heavy.

Need. Help? I asked.

He shook his head and pulled the strap higher.

The fort's brick walls, striking from the harbor, seemed

to grow more imposing with every step. Even the main door looked impregnable: solid wood, oak perhaps. It was small and well sealed, not a barrier against humans but something altogether smaller.

Rats.

Inside the fort, the harbor breeze ceased and the air smelled musty. I stood in the shade of the giant battlements and realized, finally, that this was our new home. It was the reason we'd undertaken the voyage, but until now, I'd been half afraid it might not exist at all. Now I remained rooted to the spot, savoring the quiet.

The door closed, startling me. It filled the space of the frame precisely, as impregnable as the rest of the fort.

"Impressive place, isn't it," said Chief, joining us. Ananias was right behind him. "So old, but as strong as ever. A simple design too: a pentagon, pointing to the north." He gestured to a large two-story black building about thirty yards away. "That's the battery. Runs the full width of the fort—divides it into two parts. On the other side is the esplanade. This area in front of us are the parade grounds."

I checked that I'd heard him correctly. "Parade grounds?"

"It's a military term. An old-world thing." He smiled. "The children want me to change the name, but I won't. I think it's important to keep a connection to the past. Especially when the future's so bleak."

Chief led us to the middle of the parade grounds. "To the right there are the barracks," he said, indicating a maze of crumbling walls. "Used to house officers, back when the fort was in military use. We have a rainwater harvester over there now. It's where we clean clothes, tools . . . even ourselves. There are a couple holes in the ground for toilets too. Everything runs through a sewer, but if you can wait for high tide we'd all appreciate it. The place can get pretty smelly otherwise." He chuckled to himself.

I took a moment to point things out to Griffin. He was as fascinated as I knew he'd be.

"He's deaf," said Chief when I finished.

"Yes. Do you have any deaf people here?"

"No. One of the founding members of the colony was deaf, but he passed on many years ago." He turned around to face the main gate. "Those cave-like rooms inside the perimeter wall are casemates. The ones to either side of the main gate are used for storage now. You'll see a few of the old cannons too, still dotted around the place. They used to take out ships as they entered Charleston Harbor."

"Not a very friendly welcome."

He laughed at that. "What can I say? Times have changed."

"Not completely," said Alice, eyes narrowed. "Your men still carry guns."

Rose's mother inhaled sharply. I wondered if Tarn would make Alice apologize, but one look at her daughter's defiant expression and she wisely let it pass.

There was a brief hesitation, and then Chief acknowledged Alice with a slight nod. "That's true. We're committed to the preservation of humanity at all costs. Human life is fragile, and I've sworn to do whatever it takes to protect those in my care." He cleared his throat. "If I'd found Plague on your ship, I would have asked you to leave. Had you resisted, I would have ordered my men to make you leave. However, you were honest with us, and you're under our protection now." He signaled for Kell to join us. "Tell the men to store their weapons. We'll have no need of them anymore."

Kell turned abruptly and the men fell in line behind him. They marched straight for the battery, following a shallow channel worn into the dirt, kicking up dust clouds with every step.

Meanwhile, Chief watched Alice from the corner of his eye. "She was your sister . . . the girl who died?"

Alice nodded.

"And your daughter," he added, turning to Tarn.

"Yes," she said. "How do you know?"

"Grief looks the same everywhere, I think. And there's been so much of it over the past eighteen years." Chief bowed his head. "I am so sorry for your loss. There's no explaining the world we live in now. There's only the vague hope that we can make the future brighter than the past."

Kell and his men were climbing one of the staircases that hugged the walls. They entered a room with no windows.

Chief followed my eyes. "It's an imposing building, the battery, but you'll get used to it. We sleep in dormitories, although it'll probably take us a day to clear out a room for all of you. In the winter months, we stay inside more — store tools there; eat inside too. But fall has barely started, so you'll be all right for one night outdoors, right? The casemates have roofs. You can sleep in one of those."

80

"They all look as if they're being used," I said.

"Most of them are, yes. But we'll find space for you. It's just one night, Thomas."

I hadn't meant to sound critical or ungrateful. I needed to watch my words. I was going to have to let someone else speak up too. Even though Marin and Tarn were there, Chief was addressing me as if I were in charge, not the Guardians.

"Here, let me show you," Chief continued, softer now.

As several Sumter colonists carried my father to a casemate, Chief led us to the north wall. Some of the casemates here were so deep that parts of them were totally dark. Every now and again I'd catch a flicker of movement. I tried to make out faces but couldn't. Even the people who risked a glance our way gave awkward smiles, as if they weren't used to seeing strangers.

"Look over here," said Chief. "This is one of our vegetable gardens. Rainwater is collected above us and sent through pipes to the barrels against the wall over there. Talking of walls, they help us regulate how much direct sun the plants get. They protect everything from the salt breeze too. In the winter, the bricks absorb the sun's heat, and keep the area unseasonably warm. One frost and we'd lose the plants, but we've never had a problem with that. We can grow kale, collard greens, yams . . ." He broke off. "Forgive me. I'm getting ahead of myself. You'll have time to learn all this."

As he spoke, a small group of men filled jugs from one of the barrels. They added a precise amount of water to a series of plants arranged in a row. When they were satisfied, they

81

emptied the leftover water back into the barrel. Nothing was wasted.

"So your diet is mostly vegetables?" asked Ananias.

"No. We fish too: flounder . . . red drum, if we're lucky. We mostly stick to the harbor, so there's less risk of attracting sharks." He pointed to the south. "There's also a piece of land outside the fort walls—the peninsula, we call it. We keep chickens, and there's an enclosure with goats. We have eggs and milk. We make cheese. This isn't paradise, but I'd be amazed if there's another colony that runs halfway as well as ours."

He was right about that. It wasn't just their ingenuity but also the way the colonists worked together. Kyte had kept strict control of everything on Hatteras, but that wasn't the same. Where we'd been at odds for at least a year, these people acknowledged each other with respectful gestures.

While I admired their togetherness, Dennis continued to take stock of the fort itself. "What was this place?" he asked.

Chief gave a tight-lipped smile. "A long time ago, a civil war began right here in Fort Sumter. Such a large country ours, and so many people, all forced to choose a side: north or south. By the end, six hundred and twenty thousand people had died; two out of every hundred people." He paused to let the words sink in. "And it all started here."

We were silent then. It wasn't hard to imagine the ghosts of men who had stood on this exact spot, wondering if things would ever be normal again. Or to imagine that someone might be standing here in another hundred years, wondering the very same thing.

"Our rules are simple," Chief continued. "Everything is shared; everyone is equal. We bore witness to the end of the world, but those words have kept us alive. We welcome those who wish to count themselves survivors too. But we cannot make room for any who put themselves above the whole."

A snapping sound to my right made me jerk around. Kell stood there, a wooden crossbow raised in line with his eyes. But there was no arrow. As he lowered the weapon, I followed his line of sight to a gull bleeding onto the ground about twenty yards away. The timing of his shot didn't feel coincidental, either. It was as if he was warning us what might happen if we couldn't follow the colony's simple rules.

"You'll clean that, Miriam," commanded Chief, finger pointed at a young woman walking nearby. "Our guests will be hungry."

Miriam hesitated. "But Chief, we shouldn't—"

He raised a hand, silencing her. "They are malnourished and weak. We won't prolong their suffering when we have the means to fix it."

Miriam bowed deeply and walked briskly to the gull. By the time she reached it, Ananias was already there. He grabbed the bird by the neck and pulled out the arrow in a sharp movement. When he handed the bird to the woman, she wrapped it in a fold of her apron.

Ananias admired the arrow. He ran a finger across the tip and cleaned blood off the shaft with his tunic, leaving an angry red streak across his chest. "You waste nothing, right?" He held out the arrow, forcing Kell to come to him.

Like an animal sizing up its prey, Kell approached slowly, eyes fixed on Ananias. "I think we've just found us a hunter, Chief," he said as he claimed the arrow. He nodded to himself, over and over. "Oh, yeah. Him and me are going to have some fun."

CHAPTER 12

We ate dinner together in a giant circle. Chief made sure that the Sumter colonists left gaps for us new arrivals. He wanted to integrate us, starting now.

"Over here, Thomas." Chief patted the ground beside him. "Sit down. We've got so much to talk about."

Dinner was a stew of fish and shrimp and seaweed, cooked in several pots arranged over an open fire. The food was prepared and eaten outside so there would be less cleaning up to do.

The children who served the food stared at us, wide-eyed.

I sat cross-legged and accepted a bowl gratefully. My mouth watered at the smell of the fish. In that moment, everything seemed perfect: food, warmth, safety, and a spectacular orange-purple sunset over the fort's main gate.

Beside me, Chief picked at the fish in his metal bowl. "You should slow down," he whispered.

My hand hung in midair. I'd been gobbling steaming hot mouthfuls without even realizing it. "Sorry."

"No apology necessary. It's just important to eat slowly when you've gone without food for so long."

I looked at the stew. I hadn't eaten so well in days. "How did you know?"

He gave me a sad smile. "I know you've been through hell, Thomas. But you've landed now, and things will turn around." He swept his hand through the air, indicating the circle of people eating peacefully in the twilight. "Ananias and Kell seem to have a lot to talk about. Your younger brother's made a friend too, by the looks of it."

I did a double take. Sitting directly across from me, partially obscured by the smoke from the fire, Griffin was signing to the dark-skinned girl who'd watched us from the battlements.

"Her name's Nyla," said Chief. "When you asked earlier if anyone was deaf, I couldn't help thinking of her. When she first arrived at the colony four years ago, I wondered if she heard a word we said. Everyone needs time to adjust, but some need longer than others, I suppose."

Having finished his food, Griffin was turned toward Nyla. She mimicked him as he produced one sign after another. On Hatteras, everyone but my family had been reluctant to learn his language, but Nyla seemed fascinated by him. When she repeated his signs, she was so clear that I understood her.

"The wheels are always turning with that girl. So much going on inside her head." Chief rubbed his gray beard; it was cropped unevenly, the look of a man who didn't feel the need to impress anyone. "Tell her something once, she's got it. Same with her brother, Jerren."

It didn't take me long to spot Jerren. He and Nyla looked so different from everyone else. He rested his hands on his knees, staring at someone across the circle: Alice, it looked like. His expression was serious, as if he was trying to crack a particularly challenging problem.

Alice had noticed him too, that much was clear. From time to time she'd glance up, but she wouldn't hold his gaze. He smiled every time.

The woman called Miriam handed Chief a small pot.

"Ah, the bird," said Chief. "Have you eaten gull before, Thomas?"

"No."

He raised an eyebrow. "Hmm. Well, you haven't missed much. Such fat birds, and yet so little meat. Not the most pleasant thing, but you're starving."

"Me?"

"All of you. Tomorrow, we'll fish. But for today, this'll have to do." He passed the pot to me and tapped the metal rim. "I'd appreciate it if you could distribute this among your clanfolk. But only them—everyone else here has less need of this than you."

I felt all eyes on me as I stood. The Sumter colonists would have known what was in that pot, and they were probably hungry too. But there wasn't much meat, and I wasn't willing to disobey Chief's instructions after such a generous offer.

I walked around the circle, placing a piece of meat in each

bowl. Rose smiled. Griffin signed thank you. Ananias bowed his head. Alice scowled at Jerren. I was certain everyone felt awkward about eating food that had been denied to others. Everyone except Tarn ate it anyway.

I got to Dennis and his mother last, and the pot was almost empty. When I put more in Dennis's bowl than Marin's, she craned her neck to see how much was left. She was Rose's mother too, and I wanted her to trust me, so I split the remainder between their two bowls. She didn't even reward me with a smile.

I returned to my place and put the empty pot on the ground beside me.

"How was it?" asked Chief.

"Oh. Yes, good," I said. "Thank you."

"You're welcome."

Alice was standing now. It wouldn't have been so surprising except that she was the only one. She threw some bones into the fire and walked around the perimeter of the circle, stopping beside Jerren. "Why are you staring at me? See something interesting?"

The corner of Jerren's mouth turned upward. "Interesting...yes." He stuffed more stew into his mouth. "At least, I think so. Am I wrong?"

Everyone had fallen into a hushed silence. I didn't want Alice to ruin things for us on our first night here, but Chief placed a hand on my arm before I could stand. "Don't do it, Thomas," he murmured. "They need to work this out for themselves."

Usually I would've agreed. But Alice had just lost her sister. Her father had attacked her. She was unpredictable on a good day. Today, she might try anything.

I couldn't go against Chief's wishes, though, so I stayed seated and finished my stew. Across the circle, Tarn seemed just as conflicted as me. She rocked forward as if she planned to intervene, but she didn't rise and she didn't say a word. In the quiet, I was certain that everyone was watching Alice.

If she'd expected an apology, Alice was out of luck. Jerren didn't seem embarrassed at all. So she walked straight to our casemate, and didn't look back.

"I'm sorry," I told Chief. "She's just tired."

He waved it off. "I told you Jerren is intense. Sometimes he just does stuff to annoy us. Like the way he was staring at Alice. He's like a son to me, which is probably why he feels this need to cause a scene."

I was confused. "But Alice went over to him, not the other way around."

"Yes. Just like he wanted her to." He seemed amused. "Don't worry about it. I think it's going to do him good to have you all here. And in the meantime, I'll get him to apologize to Alice tomorrow."

"I'm not sure that'll go down very well. Alice can be"—I tried to find the right word—"prickly."

He laughed at that. "Which is precisely why Jerren must apologize. And if we're lucky, we'll be around to watch the sparks fly."

The air was humid and still within the casemate. We bedded down on threadbare blankets, and waited for the rest of the fort to fall silent. I took inventory of the figures lying around me, but my thoughts always returned to the three people who would never be with us again.

"Alice." Tarn whispered her daughter's name, but the sound carried anyway. There was no reply.

I propped myself up on one elbow just as Alice batted her mother's hand away. Tarn hovered a moment longer, and then rolled away. After what had happened to Eleanor and Joven, I'd figured they would take comfort in each other. I was wrong.

Marin was sitting cross-legged, watching me. "I know you're all awake," she said, voice low and even, "and so I hope you'll listen. We have suffered great losses. We have no leader to turn to for advice. And our only hope is to become one with our new hosts, to let go of everything we were and accept the limitations of our new lives."

Rose sat up. "We don't need to let go of our elements, though."

"That's exactly what you need to do."

"Why? Because mine still works and yours doesn't?"

Marin inhaled sharply. "You call those water funnels you made an element?"

"The people here may have a use for what we can do. Maybe we should tell them about our elements."

"Don't be naïve, Rose. They're not going to trust something they don't understand and can't control. They'll be scared. And what do you plan to say about Thomas? He's only combined once, yet it cost Joven his life. You think the Sumter colonists want *that*?"

"Thomas is the reason we're here now," said Ananias in a monotone. I couldn't tell if he was taking my side, or holding me responsible.

"So why don't we ask Thomas what *he* thinks?" pressed Marin.

Everyone was silent then, but I didn't answer straightaway. I was thinking that Alice hadn't said a word in my defense. And that a weaker element meant I'd be able to hold Rose. But above all, I was thinking that if we were going to forge a new life on Sumter, our best chance was to be just like our fellow colonists.

"I think we need to adapt to our new life," I said. "We need to let go of the past."

No one spoke. I got the feeling everyone was considering what those words meant, and exactly what they were letting go. Too late, I realized that I probably shouldn't have said anything. After all, just about everyone had lost more than me.

Only Marin was still sitting up now. I watched her watching me, and though it was dark, I would have sworn I saw her smile triumphantly at the lingering silence.

As I lay down and closed my eyes, I thought of Griffin and Ananias, and Rose and Alice, and whether we would be as safe here as I hoped. Or if misfortune, like Plague-carrying rats, simply migrated to wherever it could find an easy target.

CHAPTER 13

I was the last to wake. The sun was already high, but we were shaded in the casemate.

Griffin knelt beside our father, tilting a water canister. Father's eyes were closed, his cuts and bruises still angry and raw, but he swallowed as the water trickled into his mouth.

Alice, Rose, and Dennis were there too. "Where's Ananias?" I asked.

"He left with Kell," said Rose. "Our mothers have already gone to work. But Chief told everyone to let you sleep."

I didn't need to ask what everyone had thought of that.

A shadow fell across the space. Jerren was standing against one of the large stone pillars. "I'm supposed to help you move your stuff," he said.

"Move where?" asked Rose.

"To your new room. I don't see how you're going to fit in there, but it's all we've got." He picked up the bag nearest to him, but Griffin snatched it back. Jerren laughed. "So that's where the hidden treasure's kept, huh?"

Griffin threw the strap across his shoulder.

"Oh, that's right. You can't hear a thing I'm saying."

"He's deaf," snapped Alice.

Jerren gave a salute. "That's the word I was looking for. Thanks." He cocked his head to the side. "Wait. I didn't notice you at dinner yesterday. Were you there?"

Alice picked up a bag and threw it at him, almost knocking him over. Jerren kept hold of the strap and slid it onto his back. The corner of his mouth twisted upward in a smirk. "Guess I'll take this one, then."

We traipsed after him. I wanted to bring Father along too, but I'd need Ananias's help for that. At least we were leaving him in the shade.

We climbed a set of steps in the middle of the battery and stopped at the second floor. Jerren turned left and followed a metal walkway to the end. From here the parade grounds spread out before us. "You coming?" he shouted to us.

He led us into a corridor with flaking white walls. There was a corrugated metal door at the end, which Jerren pulled open. "There are no windows in this room," he warned us, "but we'll leave a lantern for you. Actually, it's a pretty good room, all things considered. Faces north, for one thing, so it stays cool."

The room was pitch-black, so we dumped our bags and headed back out. On the way to the stairs, we passed another room. I spotted the outline of windows, but they'd been bricked up. "What's in there?" I asked.

Jerren paused to look at the wall, which seemed odd.

Surely there weren't so many rooms in the fort that he needed to think about it. "Gunroom," he said.

"Kind of a large room," said Alice. "Does the colony really need that many guns?"

Jerren shrugged. "I've never been inside. Chief doesn't like anyone except adults handling weapons."

Alice tried the door. "It's locked."

"I just told you: Chief doesn't like—"

"I know what you told me. It just seems strange you've never been inside. The fort's such a small place."

"Did you know every part of your colony?"

"Yes, I did."

He raised his eyebrows. "Yeah, I'll bet you did."

Jerren continued down the steps, but Alice didn't follow. She was looking at the sailing ship moored to the southwest of the fort. It was smaller than ours and sleek. "That's an impressive ship," she said. "Whose is it?"

Reluctantly, Jerren stopped. He didn't seem as cocky anymore. "The colony's. Everything is shared, remember?"

Alice gave a wry smile. "Good. Then it's ours too. I think I'll go take it out."

She hurried down the steps. Impulsively, Jerren reached out and held her sleeve. She shot him an accusing stare, but I wasn't fooled. She'd baited him into doing it.

For a moment, he seemed unsure of himself. I half expected him to mumble an apology. Instead, the smirk returned. "The ship is used for rescue and reconnaissance," he explained, still holding her arm.

"Reconnaissance of *what*? You ought to know this area perfectly by now."

There was silence as each eyed the other. There seemed to be a lot in that look: mutual distrust but also mutual respect, a kind of grudging acceptance. "Reconnaissance of anything we'd like to know better," Jerren said finally.

He let go of her sleeve then, and walked away. But not before I saw something I'd rarely seen before: Alice turning red. Blushing.

I'd only just returned to my father when a man joined us and explained that Chief wanted to see me. He led me through the main gate and around the outside of the fort to the piece of land that Chief had called the peninsula. It was about thirty yards across and forty yards long, covered in tufts of grass and surrounded by rocks. Below the rocks, marshland abutted the harbor water.

The peninsula was split into two parts. On one side, cages were built around a chicken coop. On the other was the goat enclosure.

Chief was leaning over one of the cages, twisting a piece of wire. He heard me approaching and waved. "Did you get breakfast, Thomas?"

I shook my head, no.

He sighed. "I'm sorry to hear that. Kell was supposed to bring you some. Instead of which, he's off playing bows and arrows with Ananias." Chief straightened slowly, hand pressed tight into the small of his back. "Kell's my right hand,

Thomas. I couldn't run this place without him. But there are times I think he hasn't grown up at all." He raised his eyebrows. "It can get a little frustrating, especially when it costs you breakfast."

"I'm fine," I lied.

He gave me a stern look. "You're the leader of your colony. Starving yourself won't help."

"I'm not the leader."

"Yes, you are." He sat on the cage. "You had the chance to give yourself the largest portion of gull meat yesterday; instead you took none. Kell would've kept most of it for himself and hoped no one noticed." We both laughed at that. "You say you're fine, but you're not. So why don't you tell me what's really been going on these past few days."

I wasn't sure where to begin, or what to tell him. When I didn't immediately answer, he handed me a tool and patted the cage. One of the strips of wire running across the top had snapped.

"After people, animals and birds are this colony's most valuable resource," Chief explained. "One hole and we'd lose our chickens. So what do you suggest?"

I studied the wire, grateful for the change of subject. Surprisingly, my first instinct was to join elements with Ananias—we could melt the two ends together again—but elements were out of the question. Which left me with only one choice: "We use a small piece of wire to cross the gap."

Chief frowned. "You're not afraid it'll be too weak? What if it gives out?"

"It's at the top of the cage. Unless you have really agile chickens, we'll be all right."

He raised an eyebrow. "And what if I tell you we're out of wire?"

I puffed out my cheeks and looked at the cage again. The wires crossing the top seemed particularly close together. "We could just spread out the other wires so they're equally spaced."

"And do what with the broken wire?"

"Save it for future repairs."

Chief clapped me on the back. "Then get on with it."

As I began the process of detaching the wires from the ground and sliding them along, Chief took a water canister from his pack and sipped from it. "Why do you think I'm chief of this colony, Thomas?"

I moved the first wire into place and twisted it tight with the tool Chief had given me. "Because you're experienced."

He laughed. "Experience is code for *old*. Which I am, I suppose. But no—I'm chief because I care. Not about me, but about *everyone*." He stared up at the fort. "I have no direct family here. The way I see it, every person on this island is my family. And I've discovered that the key to being a leader is the ability to listen. Listen hard enough, you might even hear things that people haven't said."

I stopped what I was doing. "What do you mean?"

"Let's take your group, for example. Your father is the oldest male—natural choice for a leader, but no one refers to him that way, which means he wasn't chief even before he got

97

injured. Ananias would be the next logical choice, but he's in shock. My guess is that he was connected to the girl you dropped overboard yesterday. And that's an interesting situation too. Father and daughter die on the same day, but only one of them got a funeral."

"He fell overboard."

"That's what Alice told me, yes. But she also has bruises on her neck like she's been strangled. Still quite fresh. Two days old at most. She looks like the kind of girl who can handle herself, which means the person who attacked her was a man. And I know for sure it wasn't someone from your family, which means it was her father. Who mysteriously died."

I moved the next wire into place, but my hands were shaking. Chief noticed, and placed his hand on top of mine. "I've made you nervous. I'm sorry." He eased the tool from me and continued what I'd begun. "You look as old as me right now, Thomas . . . carrying the weight of the world on your shoulders. My father used to say 'a burden shared is a burden halved.' I'm not trying to alarm you. On the contrary, I'm trying to show you that you don't need to carry the burden alone. Tell me how I can help you all. Please."

It was the last word that got to me—the way he said it as if he craved my trust. So I told him about the pirate attack, and how we'd stolen Dare's ship during the hurricane. How the pirates had claimed our island as their own, and Kyte had died because we were too slow to escape. How I'd heard Chief's message and knew that it was the answer to everything, even though not everyone had been sure. I told him that Eleanor fell, and her father threw himself overboard.

I didn't tell a single lie, but I left out a lot. And all the time I hoped that no one would ever contradict me.

When I was done, Chief was quiet for a while. "You're a brave boy," he said.

"No, I'm not. Not everyone wanted to come here, but I promised them it would be all right. Now mine is the only family that hasn't lost a member. I can't stop thinking it's my fault."

He didn't tell me I was wrong, and I was grateful for that. He just kept sliding the wires along and twisting them and saving the chickens for one more day. "I'd like you and your friends to form a food-gathering group. Sumter's resources aren't enough to provide for everyone."

"We'll do whatever you need," I assured him.

"I know you will." He moved the tool from his right hand to his left and flexed his fingers. The joints were red and swollen. "I've seen so many people die since the Plague started, Thomas. And with every death, I remind myself that here was a person who trusted me. It never gets easier, and I can never reason my way out of it. I'd like to tell you that you'll get over what you're feeling now, but you won't. Not really. You'll be reminded of it every time you look at Alice and her mother. Just as I'm reminded of death every time I look at Jerren and Nyla."

"How so?"

He stared at the outline of Charleston, a few miles to the west. "They came here four years ago. Beautiful children.

Hard workers too. And their parents were the best of any of us. But they contracted the Plague during a trip to one of the harbor islands."

I surveyed the harbor and wondered which of the thin strips of land it had been. "If there were rats, what were they doing there?"

He handed the tool back to me. "Gathering food," he said matter-of-factly. "Just as you will be tomorrow." He paused to let the words sink in. "There's a reason we call them suicide squads."

CHAPTER 14

I stayed on the peninsula for most of the afternoon. It was hot, hard work, but Chief brought me food and a canister of water to drink. I'd have kept going even if he hadn't. All my life, I'd been told to leave the most important jobs to others. Now a relative stranger was leaving the fate of the colony's chickens in my hands.

With each passing strike, the tide fell. It uncovered more of the peninsula, mud flats that stretched a hundred yards to the south. Gulls pursued the receding waterline, eyes and beaks fixed on the turbulent water, and the fish caught in it.

"Can rats cross from over there?" I asked, pointing to the land beyond the mud flats.

"In theory, yes," said Chief, taking a break. "But that land you're seeing is tidal. Spider Island, it's called. Mostly it's marshland. Only way rats are crossing from there is if they plan the whole thing out."

I chuckled. "So we'll be fine, is what you're saying."

"No." Chief wasn't laughing. "Actually, I think it's inevitable they'll cross one day."

"But you said—"

"I know what I said." He fixed me with his eyes. "Times are changing, Thomas. Eighteen years ago, rats were as misunderstood as any native rodent. They were shy. They lived in human cities, but hid in sewers so they wouldn't be disturbed. But they needed humans in those cities. Needed food waste in order to survive. They're desperate now. And like any animal driven to desperation, they're overcoming their instinct to hide. It's not difficult to see where this is all heading."

The tide was turning. I could tell by the way the gulls began to backtrack, one step at a time.

"What will you do to stop the rats?" I asked.

Chief was watching the gulls too, perhaps making mental calculations about the width of the channel that kept us apart from Spider Island. "I'll stand on this exact spot at every low tide, just as we're doing now. And the day they cross, I'll do whatever I need to."

Chief turned to face me again. He looked as though he was prepared to say more, but then his eyes drifted past me. He wore a confused expression.

I looked too. Griffin was hurrying toward me. The ground wasn't entirely even, and his limp was pronounced. *Come,* he signed, before he even reached me.

Why? I replied.

Rose. Element.

My stomach knotted. Why would she risk revealing her element to the Sumter colonists?

Chief cleared his throat, startling me. "Everything all right, Thomas?"

I gave a halfhearted nod. "Rose isn't feeling right, is all. I should . . . you know . . ."

Chief waved his hand, giving me permission to leave.

Griffin led the way. We passed the main gate and continued following the exterior wall. When we turned the corner to the fort's next flank, I saw her.

Rose was sitting on one of the large boulders at the base of the walls. Water swirled around her legs and up to her waist. The current was fast as the tide fell. Her tunic billowed around her. She held steady against the swell and kept her hands flat against the surface of the water.

I kept my voice low. "What are you doing, Rose?"

She didn't answer. Probably didn't even hear me. It was a stupid question anyway. We both knew what she was doing.

I glanced at the battlements to make sure that no one was watching. "We mustn't use our elements here. People won't understand—"

I broke off as a fish surfaced a few yards away from her. I'd seen her lure fish back on Hatteras, but I hadn't expected her to be able to do it here. Not with her element so weak.

Rose shut her eyes tight and grimaced as she channeled what little of her element remained. If anyone saw her, they would know that something strange was going on.

With the fish floundering a couple yards in front of her,

Rose eased forward to claim her prize. But as she moved, her concentration must have waned, because the fish pulled away.

"Rose!" Marin's shrill voice filled the air. When she and Dennis pulled alongside me, she pursed her lips. "Did you and Griffin put her up to this?"

I tried to keep calm. "No. I've been telling her to stop."

Rose was ignoring us both. Slowly, meticulously, she drew the fish toward her again.

This time, Marin stepped gingerly over the boulders and brushed by her daughter. The water came up to her waist and then her chest, but she kept moving forward until the fish was within reach. She slid her hand under it and grabbed tightly. The fish struggled, but Marin had done this many times before. She didn't let go.

As Rose's shoulders relaxed at last, Marin carried the fish back to the rocks. She paused beside her daughter. "No more, Rose. This is the last."

The fish struggled, silver scales reflecting in the sun, but couldn't escape her grasp. Tunic slick against her, Marin raised the fish above her and brought it down sharply. She repeated the motion until the fish was dead.

Something high above us caught my eye then. I glanced at the top of the wall in time to see a flash of bright clothing slide from view.

Someone had been watching.

I hurried to Rose's side. "We mustn't use our elements any-more. We talked about it, remember?"

She wouldn't look at me. Even worse, she was already channeling her element again. She clearly wasn't content with just one fish, and wanted to feed the entire colony. But what would they make of that?

I pulled her around. "Stop it, Rose."

She seemed to awake from a trance. "Let me be."

"No."

She slapped the water, showering both of us. "We need to do something, Thomas. You haven't seen the way these people look at us, like we're a burden on them."

"I don't know what you're talking about."

"Of course you don't. You've been with Chief all day. I'm pleased you two get along so well, but unless the rest of us can prove we're useful, they'll never welcome us. And then how long will we last?"

"They want us here, Rose."

She gave a wry smile. "Are you sure about that? Seems to me that only Chief really wants us." She glanced at the dead fish in her mother's hands. "If I can provide fish, we'll be useful to them. We'll be equals."

"Our elements don't work as well here."

"So let's combine—"

"No!" The word came out loud and scared. "If someone sees us—even if they suspect something—they're going to panic." I reached for her hand, but stopped myself. I was tense and it wouldn't feel good to either of us. "Everything is going to be different here. We're more than our elements."

"No, Thomas. *You* are more than an element." She lifted her hands and watched the water drain between her fingers. "But I'm not."

Suddenly I saw the scene through her eyes. We'd left a small, familiar colony on an expansive island for a large, strange colony in a tiny fort. Her father was dead. And now I was forcing her to give up the very thing that had always made her indispensible.

"I'm sorry, Rose," I said quietly. "We'll make this work, though. I promise."

She kept her eyes closed and gave a slight nod. I couldn't tell whether she was agreeing with me, or simply giving up fighting.

It was only then that I became aware of Marin, still standing behind us. "Rose stopped listening to her father when he was on his deathbed. But it seems she listens to you, Thomas." She gripped the fish tightly, face twisted in contempt. "I hope you'll offer her sage advice now that she no longer has any use for mine."

CHAPTER 15

I hadn't meant to fall asleep. I'd just wanted to take a portion of food to my father. One moment, I was leaning over his bunk—one of only three beds in the room—listening to the steady in-and-out of his breathing, the next I was dreaming of pirates and Plague, Fort Sumter's imposing walls and Kell's crossbow.

It was a relief when Rose shook me awake. "Thomas, come," she whispered.

I stumbled across the room after her, hoping I wouldn't wake anyone. It was dark outside and the parade grounds were empty. Rose crouched down and pointed toward the harbor. A faint glow was coming from one of our ship's portholes.

"Who'd want to check it out in the middle of the night?" she asked.

I didn't have an answer for that.

"Come on." She took my hand. "We need to find out what's going on."

"Wait. Not without help."

"You mean, more people to make noise." She gave a dismissive snort. "I say we go alone. I'm the strongest swimmer here."

"But your element's not the same—"

"I don't think I've forgotten how to swim, thanks." Rose let go of my hand. "You said I couldn't use my element anymore, not that I couldn't do anything at all."

"I just figure we could use some help."

"You mean Alice, don't you? Have you even seen her since this morning?"

I shook my head.

"She's not herself, Thomas. She was crying earlier. Ananias was holding her. They're not ready for this new world. They haven't let go of the old one yet."

"And you have, I suppose?"

Rose stared at the ship again. "If you and my mother won't let me be who I was, then at least let me decide who I'm going to be from now on."

She padded along the walkway toward the steps. She didn't even stop to see if I was following. When she got to the bottom, she headed for the main gate. No one was around to see her, and no one would be around to make sure she returned safely.

Muttering a curse, I kept my footsteps light and quiet and followed her.

Outside the main gate, the harbor wind felt fresh. It took the edge off the stifling, humid evening. Rose stood at the end of the jetty, watching the ship.

"What happens if it's someone we don't know?" I asked.

"I'm certain it's someone we don't know. But then, I'd like to know what they're doing on *our* ship."

She dangled her legs over the side of the jetty. So did I. Before she could slip into the water, though, I touched her arm. "Why are you doing this, Rose?"

She looked confused. "Don't you want to know who's out there?"

"That's not what I mean." I ran my foot through the water. "What you said just now . . . about deciding who you want to be from now on. What do you mean?"

She breathed in and out slowly. "Look, I never much liked Alice," she began. "I always thought she made easy tasks complicated. If a Guardian said one thing, Alice would want to do the opposite. I thought . . . if only she'd be more like me, her life would be so much simpler."

"But not anymore."

She shook her head. "I made it possible for my father to lie to us, Thomas. *Me*. If I'd questioned him, argued . . . things might've turned out differently. Maybe we'd hate our parents. Maybe we'd want to escape from Hatteras. But at least we'd know who we really are." She found my hand and squeezed it. "From now on, I want to know the truth. I want to search for it, and if that means taking risks, then I'll live with it. Because then I'll know I'm alive. I'll know it's all real."

She slipped into the water fully clothed and waited for me to join her.

The truth is, I already knew it was real. I'd known it from the moment the pirates burned down our colony.

I slipped into the water too. I couldn't leave my tunic behind on the jetty in case someone found it. My clothes stuck to my sides, heavy and cumbersome.

"Ready?" she asked.

"Ready."

Even without the full use of her element, Rose swam faster than me, the water sliding around her with only a slight ripple. It was a clear night and the ship appeared larger than ever as we neared it. The only sound was the water as it lapped against the curving wooden hull.

Rose waited for me beside the ship. We climbed the rope ladder, careful not to let it bat against the hull and alert the intruder. At the top of the ladder, I swung a leg over the rail and planted one foot noiselessly on the deck. I remembered that some of the planks in the middle of the deck squeaked, so I chose a long route to the stairway.

We took the stairs below deck on all fours. My heart was pounding—not just because of the intruder, still moving about in the nearby cabin, but also the memories of everything that had happened on the ship. As if she sensed it, Rose reached out and touched me, fingers glancing my bare arm.

The sounds coming from the cabin had stopped now. For a few moments, there was silence. I held my breath, wondering who it was, and how they'd react to being found.

The movements started again.

I shuffled forward, hugging the wall. When I got to the doorway, I took a deep breath and peered around the corner.

Jerren sat against the far wall, eyes fixed on the door. "I

thought you were going to wait out there all night," he said.

Rose and I entered the cabin. A tiny lantern rested on the floor.

"Lantern's waterproof," he explained. "My most valuable possession. They let me plug it into the solar panels once a month. When the charge runs out, I have to wait until the next month for it to work again. Better hope it doesn't happen now, or we'll be in the dark."

Tessa had explained solar panels to me, but I still didn't understand the concept of an object absorbing and retaining energy. I wasn't about to ask, either. "What are you doing here, Jerren?"

He nudged the lantern with his foot so that it shone brighter on us, leaving him in shadow. The only part of him I could see clearly was the white of his eyes. "I've never seen your clan before," he began. "And I guess you could say I'm curious."

"About what?"

"About how a group as sick and disorganized as yours has stayed alive so long. And how no one seems to know anything about your colony."

There was a challenge in every word. He wasn't willing to take things on trust like Chief.

"Where's your cutter?" asked Rose.

He adjusted his position. "What?"

"You're wet," she said. "Seems odd for you to swim out here in the middle of the night when there are cutters tethered to the jetty."

He smiled. His teeth were white too. "And what about you? Any reason *you* decided to swim?"

Rose didn't miss a beat. "The cutters aren't ours. We don't want to be accused of stealing. But you see, this ship *is* ours. And you still haven't really answered Thomas's question. So why are you here?"

He rested his arms on his knees and clasped his hands together. "I wanted to know where you came from. The world's a big place, what I've seen of it."

"What do you mean? *What I've seen of it.*"

Jerren studied his hands, weighing up how much to tell us. I was surprised when he continued: "Word is, there's maybe five island colonies still surviving. When I got here four years ago, there were twelve, but some of them have died out now. Normally it's a disease—wipes everyone out real quick. Plague isn't the only killer, you know."

"So where were you before you got here?" I asked.

"Fort Dauphin, just off the coast of Alabama." He picked up on our confused expressions. "It's a long way away, let's just leave it at that."

"Why did you leave?"

"My mother thought the other colonists were going to kill her." He shook his head. "Scratch that. She *knew* the others were going to kill her."

Rose inhaled sharply. "How could she know that?"

As Jerren pressed his hands tighter together, the muscles in his arms flexed. He wasn't as tall as me, but he looked powerful. "Because they told her so. Whenever the food was about to run out, they'd make everyone draw sticks from a barrel. Whoever got the painted stick died—plain and simple. No other way to keep the colony going." He closed his eyes and mouth, and seemed to disappear entirely. "My mother pulled out the stick."

The name Fort Dauphin was a mystery to me. Alabama too. "What did you do?" I asked.

"We escaped in the middle of the night. My father stole a sailboat and we set out on the ocean with almost no food or water. I figured we'd all die the moment we got caught in a storm—earlier if the water ran out—but we were rescued by a clan ship. It was a miracle. They brought us here and we joined the refugee colony."

I'd thought that nothing could be worse than our journey here, but now I realized that wasn't true. "Chief said your parents died from the Plague," I told him.

He nodded grimly. "Yeah. And now it's up to me to look after Nyla. Which is why we have to—"

He stopped speaking as Rose's open palm shot out. Slowly she lowered her other fingers until only one finger remained pointed at the deck above us. That's when I heard it too: the unmistakable sound of planks creaking.

Rose closed the door silently. We shuffled across the floor until we were as far from it as possible. Jerren turned out the lantern as multiple sets of footsteps came below deck.

I held my breath as the steps drew closer. The glow from the visitors' lantern slipped through the gap at the bottom of the door, and grew brighter until they were standing right outside.

Then they stopped moving.

CHAPTER 16

Rose found my hand and twined fingers with me, but pulled away after just a moment. My pulse was fast, energy scattered. It was *our* ship, but we were shaking. How could we explain why we'd swum out in the middle of the night, or why Jerren was hiding with us?

The people in the corridor didn't speak, and finally they moved on. Not far, though—just to the end of the corridor, and Dare's cabin. That's when it dawned on me that they hadn't tried any other doors. They knew exactly which cabin they had come to see.

They were only in there a quarter-strike at most, which surprised me. We'd had days, and still hadn't discovered everything about the room. When they were done, they wasted no time returning to the deck and climbing down the rope ladder. It seemed like only a moment before I heard oars slicing into the water as their cutter retreated to Sumter.

I peered through the porthole, desperate to know who was out there. I was some way from the window so that they wouldn't see me lurking in the background even if they had been watching. They'd put out their lantern, however, and I couldn't see faces at all. I could only just make out their figures.

"They've gone," I said.

Jerren huffed. "We're lucky they didn't find us."

"No," said Rose. "They knew we were here."

Jerren turned his lantern back on, but covered it with a fold of his tunic to keep the glare down. In the faint amber glow it was difficult to see if he was amused by Rose's announcement or intrigued by it. "How come?"

"If Thomas and I could see the glow of your lantern in the window, it figures they could too, right?" she murmured. She tugged at her tunic, which hung tight against her chest. "Anyway, we're wet, so we must've left footprints along the corridor."

I hadn't considered our tracks. But she was right: Even now we were dripping onto the wooden floor.

"Then why didn't they come in here?" demanded Jerren.

"Maybe for the same reason they didn't speak. Because they didn't want us knowing who *they* were."

"They only went into one cabin," I pointed out. "And last time I checked, the door to it was locked."

Jerren clicked his tongue. "The men in this colony can open anything they want. Some of them used to be craftsmen. They know how to make things, fix things, and destroy them real effectively." He made for the door. "As for that cabin, it's the only one they haven't seen. They might've been worried about what was inside."

"Then why come at night? Why hide?"

Rose moved to the window and tried to spy the retreating cutter. "What are you thinking, Thomas?"

I was thinking about Dare's logbooks, and the pages explaining that he was attacking Hatteras as a way to get to the solution. Most likely, the Sumter colonists had never heard of a solution, and wouldn't know it was a person in any case. They probably hadn't even read the books. But instead, I said, "I'm thinking we need to get back to Sumter and hope that no one sees us."

Jerren nodded. "Then we agree on something for once. Problem is, if Rose is right and they saw us, there'll be a welcoming crew at the main gate. We don't stand a chance of getting in without being noticed."

"So what do you suggest?"

"We swim back by a different route." He tapped the porthole. "Head to the nearest point of Sumter—the northern side. It's rocky at the base of the walls, so we can stop there. If there are no guards, we use the main entrance. If there *are* guards, we go the long way around to the animal enclosures. It'll take a while, but it's our best shot."

"Are you sure you can get us in from there?" asked Rose.

"No. But I'm sure I can't get you in any other way."

He turned off his lantern and we were swallowed by darkness. I led the way along the corridor, every plank and panel burned into my memory. We trod carefully across the deck and climbed down the ladder.

The water was calm. Quiet too, which meant that we'd

have to worry about our strokes being heard. At least the breeze was blowing toward us from Sumter.

Jerren led the way, his powerful strokes easy to follow. When we were halfway across, he took an eastward turn. I wasn't sure why until I treaded water and caught a glimpse of the men standing atop the northernmost battlements, keeping watch. I hoped they were the same ones who'd ventured on board. Otherwise, we'd have even more people to avoid.

When we reached the rocky edge of the island, we climbed out and pressed ourselves against the fort's perimeter wall. It was slow going, but at least we were difficult to see.

"You do this often?" I whispered.

Jerren paused. "More than you'd think."

No wonder he felt a connection with Alice.

Finally we turned a corner. Rock gave way to a paved path that ran beside the southernmost wall. The peninsula stretched into the darkness to our left. I could just see the outline of the enclosure, though the goats didn't stir as we stalked by.

After several yards, Jerren ran his hands across the wall. "There's a couple gaps in the brick here," he said. "Good footholds. Then you grab the bolts in the wooden planks up there and . . ."

"And what?" I whispered.

He looked from Rose to me. "There's no way you're getting up here. Not in the dark. I know where to put my hands and feet, but you don't. And if you fall, well . . . getting caught would be the least of our worries."

"So what are we going to do?"

He hesitated. "Okay, look, I'm going to climb over and create a diversion. Just something to distract the guards. Go around to the main gate and when the guards leave, get in quick. And I mean *quick*, understand? Head for the barracks. The ruins, you know? No one ever goes there at night. There should be stuff hanging up there too—maybe even blankets."

Rose took my hand. "How will we get back to our room?"

"You won't. Not for a while anyway. Once the guards have given up, make a move. But not before."

Jerren began to climb. He made it look easy, but I wasn't fooled. He was stronger than us, and knew where to put his hands and feet. When he reached the top, we approached the main gate. I didn't recognize the men keeping guard.

We lay on the grass, partly to keep low and out of sight and also to conserve energy. Now that we'd stopped moving, I felt tired and cold. Rose squeezed my hand tightly, eyes trained on the gate. For what seemed like an eternity, the guards remained still.

What if Jerren had double-crossed us? What if he was alerting the guards? My mind swam with possibilities.

Suddenly the guards looked over their shoulders. A moment later, they ran into the fort.

"Let's go," Rose whispered.

We sprinted to the main gate. Luckily the guards had left it open. Once we were sure that no one was around, we headed for the barracks. We staggered through the maze-like crumbling walls, avoiding boxes and tools and clothes hung from crisscrossing lines. By the time we were safely hidden in one of the ruined rooms, the guards were returning to their post.

Rose pulled a few blankets from a drying line and spread them across the dusty ground. "We need to get these wet clothes off," she said. "If we hang them up, they might dry by morning."

We were shivering now, and I wasn't sure it was just because of the cold. I began to take off my tunic, and Rose turned away. But only for a moment. Then she was standing next to me, helping me. My tunic fell in a heap beside us.

I helped her too. She raised her arms and the damp cloth slid over her skin. I glanced at her breasts, and fought the urge to touch her. I wanted so much to look at her, but I didn't want to make her feel uncomfortable. I wanted to speak, but I didn't know what to say.

The place was already quiet again, the diversion over as suddenly as it had begun. We hung up our tunics and removed the rest of our clothes.

Naked at last, Rose curled up in the blankets.

"So was it worth it?" I asked, joining her.

She gave a nervous chuckle. "I must admit, I do feel alive right now."

"We still don't know what Jerren was doing there tonight."

"No," she agreed. "We don't."

"And I can't stop thinking about—"

"Shh." She placed a finger against my lips, silencing me. She ran the finger down my chin and across to my bare arm. "You have nice arms," she said. "I like how I can feel every muscle."

I felt the progress of her finger, sliding toward my hand, so light I couldn't tell whether she was touching my skin or just the hairs on my arm. All my senses focused on that one finger. By the time she reached my hand, my pulse was racing, each heartbeat so strong, I figured she could probably hear it.

We twined fingers. She was shaking. I wanted to pull her close to me, let us warm each other. I was as scared now as I'd been on the ship.

Rose let out a long breath. For a precious moment, I allowed myself to believe that it was a contented sigh, a sign that we could stay like this. But then she released my hand, and I knew that she still felt my echo. Felt the pain of my element flowing into her. Even weak, my element could be powerful enough to divide us.

We lay side by side, facing each other but not speaking. My pulse slowed completely, but it was too late for us to touch again. Finally, Rose turned away from me and pulled her blanket around herself.

We were apart once more. And Rose wasn't the only one crying.

CHAPTER 17

I barely slept at all. The ground was hard and I was afraid that I wouldn't wake up before the colony came to life in the morning.

I nudged Rose while it was still dark. We dragged our wet clothes back on, shook out the blankets and hung them back up where Rose had found them.

I peered over the crumbling walls to see if the coast was clear. The guards seemed to have left their posts, so we slipped out as far as the entry to the barracks. Then I checked again. It still seemed clear.

We didn't see anyone as we crossed the grounds and padded up the metal steps. Beyond the walls, the ship was still. Going over had been a mistake—one we couldn't repeat. We needed to embrace our new life and win the trust of everyone at Sumter. And we had to hope no one woke up as we crept back into our room.

At the end of the walkway, we turned into the corridor and stopped abruptly. Griffin and Nyla were sitting together, backs against the wall, a lantern between them and a small book in each of their laps. They startled as they saw us, and snapped the books shut.

Even in the low light I recognized the books. They were the journals we'd found back on Hatteras Island, hidden inside the Guardians' dune boxes. Before we'd left Roanoke Island, the journals helped Griffin uncover some of the colony's secrets. From the way he kept the book pressed against him now, I figured he'd discovered something else that interested him.

But why had he shown them to Nyla?

What. You. Doing? I asked him.

He placed the book in his lap deliberately. *Reading.*

Why. With. Her?

"Because you weren't around," muttered Nyla, before he could sign again.

I froze. "Wait. Did you really understand all that?" I asked her.

Nyla shook her head. "One or two signs, that's all. But I read your face well enough." She added her book to the one in Griffin's lap. "Look. I get that you and Griffin are close. He's told me about you. But, you know, Griffin is the closest I've come to having a friend since I got here. So there's no way I'm going to tell anyone about what's in these books, all right? I promise."

It still felt wrong to me. But from the way Griffin was avoiding my eyes, I was fairly sure he wasn't in the mood to discuss it. Besides, Nyla was probably the closest *he* had come to having a real friend too.

Rose pointed to the journals. *What. Find?* she asked Griffin.

Glancing from Rose to me, he opened the first journal and held it up. At the top of the page was a single word: *CROA-TOAN.*

Nyla pulled the journal around so that she could see it too. "What's Croatoan?" she asked.

I wished I knew exactly how much she'd already learned. "It was written on an old bridge column in the region we came from," I explained. "Alice saw *CRO* written on the wall of a cabin over on the mainland too."

Nyla never took her eyes off me. "But what does it *mean?*"

"Tarn says it's a legend—an ancient colony that disappeared."

Griffin was still holding up the journal, his finger pressed against another line of text farther down the page. The handwriting was faint, the glow from the lantern barely enough to read by. But the words were all too familiar: *union of Ananias and Eleanor.*

"Why does it say *that?*" Rose's voice shook. "I don't understand."

Neither did I. Had Ananias and Eleanor been promised to each other? Had an arrangement been made without them knowing?

Griffin leafed through the pages again, stopping at one that featured a strange diagram, like the branches of a tree connecting different names. Ananias and Eleanor were joined by a straight line; another smaller line hung down from it, and beneath the line was the word *Virginia.*

Virginia. I'd read that name before, but I couldn't remember where.

Nyla handed Griffin the second journal—the one from our father's dune box. He opened it to a page I'd seen back on Roanoke Island. It was an illustration of a little girl with giant flames shooting from her fingertips. Beneath the drawing was the same word: *Virginia*.

Nyla must have seen this page too, but if so, she didn't seem to make anything of it. Maybe she thought it was just a picture, nothing more.

I studied the journals side by side. I had an inkling what it must mean, but it seemed impossible that there had been another Ananias and another Eleanor. And that they, too, had been connected.

Griffin tried to get my attention again. He was pointing to Ananias's last name: Dare. Before I could process this, he slid his finger above Eleanor's name. Her father was named John White.

I looked at my brother, confused. The name meant nothing to me, and yet Griffin behaved as though this name, not Dare, was the one I should be focusing on.

Exasperated, he stabbed a finger against the picture of Virginia in the other journal. Below it were two letters, presumably the initials of the artist: *J.W.*

John White.

"What does this mean?" asked Rose.

I struggled to piece it together. "Tarn said Croatoan was

a legend. But what if that ancient colony *didn't* disappear? What if these people were our ancestors?"

Rose continued to stare at the page. "The Guardians reused their names and possess their journals. I'd say we're definitely related."

Griffin watched us carefully. He no doubt had ideas of his own. When he had my attention, he put down the book and signed: *Need. All. Dare. Logbooks.*

No, I responded, the motion short and sharp. *Dangerous.*

"What's he talking about?" demanded Rose. "What Dare logbooks?"

Griffin was already annoyed at me. So was Nyla. But Rose would be angriest of all once she knew the truth.

"Answer me, Thomas," she pressed.

I rubbed my eyes, heavy from tiredness. "Alice found a key to Dare's cabin. Griffin's been reading Dare's logbooks."

Griffin waved a hand. *When. Get. Logbooks?*

No, I signed again. I pointed in the direction of the ship. *Much. Dangerous.*

"He's trying to work out who we are," snapped Rose.

"Doesn't matter." I shook my head vehemently. "We have to stop this now. We could've been caught last night. We risked everything . . . and for *what*?"

Griffin slapped his palm against the book. *Sign!*

I knelt down beside him, wishing so much that Nyla wasn't around to see all this. *No. More.* I picked up the two journals and laid them gently on the ground. *Everything. Different. Now.*

I didn't expect him to agree, but I at least hoped that he'd understand.

We. Safe, I tried again. He watched the signs, but I may as well have been speaking out loud for all the effect they had. *Safe.*

Nothing. Safe, he responded. He picked up the journals and pulled to a stand. With a nod to Nyla, he limped into the room where the others were still sleeping.

There was no mistaking the look Nyla gave me then. I'd broken up their meeting, and let Griffin down. Both were unforgiveable. She took the lantern beside her and turned it off, so that I could barely make her out as she retreated to her room.

Rose moved in front of me. "What's going on, Thomas?"

"I'm sorry. I should've told you about Dare's cabin—"

"I don't care about Dare's cabin," she hissed. "When you first discovered your element, you said you wanted to know who you really are. Now you won't even let Griffin find out about himself. If he's the solution—"

"We didn't come here to find out if Griffin can cure the Plague."

"I know. We came here to start a new life. But what about the old one?"

"The old one was a lie. You said so yourself."

"That doesn't mean we can ignore it. If we pretend our life on Hatteras never happened, this place will be a lie too." She crouched down beside me. "We can't ignore what we are, Thomas. We're elementals. What else do we have to offer this place?"

126

"There are other ways we can help."

"Like what?"

I hesitated. "Food-gathering squads. Chief sends groups out to get food from other islands in the harbor."

Rose leaned against the wall. "Tell me there aren't any rats."

I wasn't willing to lie, so I said nothing.

"Let me get this straight," she continued. "You'd sooner risk your life on a rat-infested island than let me use my element to catch fish."

"We can't just live on fish, Rose. Chief says there are vegetable gardens on the islands. This is how life has to be here. We're part of this colony now."

"Is that how it felt while we were hiding on our *own ship* last night? Like we were *part of it*?" She folded her arms. "Seems to me, Chief has you saying all the right things already."

"He's a good man, Rose."

"I hope you're right about that." She looked over her shoulder at the empty parade grounds. Or maybe she was looking beyond, to the harbor, and the islands, and whatever might be on them. "At least tell me you'll take Griffin. If he's the solution, he can protect you—"

"No! Our elements are done now."

She flared her nostrils. "Not using them doesn't mean they're done. We are what we are. Denying it doesn't change a thing."

"I just want to keep him safe," I groaned.

"So do I. But sooner or later you're going to have to let Griffin decide what he wants for himself. And whether or not there's such a thing as safe anymore."

CHAPTER 18

G rab your pack," Kell shouted. "Tide's rising. Time to sail."
Breakfast was over and Rose hadn't joined me. I
wanted to see her before I left for food gathering.

"Pack, Thomas!"

I picked up the canvas bag. Someone had filled my water
canister for me, and wrapped my lunch portion inside a piece
of freshly washed cloth. The smoothness of the whole opera-
tion was comforting. It reminded me that the colonists made
these trips regularly.

They almost always came back alive.

Kell headed for two sailboats tied to the jetty. I'd been too
distracted to pay much attention to them before, but they were
extraordinary: two slender hulls instead of one, connected by
a metal frame. There were no seats, just a piece of canvas
strung tight across the frame.

Jerren climbed aboard and rapped his knuckles against the
mast. "Ever seen a catamaran before?"

I shook my head.

"Then you're in for a treat."

As he rigged the first boat, Alice copied him in the second. The process quickly turned into a competition, Alice's fierce determination to be first in everything against Jerren's familiarity with the sails.

When they were done, Alice took the helm of her boat, and Jerren, his. Ananias and Kell joined him, so he made sure to tell Alice that his crew was heavier. Alice didn't respond, but raised an eyebrow, recognizing the excuse for what it was.

Jerren pointed to Charleston. "I'll see you over there, then."

"Where?" said Alice, sounding impatient.

"Over there," he replied with deliberate vagueness. "As long as you don't fall too far behind, you won't get lost."

For a boy who'd only met Alice two days earlier, he sure knew how to get under her skin. Before the words were even out of his mouth, the race was on.

Jerren set off first. He understood the harbor conditions well and began to pull away from us. As she struggled to make up ground, Alice wore the same grim expression she'd had ever since Eleanor had died. Griffin and I sat beside her in awkward silence, spectators in her personal battle with Jerren. Behind us, Sumter faded from view.

"We're closing in," muttered Alice. She seemed to be speaking to herself, not to me, but she'd said so little the past two days that I leaped on the words.

"What can I do?"

"Nothing."

We caught Jerren after a mile. When we were only a few

yards back, he eased the tiller toward himself, blocking our path. Alice baited him into changing his course even more drastically and then slipped under him. The breeze was blowing from the south and too late Jerren realized that we were going to steal his wind. We glided past as though he wasn't even moving. The only sounds were the water lapping against the bow and Kell's laughter.

I stole a glance to see if Alice was smiling too.

She wasn't.

A couple more miles and we were bearing down on Charleston. It was the largest place I'd ever seen—a mish-mash of battered buildings, crammed together so tightly that it seemed they'd had nowhere to go but upward. It must have looked beautiful once. Hard to imagine that such a place could be uninhabited. And uninhabitable.

We overshot our target because we didn't know where we were headed, but after turning about we joined Jerren and beached our catamaran on a long, slender island about a half mile east of Charleston. A ruined wall ran around the eastern tip; tree branches emerged tentacle-like from every hole. It had a similar feel to Sumter—a stronghold from a past too distant to imagine.

"Welcome to Castle Pinckney," announced Jerren. "Glad you could join us."

I scanned the land for rats but didn't see any. Neither Kell nor Jerren seemed concerned at all. Maybe that's what happened after years of food-gathering trips—you let down your guard. Did that make you more efficient? Or more complacent?

"This way," said Kell. He stepped through a blanket of weeds, heading straight for an arch in the nearest wall. "This place is even older than Sumter. Not as strong or stable, but you can't have everything."

We passed under the archway and into the ruined castle. Then we stopped in our tracks.

Plants ran in several orderly rows, green and healthy. There was weeks' worth of food here. About twenty barrels too, arranged neatly against the walls. Pipes connected them to the top of the walls, where a series of sloping wooden panels diverted rainwater.

Jerren took a seat in the shade beside a barrel. He rapped his knuckles against it. "Sounds full," he said. "Got to love storm season."

Kell looked up at the clear blue sky. "Easy to say when you're on dry land." He turned to Ananias. "You were on the ocean when the last storm came through, right?"

Ananias took a sip from his water canister and gave a curt nod.

"How'd you handle such a large ship with your crew?"

The questions seemed innocent, but it was the answers that worried me. Ananias didn't seem fazed, though. He just tilted his canister toward Alice. "Same way her crew handled us on the way out here. With her on board, anything's possible."

Jerren grabbed a metal bucket sitting beside the barrels. He placed it under a tap protruding from the barrel and turned a lever. Water gushed out.

"We'll start with the top rows," Kell told him. Turning to

131

us, he added, "Don't drink this water. We can't purify it out here, and we've lost too many days to sickness after someone drinks this stuff."

I thought of Rose and how she used to be able to tell the purity of water from a single drop. She'd be able to do it on Sumter too if we combined elements. But who would trust her? And if they found out about our elements, how would they react?

I pushed the thought aside and joined Griffin as he wandered along the rows. With the element of earth, he knew better than any of us how difficult it was to keep plants alive. *Who. Plant?* he signed.

I relayed the question to Kell.

"Chief did," he told us. "He was a botanist; a plant expert. A survivalist too. While everyone else was leaving Charleston, he put down the master plan for the colony. Enlisted the help of a fish expert and a water and sanitation specialist. They died a long time ago—old age—but Sumter was sustainable by then."

Griffin watched intently as I passed along as much of the answer as I could. *Where. Plants. From?* he asked next.

Kell seemed to enjoy having all the answers. Or maybe he just enjoyed the stories of how they'd survived. "During the evacuation of Charleston, there was looting, just like in every other city. But people always took the same things first: water, food, and fuel. Chief took live animals, seeds, tools, and a couple of weapons for protection. Wasn't long before Charleston was a ghost town. After that, we began expanding our plantings and water collection to the other islands in the harbor."

"You keep saying 'we,'" Ananias pointed out. "You were, what—ten years old? Maybe less. So what exactly did *you* do?"

Kell licked his lips. "Chief sent me into abandoned houses and stores to grab stuff. I was the fake-out." He was obviously proud of the title. "People were killing each other over nothing, but no one wanted to shoot a kid. They'd just tell me to get out instead. So I'd pretend to leave and then pop them. One bullet in the head for them, one fully loaded weapon for me. Can't beat that exchange."

I waited for him to tell us it was a joke—a sick one, sure, but I wouldn't put that past Kell.

He curled his lip. "Don't act so surprised. Any adult who's still alive today has killed. Even your parents. Maybe they didn't pull a trigger, but no one survived unless they were prepared to see someone else die."

Jerren was about to fill another bucket, but Alice snatched it from him. She wasn't content with being faster in a boat; she wanted to outwork him too. Or maybe she just couldn't bear to listen to stories of people dying so soon after losing her father and sister.

Alice splashed water across her face as it gushed into the bucket. "So where are the rats?" she asked.

Kell and Jerren exchanged a knowing glance. "There aren't any," said Jerren.

"But I thought . . ."

Kell snorted. "No way Chief's sending you to a rat-infested

133

island when you don't even know what vegetables and roots you're looking for yet." He tapped his head. "Suicide squads move in pairs. Quickly. One person picking food, the other keeping lookout. Today is about learning the process, not about taking risks."

Ananias wandered toward the nearest plot. "Why not tell us that?"

"Chief wants you to know the danger is real. If you'd freaked out on the way here, better for us to find out when there's no risk to anyone. Jerren and me . . . we don't want one of you accidentally costing us our lives, know what I'm saying?"

Alice looked Jerren up and down. "I can think of worse outcomes."

Jerren fought back a smile. "Well, here's your chance. You're pairing up with me today."

Alice gave a nonchalant shrug, but as he brushed by her, she moved the bucket to her other hand, trying to catch him with it. He sidestepped quickly, and grinned so large, all his teeth showed.

Kell took the rest of us over to the farthest plot and began listing the vegetables. He showed us how to tell if they were ready to be picked, and how to check the leaves for signs of blight. Insects were a problem, but couldn't be helped, he said, directing all his remarks to Ananias.

When Kell was done explaining, Griffin and I broke off as a pair. As Griffin carefully selected leaves from a spinach plant, I took the role of lookout, imagining what it would be

like to stand on a tiny island in the middle of the harbor, surrounded by rats.

Alice stood beside the opposite wall; on lookout, just like
me. Only she wasn't surveying the ground at all. Her eyes
were fixed on Jerren as he poured water in a steady trickle. She
seemed to be in a trance, just staring at this boy who was so
unlike any she'd known before. When she finally looked up,
she saw me watching her. Her expression, so calm a moment
before, turned fierce, as though I'd uncovered a deep secret.

It wasn't difficult to guess what that secret might be.

CHAPTER 19

Alice and Jerren were still busy when the rest of us filled our packs with fresh vegetables and returned to the boats. We tied the packs to the masts to make sure they didn't fall overboard.

While we waited, Ananias pointed to Charleston. "Why don't the rats cross over here?"

"Too far," answered Kell. "One or two out of a whole pack would make it, but not enough to populate an island."

"So why didn't the people from Charleston come over here to live?" I asked. "There's plenty of food."

Kell pushed the boat out. "No shelter, for one thing. And we didn't plant here for almost a year. We needed to be sure no one would steal from us."

"You're a refugee colony."

"So? We wanted survivors, not hangers-on. Not the ones who were too stupid to keep themselves alive." Kell ran his hand over his bald head. "It sounds cruel, I know. But we couldn't let them in and watch the colony collapse. We started taking refugees after six months, when we knew the fittest had survived. By then, anyone still alive had something special. A gift, or a quality." He nodded to himself. "Like you, Thomas. You've survived sixteen years, right? So what's your special ability?"

I resisted the urge to look away. "Nothing. The Guardians were well-organized, is all."

"Hmm." He planted his hands on his hips. "Well, you better find a skill quickly. Today was a practice run, you understand? Tomorrow, we'll be heading to Fort Moultrie. It's less than half the distance we went today, but a thousand times more dangerous."

My pulse raced. "Rats, you mean."

"Sure. It's an island, but closer to the mainland, so the rats crossed over a long time ago. It's where Jerren's parents died." He paused to let that sink in. "Unless the lookouts are working harder than the gatherers tomorrow, they won't be the last, either."

It was three miles back to Sumter. I figured Alice would want to race, so I pushed off quickly to give us a head start—anything to help her feel like herself again.

Griffin sat across from me, legs splayed out on the stiff canvas sheet pulled taut across the catamaran's metal frame. I tried to make eye contact a few times, but he was obviously angry about our early-morning conversation, because he wouldn't look at me.

Halfway across the harbor Alice had built a big lead. Satisfied that he wouldn't have anything more to do until we reached Sumter, Griffin reached into his bag and pulled out a piece of paper. He began to draw.

What. Doing? I signed.

He didn't respond at first, but when he finished the image, he showed it to me. It was of a pair of hands forming the sign for *water*. He noticed my startled expression and finger-spelled the name N-Y-L-A. By the time he reached the last letter, he'd turned red.

She. Sign. Good, I continued.

He gave a halfhearted nod. *She. Smart*, he returned, admiration coming through each decisive sign.

What. You. Talk. About?

He held up the paper again. *She. Learning.* He shrugged. *Not. Many. Signs. But. Try.*

I was about to remind him that she'd followed our signs pretty well earlier that morning, but stopped myself. At least she cared enough to learn his signs at all.

How. Echo? I asked.

From the way he furrowed his brow, it was almost like he'd forgotten what his echo was, or at least had to think hard about his answer. *Echo. Good*, he decided. *No. Pain.* He smiled for a moment, but then his face darkened again. *Me. Not. Solution.*

Maybe, I hedged.

He looked me right in the eye at last. *Not. Solution. But. You. Save. Me.*

Save. You?

On. Roanoke. He paused. *You. All. Save. Me.*

I raised my hands to sign, a word or two to play down what we'd done for him. But he was already shaking his head, warning me not to do it. I'd been worried that learning he was the solution would change Griffin. I hadn't considered that the hardest part would be realizing that everything had happened because of him. Everything we'd risked and lost was a burden he had to carry. A debt he couldn't repay.

I leaned forward to take his hand—without our echoes, it would have felt different than ever before—but Alice interrupted us. "Useless," she muttered.

I turned to face her. "What?"

She flicked her head at the boat trailing in our wake. "Jerren." She seemed to enjoy saying his name, though she didn't smile. "He just got caught in our wake. Such a small wave, but he didn't see it coming. He's lost another few yards."

"You like him, don't you."

Her face tightened. "What do you mean?"

Reconciling with Griffin had lulled me into a false sense of security. I'd approached Alice all wrong. "He seems all right," I said, trying to backtrack.

Alice raised an eyebrow. *"Seems?"*

I shrugged. "I found him on board the ship last night. He was searching our cabins."

"You went to the ship during the night?"

"Yes."

"Alone?"

There was no use in lying. "With Rose. I . . . didn't want to wake you."

"Right," she said, like she didn't believe me for a moment. "And what did you two do after you got back?"

I could hear the judgment in her voice. "*Nothing.* We hid, so we wouldn't get caught." I sat up again. "What's your excuse? I notice you weren't around the room this morning either."

She gritted her teeth, but didn't answer.

"Don't you wonder why Jerren was on the ship at all?"

"Keep your voice down," she hissed. "Sound carries on water. And no, what I really want to know is why you're telling me this now."

"Because you should know."

She dragged her mouth into a smile. "Should I have known this morning? Or on the way over today? Or should I only know when you think I like him?"

"This isn't personal, Alice. I don't know if we can trust him. And since you're spending all your time with him, that's important."

She blanched. "All my time? Or is this really about nights?"

Jerren cruised by, pumping his fist in triumph. Alice didn't care, though. Normally, she would've responded by trying even harder, working the boat for every yard of advantage. Now she just stared straight ahead, as if nothing mattered at all.

"The reason I've been leaving each night is because I need to be alone," she said. "Every time I close my eyes, I see Eleanor. I remember the way she looked at me. The way she fell." Alice raised a hand to her neck, ran her fingers across the red marks. "I have nightmares too. My father, strangling me. I feel his hands around my neck. I can't block it out. I can't...breathe." Suddenly her eyes welled with tears. She stared at the sail above us. "He wanted to kill me."

"He was crazy, Alice. Eleanor had died and—"

"He wanted me *dead*." The word punched the air, left no room for explanations or excuse. "And then you stepped in and . . . I think you saved my life." She swallowed hard. "No. I *know* you saved my life. And I don't know how that makes me feel."

I placed a hand on her knee to comfort her. "He wouldn't have done it, Alice. He couldn't."

From thirty yards away, Jerren watched us fall farther behind. He wasn't racing anymore. He already knew Alice well enough to realize that something was wrong. He looked genuinely concerned. So did Ananias.

Alice didn't see them, though. She was looking at me, her expression tired and frustrated. "It doesn't matter, Thom. You and me, we rescued them all, remember? They were as good as dead and we *saved* them. And after all that, my sister couldn't face me, and my father killed himself so he wouldn't have to live with me anymore." She fed the mainsheet through a cleat, as if simply holding the rope was too much effort. "All my life, I dreamed of getting away from Hatteras. But now I'm here, and I can't see the future at all." She surveyed the harbor, eyes constantly shifting. "The only thing left is loss."

»«

Chief sat on the jetty, waiting for us. As I clambered off the boat, he handed me a water canister. "Drink up, Thomas. I need a word."

The others went on without me. "What is it?" I asked.

He flicked sweat from his forehead. "You probably smelled me from Pinckney. I've been cleaning poop from the enclosure. Figure it's hard for anyone else to complain about their work while I'm doing the worst job of all." He lifted a hand to his nose and grimaced as he sniffed it. "Might be time to revisit that idea, though."

He laughed. Even though it seemed rude, so did I. Every time the breeze calmed for a moment, he stank.

"That's why we keep the enclosures outside, of course. On still days, it can get stifling inside those walls. The fumes would be dangerous."

"Makes sense," I agreed.

"Indeed." He wiped the back of his arm across his forehead. "Life has to be symbiotic: We work *with* nature. Wasn't that way before the Plague, of course. Back then, we'd fight the earth, the water, the wind, then find ways to undo the damage." He pursed his lips. "Sometimes I wonder if the Plague wasn't nature's way of reclaiming the world."

He massaged his back as he took a seat on the jetty. "Tell me about life in your colony."

It was my cue to join him, but I didn't want to. It was late afternoon and I was hot and tired. I wanted to check on my father and Rose.

"Please, Thomas. Sit down."

Reluctantly, I sat. "Our colony wasn't that different from yours. Rainwater harvesters, vegetable gardens, a grove of fruit trees—"

"And fish." He made it sound important. "Marin caught a beauty yesterday. Didn't exactly feed the whole colony, but every little bit helps. Is she going to be able to do that often?"

Panic rose inside me. "I don't think so. It was probably just luck."

Chief scratched his chin. "Well, you'd know, of course, since you were there. But I think you might be wrong, all the same."

"Really?"

"Yes. See, one of the colonists saw her catch it. He described the whole thing to me. Many years ago, I saw a woman use the very same technique. She'd tickle the fish's underbelly, make it still, and then grab it." Chief nodded to himself. "If Marin has the skill too, she'll be a real asset to us."

There was nothing for me to say to that. All I could think was how fortunate it was that the colonist had misunderstood the situation with Rose and Marin completely. Otherwise we'd be having a very different conversation.

"Does Marin seem happy?" Chief asked then.

Again I sensed that the question wasn't completely innocent. Again I had no good answer. "I think so."

"Good. I want everyone to be comfortable here." He peered up at the battlements and waved at the children who were watching us. "Poor things," he murmured. "This fort is their salvation and their prison. I can't imagine spending my entire life in such a small place."

"They seem to be doing all right."

"I suppose so." He gazed at the harbor, a view he must have taken in a thousand times. "Do you have any idea about the history of this place, Thomas?"

"Only that the people here used to destroy ships entering the harbor."

He chuckled. "Not all ships. But yes, Fort Sumter was a military installation. An attack on this place started a civil war. Depending on whom you ask, it was either the moment that our country died, or was truly born. When the dust settled, they rebuilt from the battered remains of the old fort." He looked me squarely in the eye. "I don't believe it's an accident that we've been able to survive here. I believe in a higher power, a God if you will, that wants our nation to be reborn. Our civil war is not man against man, it's man against rat. But we have battled the Plague and won for eighteen years. And we'll continue to fight."

I could tell he meant it, but it was hard for me to share his faith. "Do you think you'll win?"

He looked suddenly tired. His eyes drifted back to Charleston, tantalizingly close but completely uninhabitable. "I don't know. I've never lost faith, but I'm an old man and I fear I may not live long enough to see a solution."

Hearing that word made me shudder. He didn't mean anything by it, didn't even register my startled response, but the meaning of *solution* had changed forever.

"Please help us, Thomas." Chief patted me on the shoulder and stood. "The truth is, time's running out for all of us."

Then he walked away, leaving me to wonder what he meant.

CHAPTER 20

We had an hour before dinner and everyone was resting. Jerren had said he didn't think we'd all fit into the room, but he was wrong. A few weeks ago, Hatteras Island itself had felt too constraining for our colony. The nine of us who were left now fit inside four walls.

The tiny lantern that Griffin had been using that morning cast a feeble glow against one corner of our room. It was just enough light for me to see that Father was sitting up in his bed, back against the wall. He tried to smile as he saw me, but his face was still too scabbed for the expression to come naturally.

I sat beside him. "You seem better."

He raised an eyebrow. "Everything's relative. But Rose has been making sure I eat and drink."

I was about to thank Rose when I noticed her mother watching us. From her expression it was clear how much Marin disapproved of the way Rose had ignored Kyte's dying wish to avoid my family.

"Have you been working with your element, son?" Father asked.

He took my hands in his. I responded by sending energy into him. It was a foolish thing to do, to try to impress him like that. Especially after I'd told Rose to stop using her element.

"Yes, I can feel you have," he said.

The pride in his voice crushed me. I didn't deserve it, and I didn't want it—at least, not for my element. "We have to let our elements go now, Father. We all discussed it."

"Well, I didn't. And I never would've agreed to it." He looked confused. Winded, even. Hands still connected to mine, he furrowed his brows in concentration. He was trying to summon his element—to return power to me, and show me what we shared—but there was nothing passing between us now.

He loosed my hands and gave a melancholy smile. "All those years I kept wishing for it to go. Now it's gone, and I feel empty." He leaned closer. "Elements peak early, Thomas. You have power now, and you need to use it."

I felt Rose watching me. "No. Not here."

"Especially here." His face hardened. "You know nothing about these people."

"And I know nothing about *you*. If my element is so important, why did you hide it from me all those years?"

He sighed. "I made a promise. They were going to make us leave the colony, Thomas."

"But why?" I was almost shouting and couldn't stop myself. "*Why?*"

Marin produced a humorless laugh. "Go ahead and tell

him, Ordyn. How we're godless. How we'll die for our sins, every last one of us."

"That's enough," Father muttered.

Rose's mother was undeterred. "No, it's not. It's time everyone knew what we are, what we've done. Just don't leave anything out, Ordyn. Especially not the story of the boy you killed."

My heartbeat flew, as sudden as a sail catching the wind. I waited for Father to deny it. He didn't, though. Just tugged at his tunic's bloodstained cuffs.

Silence fell over us. Then, to my surprise, my father spoke: "It happened just after you were born," he said softly. "The boy was a refugee from the mainland. About Griffin's age. Probably got left behind when his family evacuated." He opened his mouth, then closed it. Once again, a conversation that he'd had years to prepare for seemed to have caught him by surprise. "We still had some working machines on Roanoke back then. One of them was a saw. It was a great big powerful thing, could slice through lumber in no time. The boy was playing with the blade, trying to make it start." His jaw twitched. "And I panicked.

"I grabbed him. But it was the blade I was worried about. My heart was pounding and—" Father stopped as his eyes welled up suddenly. "My energy went straight through him. The blade turned, pulled him in and sliced straight through him. He bled out so fast, I'm still not sure he realized what was happening to him. But I did." He shook his head, trying to shake the image. "I saw his life slip away."

More silence. I handed my father a water canister. He took a sip.

"The colony was larger back then," he continued. "Not just elementals, but regular folk too. None of the non-elementals knew what happened. They thought it was an accident, and we were used to tragedy. Life moved on." He blinked away tears. "But I knew. And so did the other elementals. You'd just been born, Thomas, and revealed the same element as me. Everyone warned me I could hurt someone again. Even worse, *you* might, without realizing it. I had to ask myself: How would I feel if you had blood on your hands too?"

I thought of Joven, and what my element had done to him. "It was an accident."

He swallowed hard. "Doesn't matter, son. When you see something like that, blame is irrelevant."

Griffin was sitting on the end of our father's bed, his attention fixed on us, just like everyone else. Ananias had been signing for him, but I'd have to tell him everything later. There weren't even signs for some of the things my father was telling us.

Seeing Griffin reminded me of something. I grabbed his bag and pulled out the two journals. "Who is Virginia Dare?"

Alice's mother, Tarn, turned white. "Where did you get those?"

"From your dune boxes."

"Where's the third?"

"Kyte's box was left on the beach at Hatteras."

Tarn sat on the floor and hugged her legs. I couldn't tell whether she was distraught or relieved.

"Who is Virginia Dare?" I growled.

No one answered.

"Who is John White?"

Still no answer.

"Just tell us the truth!"

In the silence that followed I felt everyone watching me. Ananias, Alice, Rose, Griffin, and even Dennis. But I also felt their expectation, their need to know who we were at last.

Tarn walked over to the door and closed it. It didn't fit the frame and there were gaps around it. As she returned to her place, she moved slowly, not at all like the proud, confident woman I'd known back on Hatteras. The loss of Joven and Eleanor was weighing on her like it weighed on Alice, and it was hard to imagine anything that might lighten their loads.

"The *truth*," Tarn murmured. She made the word sound ugly. Deceitful. "The truth is that hundreds of years ago, white settlers crossed the oceans in search of new colonies. They built the first on Roanoke Island. But they weren't self-sufficient. They didn't understand the land and the climate and the native tribes that already inhabited the region. They needed additional supplies, so their leader returned home to request help. His name was John White."

She licked her dry lips. "Back in his home country, everyone was preparing for war. By the time it was over, years had gone by. White brought a supply ship to Roanoke, but most of the settlers had left by then. And those who remained weren't the same."

She paused as wind nudged the door. She didn't want us to be overheard.

"The youngest children had developed the ability to control the elements," she continued. "White was amazed. He'd gone in search of a new world, and he'd found one—a land in which the accepted laws of nature no longer applied. But he also knew that others would see things differently. He suspected that the other colonists had left because they were scared of these elementals. He was afraid his crew would accuse the children of witchcraft, and attempt to free them of evil spirits by drowning or burning at the stake, as was the custom. So White lied to the members of his expedition; he said he'd found no one on the island. The crew returned home, and a legend known as the Lost Colony was born. It's a legend we've maintained ever since."

I wanted to feel something—relief, maybe. Our long-kept secrets were out in the open now, but as I looked at Griffin, I knew the biggest question still remained: "Why is Griffin the solution?"

"We're all solutions," explained my father. "Or the descendants of one. It's just the name given to the first person who reveals a new element."

"Why *solution*, though?"

He rubbed his chin. "When the first colony faced extinction, they received the gift of the elements—earth, water, wind, and fire—to keep them alive. When the world changed, driven by engines and machines, our power emerged—yours

151

and mine, Thomas. And when the world was consumed by Plague, Griffin was born."

"So why aren't I a solution too?" asked Dennis.

"No one knows. Elements are passed from parent to child. I passed my power to Thomas, and my secondary element, fire, to Ananias. Their mother was a seer, and so is Griffin. I can't say why he's the solution, though. I suppose it's a kind of evolution, just like the way some elements that existed in the past have died off."

"What kind of elements?" Ananias asked.

"All sorts. Back in the era of steam-driven machines, there were people who could boil water with just their hands. It sounds like a water-fire hybrid, but it wasn't really. It was a unique element. And then the machines changed, and those elements naturally phased out."

"Except for earth, water, wind, and fire," said Alice, speaking up at last. She sat in the corner of the room and rested her head against the cold stone wall. "Just before he was shot, Kyte said: *Four boys, four elements*. How did they get the first elements?"

Father adjusted the blanket pressed into the small of his back. He'd been lying down for days, and it showed. "No one knows for sure. Legend says the boys visited one of the tribes on the mainland. They stole food and other goods. Someone sounded the alarm, and in their haste to escape, the boys destroyed an idol of the god Kiwasa. The natives gave chase, followed the boys to their Roanoke Island colony. A battle seemed inevitable. But as tribesmen neared the shore, one of the boys caused a wave that overturned their canoe. Another summoned a wind that pushed them out into the sound. The third boy created a flame, and in the light the natives saw the final boy touch the earth and make it shake." He shrugged, as if he wasn't sure whether to believe it himself. "Some say it was Kiwasa's revenge. From that day onward, the boys were outcasts, as was every one of their descendants. They had the power to survive almost anything, it seemed, but they were destined to do so alone."

Marin cleared her throat. "So now you know." She sounded disappointed, as though the fault was with us for wanting answers, rather than with her for keeping them from us.

"No, Mother," said Rose. "You still haven't explained why you kept this a secret from us all these years."

Marin's eyes flickered to me as if I had spoken, not Rose. "You have no idea how hard it used to be for us. When we were young, people were as superstitious as they'd been in John White's time. We lived in constant fear that one of us would reveal an element." She took a calming breath. "When the world changed, we had a choice: Tell you that you're nature's mistake, or allow you to be the perfect humans you are. We gave you the one thing we'd always dreamed of: a colony free from non-elementals, where we could be truly ourselves."

She sat up straighter now, confident in the truth of her words. "But now we're living with non-elementals again. And while the world may have changed, attitudes haven't. If any-one finds out what we can do, they'll kill us without hesitation, simply out of fear. Which is why we've promised to put our elements behind us."

"No." My father smacked his fist against the blankets. "They need to practice."

"So someone can give our secret away? Or maybe Thomas'll accidentally kill someone else." She stood and placed a claw-like hand on Dennis's shoulder. "Think we'd survive that, do you, Ordyn?"

"The elements are more important now than ever," he insisted.

"Not to us, they're not." She nudged Dennis toward the door.

"Where are you going?" demanded Rose.

"Our colony is no more. Your father is dead, and our elements are done. Chief has found a different room for us, Rose. If this is home now, we should be looking forward, not back. We should be joining our new family, not staying with the old." She picked up Dennis's bag and paused beside the door. "Come along."

Rose seemed frozen in shock. There was no ignoring the finality of what her mother was doing. Dennis sensed it too, and hesitated, torn between the people he'd always known and the mother he trusted above all of us.

My thoughts returned to the conversation with Chief. When he'd asked me if Marin was happy, he already knew the answer. Which meant that he wasn't really asking for my opinion at all. He was trying to work out if he could trust me.

"Rose?" Marin said her daughter's name without enthusiasm, a question she didn't much care to have answered. When she received only silence in return, she didn't even seem disappointed. "Your father would be ashamed of you."

She left without a backward glance. The door swung shut behind Dennis. In the quiet of the room I counted seven people. Our colony—fractured and decimated—was no longer a colony. It wasn't even a cohesive group, just the residue from centuries of lies.

CHAPTER 21

claimed two portions of dinner and carried one to my father, grateful for a reason to avoid Chief. Father was sleeping, so I ate one bowl and left the other beside his bed.

Outside, I climbed the metal staircase that ran against the battery and wandered across the roof. Beyond the roof was the esplanade, a large area on the same level. The flat grounds were covered in rows of plants. There was grass too, brown, worn thin by the long summer. A stone monument rose a yard above it all.

I took a seat on the monument and surveyed the harbor. It was dark now. Stars glittered to life above me. Waves brushed against the tiny island, soft and hypnotic.

Footsteps on the staircase broke the quiet. It took me a moment to recognize Dennis's figure, and longer for him to recognize mine. He stopped a few yards away, and turned to leave.

"Don't go," I said. "Please."

He hesitated, then shuffled onto the stone beside me.

"My father made me promise not to talk to you."

"I know. I'm sorry." I wasn't sure why I said that, but I meant it. Dennis had lost his father. Maybe his sister too, if things didn't get resolved between Rose and Marin. "Your father was probably trying to protect Rose. You've seen what I can do. Or maybe it was because Dare was my uncle."

He raised his hands. "So? You never knew that before. It's not fair." He dangled his legs from the monument. His feet bounced against it. Seeing him like this reminded me how young he was—still only nine.

"How's your new room?"

"Weird. Mother was so pleased to get away from you all. But no one in that room will talk to me. They smile and nod, but . . . something's not right."

"They're probably just not used to you yet."

"No. It's more than that. Chief made two of the adults give us their beds. It doesn't make sense. If this is home now, why should I get a bed? Why should adults sleep on the floor?"

"It's strange," I agreed. "Do you want to move back to our room? It's all right if you do."

He thought about this. "No. I want my mother to stay with you. Then I'll come back too." The answer seemed to satisfy him. "Do you like Rose?"

I hesitated. "Yes. Although . . . it's more than that. It's kind of difficult to explain."

Dennis nodded sagely. "That's okay. You can try now. She's standing right behind you."

I spun around. Rose met my eyes, flushed red, and looked

away again just as quickly. As Dennis left us alone, she wandered over to the perimeter wall, tiptoeing the edge.

"Planning to jump?" I asked, joining her. The sheer wall plunged into stacked boulders. Waves lapped against them.

"No. Just realizing how much water there is in the world." She crouched down, hair blown about in the wind, and tightened the blanket wrapped around her shoulders. "It's strange, but I've never really *thought* about water until now. It just existed, like my element. Now I realize what I'll lose if I let it all go."

I suspected this wasn't just about water and her element. "Dennis is going to be all right."

"Only if my mother comes around. And I don't think that's going to happen."

She raised a hand and I helped her up. We wandered past the rows of plantings. When we reached an open area, she laid her blanket on the ground. "Stay with me?"

I put my water canister down and lay beside her. Side by side we stared at evening sky.

"Do you trust the Guardians now they've told us everything?" she asked.

"*If* they've told us everything. That's the problem, I guess. We'll never know."

"True. I heard Alice and Tarn arguing outside the main gate during dinner. They stopped when they saw me, but I don't think Alice trusts her mother anymore."

"I'm not sure she trusts anyone anymore."

"You're probably right." Rose sighed. "Do you trust Chief?"

Maybe it was the way she asked, her voice uneven, but the question felt awkward. "Why are you asking?"

She glanced toward the battery steps before continuing. "As soon as you all left today, he stopped what he was doing and disappeared. One moment, he was tending to the goats. The next, he'd gone. I kept an eye out for him, but didn't see him until a couple strikes later. He was coming out of the room that Jerren says he's never seen."

"The gunroom, he called it."

"Exactly. It might mean nothing," she added hurriedly. "Or it might be important."

I almost wished she hadn't told me that. "I don't know who to trust, Rose."

She tilted her head toward me and smiled. "Yes, you do. You can trust me."

She'd rolled up the sleeves of her tunic, revealing her bare arms. The skin was slightly pink, sunburned, but perfectly smooth. I ran a finger along her right arm and she stiffened momentarily, then let out a long breath. I was relaxed for once, and the discomfort she'd braced for wasn't there. She shuffled closer to me so that our bodies were touching.

"What does it feel like, your element?" Her words were tiny breaths punching the air. I felt them as much as I heard them.

"Like tiredness. Like ache." I propped my head up on my arm. "Used to, anyway. It's not as bad now, but I wish it would fade faster."

Rose didn't hide her disappointment. "I don't want to lose

159

my element. When we were on the ship, I couldn't tell for sure that the water was fresh. We might've gotten sick. Someone might've died. And I would've felt like it was my fault."

"You can do other things—"

"Anyone can do other things, Thomas. That's not the point. I don't see what's so wrong about being special."

I let my finger slide off her arm. "Being here with you . . . I couldn't have done that at Roanoke."

"I guess so. But you could learn. Like you learned to channel your element." She bit her lip. It looked nervous and cute all at once. "Would you do it to me? Take over my element, I mean."

Just thinking about it sent me back to our last night on the ship—how I'd seized control of Ananias's apologetic sparks and propelled them into flames. How I'd sent a man to his death.

"Hey," she whispered. "It's all right." She stroked my cheek as if she were calming a wild animal. "Everything is all right."

She reached for her canister and sniffed the contents, challenging herself to connect with water the way she used to. But she couldn't do it. I could see it in her eyes.

Before I could change my mind, I wrapped my arms around her and focused on the water inside the canister. My pulse was quick, but as long as I focused on the water, the energy surged right through her.

Rose didn't pull away.

I could feel her regaining control of her own element, forcing the liquid out of the canister in a slow, perfect arc.

She opened her mouth, ready to drink. Her eyes shone with the miracle of it. At least until the water touched her lips. Then I sent a rush of power that spattered the liquid across her face.

She gasped. "You . . . pig!" She tried to brush the water off her suddenly wet tunic, then burst out laughing instead. "I was actually thirsty!"

"So try picking up the canister with your hands. It's what I've been doing all these years."

I meant for it to come out as a joke, but it fell flat. Maybe deep down, I kind of meant it.

Rose lifted the canister and drank. "You're right," she said. "It works this way too."

She lay back down then, wet tunic and all, and reached for my hands. She dragged my arms across her. "It's your job to keep me warm now. You know, since you're the one who got me wet."

She held my hands and pressed them against her chest. I couldn't decide what was more amazing: the feeling of holding her, or that she'd forgiven me for being stupid.

We were still after that. Nothing but our breathing and heartbeats to tell us apart. Concentrating so hard on my element had left me tired. My pulse wasn't racing anymore.

"I felt you, Thomas." Rose swallowed hard. "Felt your element running through me. It was gentle and warm. I was controlling the water, but you were controlling me." She closed her mouth, then opened it again. Her breaths were fast and shallow. "There was no pain. I . . . I liked it."

For a moment, the words hung between us. They were more than words, though. In them was a promise.

There was so little distance between us. I studied the arch of her eyebrows and the way the breeze toyed with her hair, each loose strand silhouetted by the setting sun. As she played with the glass pendant around her neck, her hands shook.

Rose lifted my hand to her cheek. I ran my fingers over every part of her face and lips. She closed her eyes, and I closed mine, and when our lips came together it felt completely natural. I still half expected her to pull away, for closeness to shift toward pain. But the energy, or adrenaline, or fear, or whatever usually came between us wasn't there this time.

I ran my hand behind her head and pulled her closer. Kissed her over and over, madly, fumbling for everything at once. She dragged me on top of her and I felt her legs and her chest. The moment I'd dreamed of was finally—impossibly—here.

I was as alive as I'd ever been.

CHAPTER 22

We woke up as the sun rose. My clothes were damp from the grass and I was sore from the hard ground. Cold too. Rose and I came together for a moment and shared body heat while I ran my fingers in slow circles around the small of her back.

A strand of hair fell across her face, so I eased it away. Eyes still closed, she batted at it as if it were an insect. I couldn't help smiling. There was something so instinctive about it. I was reminded that everything had felt that way until a couple weeks ago.

"What are you thinking about?" I asked, breaking the silence.

She opened her eyes halfway and ran the backs of her fingers across my right cheek. "Hatteras. I thought what we had there was real, but it was a lie. Now I want to believe that this is real, but . . . I don't know. It's just this feeling I have. You know what I mean?"

I rolled onto my back and sighed. "Yes, I do."

163

Scanning the area around us to make sure no one was there, Rose leaned across me and planted a kiss on my lips. "So what's bothering you?"

"Right now? Well, Chief told me that Kell is his right hand. He also said Jerren is like a son to him. But those two are hiding things from each other, and maybe from him too." I fought to concentrate; it wasn't easy with Rose so close. "I'm worried that they were both so interested in Dare's cabin."

Her eyes opened wide. "You think it was Kell who disturbed us on the ship?"

"I'm sure of it. What I don't understand is why he and Jerren were there at night in the first place. What's ours is theirs, right? They could've just gone during the daytime." I took a deep breath. Saying everything out loud was making my concerns feel more real, not less. "No. There's something more. What if neither of them is playing by Chief's rules anymore?"

"Then we stay out of it."

I gave a wry laugh. "Try telling Alice that."

"Are she and Jerren . . ." Rose raised an eyebrow questioningly.

"If they're not, I reckon they will be soon. Anyway, staying out of it might not be an option. Griffin noticed that Dare's logbooks were missing some pages from about a month ago. He traced the ship's course to Hatteras, but we don't know where Dare came from. What if he visited *here*?"

Rose rolled her eyes. "Dare could've come from anywhere. And even if you don't trust Kell and Jerren, do you really think Chief would keep something like that from you?"

"I don't know anymore." I puffed out my cheeks and let the air out in a steady stream. "I just want this place to be perfect, you know? Without all the stuff that tore our colony apart."

"Sumter doesn't have to be perfect to be good, Thomas. I mean, I know one person I can always trust." She leaned in to kiss me. "And we couldn't do this on Hatteras. Or . . . this."

She opened her mouth, and so did I. The energy that flowed between us then had nothing to do with an element. It was more powerful than that, more all-consuming. And still I needed more. I slid my hands down her back and found the hem of her tunic. I pulled it upward, her bare skin perfectly smooth against my fingertips. When I reached her chest, she pulled away from me slightly so that I could lift it over her shoulders.

We heard the footsteps at the same time. Slow and heavy, coming from the battery.

Rose sat bolt upright and adjusted her tunic back down. The footsteps stopped at the first level. She reached out and took my hand, relief written all over her face.

Then the footsteps started again. Someone was climbing the stairs to the esplanade.

There was a bank about ten yards away. It looked like the other side was only a yard or so lower than where we were, but we crawled over and hid behind it. I didn't stop to think about why we were hiding, or how guilty it made us look. I just knew that I didn't want us to be seen.

The new arrival paused at the top of the steps. At first, I was relieved because it meant we probably wouldn't be found.

But why climb the steps at all, then? Unless he or she was looking for someone.

Or making sure that no one was around.

As the footsteps receded, I pulled myself up and stole a quick look. I didn't see much, just the top of his head, but as the light caught the wisps of gray hair, I knew it was Chief.

Several footsteps later there was the sound of a door opening. There was a click as Chief closed it behind him.

Rose exhaled slowly. "Please tell me that wasn't Chief."

"At least it wasn't your mother."

She wasn't amused. "He's in the gunroom again. All those weapons—it scares me. Why is he visiting at dawn anyway?"

"I don't know. But I do know he didn't want anyone to see him."

We lay side by side again, but apart now. Kissing Rose already felt like a distant memory.

"We need to know what's in there," she said. "And soon."

The words could've come from Alice, but Rose's tone was different. Where Alice would've been looking to prove someone's guilt, Rose just wanted to reassure herself that everything was all right. At least we were in agreement about that.

"There's no way we're getting in that room, Rose."

"We won't have to." She wrapped her fingers around her pendant. "Anyone would notice you or me sneaking in. But what about Dennis?"

"No."

"He's small, Thomas. If someone were to leave the room in a hurry, he could slide in before the door closes."

"He shouldn't get involved in this—"

"He's already *involved* in this." She huffed. "He's split between us, my mother, and everyone new at Sumter. He doesn't want to leave us. Anyway, has it occurred to you that he might want answers too? He's not stupid, you know."

"I know." I wasn't sure what I felt worse about: getting Dennis mixed up in everything, or telling Rose she didn't know what was best for her own brother. "How can we make someone leave that room in a hurry?" I asked finally.

"Oh, I can think of a way." She smiled to herself. "Want to hold my hand again?"

CHAPTER 23

Rose told Dennis what we wanted him to do. I almost hoped he'd say no, but he didn't. After a lifetime of open spaces, he felt cooped up in Sumter. Checking out a room that no one else had seen was irresistible to him.

That's what he said, anyway. But from the way he watched Rose the whole time, I wondered if he would've agreed to anything just to be with her again.

Two strikes after sunrise, Dennis hid in a shadowy space beneath the battery stairs, exactly as we'd told him. Down on the parade grounds, Rose and I stood beside the sewer entrance.

"Ready?" she asked.

"No," I answered truthfully. But I took her hand anyway.

I didn't think the diversion would work. The water level was at least a couple yards below us and our elements were as weak as they'd ever been. People wandered back and forth, a constant distraction. But my heart was pounding and so was hers. So I sent my energy through her and watched.

168

The stench grew worse as the waste reversed course. I closed my eyes and felt her element respond to my touch. I was vaguely aware of the liquid's progress, but when I heard a shout, my first thought was that we'd been caught.

Rose let go of my hand and we split, taking separate staircases up the battery. Behind us, the colonists were gathering, staring with alarm at the filth strewn across the ground. It formed a dark circle in a yard radius around the sewer entrance.

Kell joined them momentarily and slipped away, making a direct line for the gunroom.

I retreated to the corridor just outside our room and spied from the shadows as Chief accompanied Kell outside. I would have kept watch too, but Griffin and Nyla were in the corridor and I didn't want them to be suspicious.

They sat cross-legged opposite each other, signing in the half-light. Amazingly, Nyla already signed better than some of the Guardians ever had.

Good. Signs, I told her.

She accepted the compliment without smiling. *Useful,* she returned, the gesture too small, like she was still afraid of getting it wrong. "Imagine how this'll change the food squads," she said. "Jerren says the gatherers work in the same area so they can hear each other. But with signs, they could move anywhere, as long as the lookouts still see each other."

The more she spoke, the more excited she became. Even though he couldn't hear her, she looked at Griffin from time to time like she was seeking his approval. Her signs were more natural and confident with him around too. She smiled, which I hadn't seen before.

I peered around the corner to see if Dennis had left the gunroom, but he hadn't. He needed to get out. He was only there to look around and report back to us.

As I turned back to Griffin and Nyla, a young child's cry split the air. It was loud enough to startle Nyla. The others flooded out from our room and joined me on the walkway.

Kell was marching Dennis toward us. Rose was running up from behind them. Her mother too. Even the people working on the parade grounds paused what they were doing to watch.

"What's going on?" cried Marin. "Are you all right, Dennis?"

Kell stared at every one of us, weighing our guilt. "Dennis decided to pay a visit to a room . . . a *private* room."

Under other circumstances, we might have been able to pass it off as an innocent mistake. But from the way Dennis was shaking, it was obvious he knew he'd done wrong.

Marin was desolate. "Why did you do such a thing?" she asked him. "Did someone tell you to go in there?"

Dennis didn't answer. But his eyes shifted to Rose as if he was waiting for her to save him.

Marin understood well enough what the look meant. "What have you done, Rose?" she hissed.

"I didn't know what was inside the room," said Rose. "It scared me."

"Is that so?" Kell sneered. "Well then, ask your brother what's in there. Ask him what we have lined up against the

170

walls. What horrible little secrets have we been keeping from you all, Dennis?"

Dennis shrank back from him. "There were guns. Lots of guns."

"Lots of *loaded* guns," corrected Kell. "The kind that might accidentally kill a child if he got hold of them. The kind that any responsible colony would kept locked away." He gritted his teeth. "If you think you need one of those guns, Rose, you should've asked. Although I'd like to know what you plan to do with it."

Chief had joined us now. He looked from one to another of us. "I don't understand," he said. "One moment, I'm on the parade grounds dealing with a serious health issue, the next I hear that you took advantage of the situation to spy on us. If you'd just asked me, I would have told you what was in that room." His voice had an unfamiliar edge. "Please, tell me what we've done to make you so distrustful."

I should have held my tongue, but I couldn't stand the way that everyone was turning on Rose. "Kell boarded the ship the second night we were here," I told Chief.

He hesitated. "Is that true, Kell?"

Kell didn't miss a beat. "Yes. I saw a light through one of the portholes. I got to wondering who'd board their own ship in the dead of night. And why."

"You went into the captain's cabin," I snapped.

"As did *you*, even though you told us you hadn't. How else would you have heard our radio transmission?" He paused to let the words sink in. "The thing I really want to know is

how you got back into the fort that night without me notic-
ing. Seems that if anybody has been keeping secrets, it's you,
Thomas."

Chief was hunched over now. He looked older than before.
"I trusted you, Thomas," he said quietly. "I really did. But trust
works two ways. I sincerely hope you'll think ours is worth
winning back. If not, I'd urge you to find another home."

He turned to leave. Kell stayed right beside him, his alle-
giance unquestioned.

No one else moved.

"There was something else," began Dennis, but Marin cut
him off.

"Enough!" Her eyes roamed from Rose to me as though
she couldn't decide which of us she hated more. "Stay away
from Dennis. You told us not to use our elements anymore,
Thomas, yet from the mess over there, I can see you dared to
combine with Rose. In full view. Never mind the dangers of
having human filth strewn across the ground." Her voice was
quiet but venomous, anger visible in every twitch. "As for you,
Rose, a real sister would never have done what you did today."
She pulled Dennis toward her, hands draped over his shoulders possessively as he tried to wriggle free. "Do whatever you
like, but understand this: Dennis and I will be staying here. I
will not let you jeopardize his future."

As Marin dragged Dennis away, he kept his head turned
back and eyes fixed on us. I expected him to appear as angry
as his mother did. Marin was right. We'd taken advantage of
his trust. Instead, he looked conflicted about the side he'd

been made to choose. Or was it more than that? He mouthed a silent word as he retreated, but I couldn't make it out.

Ananias placed a hand on my shoulder. "What were you thinking, Thomas?"

"Look, something's going on between Kell and Jerren—"

"So? That's their problem, not ours." His voice rose with every word. "What'll happen to Father if they throw us out? What'll happen to any of us? There's no food on that ship. If they make us leave, not one of us will survive—"

"I'm sorry," I snapped. "All right? I'm sorry."

There was a flash of anger in Ananias's eyes. He was bigger than me and stronger. If he wanted to hurt me, it wouldn't be a close fight, especially without full use of my element. But the anger didn't last. "*You* brought us here, Thomas. *You* were the one who said everything would work out. We doubted you, but it turns out, you were right. And now that we're safe, you're risking everything to prove you were wrong. If they knew that *you* had done that to the sewer . . ." He squeezed my shoulder. "We have friends now. Allies. You can stop doubting that everything is real."

Alice and Tarn watched me with looks of disappointment and confusion. Griffin and Nyla too. Chief had opened up to me more than to anyone else. Of all of us, I was the one who should have trusted him. If I still had doubts, how could anyone else be reassured by what they saw all around them?

Rose hurried past them, heading toward our room. I ran after her, and caught up to her in the corridor.

"This is all my fault," she whispered.

"No, it's mine too."

"I have no one now." She drew a quick breath. "I have nothing left."

I wrapped her in a hug. "You have me."

She was shaking. "Dennis mouthed a word as he left. It looked like *rat*." She must have felt me sigh, because she added, "That's what I *think*, anyway."

I wiped away her tears. "We'll ask him, all right? Later on, when your mother isn't around."

She nodded then, and we hugged. And in the silence of the corridor, I realized at last that Ananias was right: There was no need to doubt that everything was real, when the most real thing of all was right in front of me.

CHAPTER 24

I hid out in our room for the rest of the morning. Maybe it was cowardly, but I couldn't stand the thought of everyone staring at me, knowing what I'd done.

Away from everyone else, I tended to my father. I collected water so that he could wash himself, and helped him pace slowly around the room to get his muscles working again. Someone, Tarn maybe, had left a pile of clean clothes beside his bed. I turned away while he dressed. In a fresh tunic, he looked almost human again.

It must have been around lunchtime when Ananias joined us. He carried a small wooden object in one hand and a bowl of water in the other.

"I'm not thirsty," I said.

"It's not to drink."

He placed the bowl on the floor beside Father's bunk. Then, with a flick of the wrist, he opened up the wooden object. A razor-sharp blade emerged.

"What are you doing?" I asked.

He studied Father's face. "Shaving him. At least, I was going to, but it can wait until he's up again." He gave the razor to me handle first. "For now, you can shave me."

The razor felt surprisingly light in my hand. "Whose is it?"

"Kell's."

"So why don't you get him to shave you?"

"Kell?" Ananias raised an eyebrow. "I'm not stupid enough to let him near me with a blade. His idea of fun is shooting birds with a bow and arrow. I'd hate to think what he might do to my neck . . . especially after Dennis's adventure this morning."

The blade was so clean and shiny that I caught a little of my reflection in it. It was the first time I'd seen myself in days. My face was bruised, just like Alice's. I had a thin coating of stubble, just like Ananias. I looked older than before.

"I'm sorry," I said. "I've made things difficult for everyone."

Ananias nodded. "Well, I'm sorry for what I said to you. I panicked. I was scared about being thrown out of the colony. I was scared for Father. For all of us."

He pulled a small tub from his pocket and popped the lid off. Once he'd splashed water on his face, he took a glob of the stuff inside and smeared it across his cheeks, chin, and neck. "Kell says this helps."

"What's it made of?"

"I don't know. Don't want to know, either. Anything that smells this bad can't be good."

Usually we'd have smiled at that. Now it just melted the ice a little.

"So start," said Ananias.

"Start what?"

"Shaving me. And telling me what's really going on in Sumter."

He clamped his mouth shut and waited. I didn't know where to begin. Rose and I had made a mistake and paid for it. Shouldn't we be looking forward, not back?

"I trust you, Thomas," murmured Ananias. "You're the reason I'm still alive, remember? So please, help me understand what's going on here."

The words poured out of me then. Over several careful blade strokes, I told him how we'd boarded the ship and found Jerren there. I mentioned Jerren and Kell's rivalry, and the gunroom.

Ananias didn't speak at all, or move, or even blink. His breathing was steady. I wanted him to have questions, if only so that I'd know he wasn't as anxious as me. But even when I'd finished shaving him, his mind seemed to be elsewhere.

I rinsed the razor in the bowl and handed it to him.

"You haven't got much to shave," he said.

"No. But something tells me you've got something to say as well."

We were both holding the razor now. Finally, Ananias gave a slow nod.

I washed my face and applied the goo just as he had done. Then I sat perfectly still before him and watched flashes of lamplight reflected in the blade.

He didn't speak for the first couple sweeps. The blade

scraped down my cheek. He rinsed it and started again. "It's Eleanor," he said finally.

Another sweep, this time all the way to my chin. He was shaking. I felt it in every tiny vibration. His eyes filled with tears.

My instinct was to say something reassuring, but I couldn't move with the blade against me. This was the way he wanted it too. Ananias didn't want any interruptions.

"I don't know what happened the night she fell," he continued. "When I climbed the mast, I thought she was still on the ladder. But when I got to the top, she was out of reach, hanging from the rope."

Another rinse. Slow and methodical. Something to distract him from what he had to say.

"I made a flame. I needed to see her face clearly, and I wanted her to see me too. I thought, even with everything that had happened to us, it would reassure her. But the look in her eyes . . ." He pulled the blade away from my neck and exhaled deeply. "It was like she'd never seen me before. She was frightened of me, I think. Truly frightened."

Ananias eased my chin up so that he could reach the curve of my neck. I swallowed hard.

"Then Alice joined us. I stopped the flame because I thought I might be able to grab Eleanor, and I needed both hands for that. But when my eyes adjusted to the darkness again . . ." He blinked, sending a stream of tears down his face. "I figured that seeing Alice would calm Eleanor down. But it didn't. The way she was looking at us . . ." Ananias wasn't even watching me anymore, but the razor still continued its course. "Eleanor didn't fall, Thomas. She jumped."

I flinched. The blade stopped moving, a sudden adjustment that nicked my skin. I felt the coolness of it, then the heat of blood rushing to the surface.

Ananias lifted the razor and held it in front of him. The blade was tinged with red. "I'm sorry," he mumbled. "I . . . I'm—"

The door creaked opened. I hadn't heard anyone outside, and the timing of the arrival felt too convenient to be an accident.

It was Rose. She padded over to us and took the blade from Ananias. He didn't try to stop her. And once he was free of the burden, he seemed to awake from a trance.

He left without a word.

Beside us, my father didn't stir.

Rose dabbed the sleeve of her tunic in the water and cleaned blood from the cut.

"You were listening, weren't you?" I asked.

She nodded. Blade ready, she continued what Ananias had started. Her strokes were calm and steady, but I could see in her expression that his news had shaken her up just as much as me.

"Ever since we got to Sumter, Alice has been so quiet," said Rose. "So lost. We should've been there for her, Thomas." She removed the razor and rinsed it.

"I thought she was grieving."

"Sure she was. But I don't think that's why I've been stay-

179

ing away from her." She ran the blade over my cheek one last time. "I've spent so long seeing her as a rival . . . it just never occurred to me that she might need my help. My friendship."

Rose rubbed the remaining goo off my face with her sleeve. My skin felt even more alive at her touch than it had earlier.

"Do you think Eleanor really jumped?" I asked.

"I don't know. But Alice clearly thinks so. That's probably why she was arguing with Tarn last night—she's looking for answers again. And I don't think she's getting them." She finished cleaning the blade and handed it to me.

"Talking of answers, have you spoken to Dennis yet?"

"No. He's closely guarded. It'll be a while before I can get him alone." She rolled up the sleeves of her tunic. "Your turn now."

"To do what?"

"Cut my hair."

I was about to fold the blade away when she stopped me.

"I'm serious, Thomas. I want it gone." Her hand rested on mine. My pulse was growing faster, but she refused to let the pain show. The fierceness of her expression reminded me of someone else in our colony.

"Just because Alice has changed, doesn't mean you need to take her place, Rose."

"I've lost my father. My mother hates me. I betrayed my brother. This isn't about becoming Alice. It's about not being me anymore." She gave a tired sigh. "If this is our new home, then let it feel new to me. Give me the chance to be who I want to be, not who I was."

She let go of my hand then, but her eyes remained fixed on me. She was imploring me to do this, to be the one person she could still count on.

I liked Rose's hair. But I loved Rose. So I tugged the blade through the blond locks until the uneven strands fell tight against her neck.

When I was done, she didn't ask to see her reflection in the blade. She didn't ask me what I thought, either. She just gazed at me once more. Maybe she was deciphering my feelings from the way I gazed back.

Rose had wanted to change. Well, now she was different. And from the way she was looking at me, it was about much more than her hair.

CHAPTER 25

Alice and Jerren were rigging the catamarans in preparation for our journey to Fort Moultrie. Unlike the day before, they moved slowly, half their attention on the job and half on each other. Alice had taken to wearing a tank top that scooped low at her chest and ended a couple inches above her waist. Her tanned skin glistened with sweat. Sunlight caught the ripple of muscles in her arms and stomach.

Jerren noticed me watching him and turned away. He was embarrassed too—I could see it in the way he fought to make a simple knot—but he shouldn't have been. Even I found it hard not to peek as Alice paused to lick the sweat off her upper lip.

Now Jerren was watching me, and I was the one turning red.

"Have you seen Griffin?" Alice asked.

Hearing her voice startled me. After what Ananias had told me, it was hard not to look at her differently. "Not since this morning."

"He wanted to tell you something."

That was strange. I hadn't been hard to find. I began to walk back toward the gate when Kell emerged, Nyla beside him.

"Where's Griffin?" I asked her.

She wouldn't look at me. "He's resting. Spent most of the night reading."

"How would you know?"

She coiled a loop of hair around her ear. "I was with him."

"What about Ananias? Why isn't he here either?"

Kell leaned closer. "Turns out, Chief has a new favorite, Thomas. Can't think what the old one did to offend him. Can you?"

Before I could ask him what they were doing, Rose passed through the main gate and headed toward us, a pack slung across her shoulders.

"Are you coming too?" I asked her.

"Yes. Chief wants me to fill in for Griffin."

"Why?"

Nyla scraped her foot across the dusty ground. "I told you. He's resting."

Everything felt off-kilter. I wanted to see my brother, just to check that everything was all right. But Kell stopped me with an outstretched hand. "Where are you going?"

"To see Griffin."

Kell spat on the ground. "Tell him, Alice," he shouted. "No way Thomas will listen to me."

Alice peered over her shoulder. "Griffin can't come," she

said. "We'll be using a series of shouts to let each other know if we see rats. He wouldn't hear anything."

"But he can sign," I said. "Nyla had an idea for how we can work farther apart—"

"No." Kell brushed by me and headed for the boats. "Nyla's idea needs all of us to learn the signs. We don't play with lives on Moultrie. He'll get plenty of work during gathering trips to other sites, just not this one. But Rose has agreed to take his place." He raised an eyebrow. "If that's okay with you?"

As Rose approached her, Alice stopped what she was doing. "Interesting haircut," she said. "Tell me who did it and I'll get them for you."

Rose broke out in a smile. Alice did too.

Nyla began to walk to the boats. "What are you doing?" Kell asked her.

"Going with you," she replied. "You're a person short. Can't make pairs with five people."

"It's all right," Jerren shouted. "She can help me. It's time she learned the drill. Besides," he added, fixing Kell with a stare, "something tells me she may be helpful to us."

Kell didn't speak for a moment. "Fair enough," he said with a forced, icy calm. "Come on, Thomas. Time to leave."

Again, I stared at the main gate. Through the small doorway, I noticed that the grounds were unusually empty. Children peeked above the battlements until their parents dragged them away.

Kell rejoined me. "Don't mind them," he said with uncharacteristic softness. "Poor things always know when we're heading to Moultrie. They tell stories to give each other night-mares: a hundred dead. A thousand. Rat bites, snake bites, ghost bites . . . in their minds the place is a giant graveyard." He sighed. "Heaven help them when they have to start going over."

It wasn't just the children watching us, though. Even the parents cast anxious looks in our direction.

"Jerren's parents really did die, though," I reminded him. "It's not all make-believe."

He grabbed my arm. "You can keep thoughts like that to yourself. This is Nyla's first trip to Moultrie. I don't need her panicking. Understand?"

Kell pulled a map from his pack and spread it out on the jetty. He pointed out the fort itself, and the landmarks inside its walls. He told us about the land that lay between the fort and the water, and the plants we'd find there. Once we had a mental image of the area, he folded it back up and left it in a box. He never mentioned rats, because he didn't need to.

Jerren untethered the rope that connected us to the jetty and we pushed off. The breeze nudged the sail, but Jerren held the mainsheet fast, at least until we were twenty yards away. Then he loosed the mainsheet and the sail kicked out, driving us across open water.

The wind was stronger than the previous day and we made quick progress. Behind us, the rust-colored walls of Sumter grew smaller. I squinted at the battlements, hoping that I'd catch a glimpse of Griffin and Ananias. Neither of them was there.

Ahead of us, Alice's boat sliced through the water. I imagined her shouting instructions to Rose and Nyla, anything to ensure that they arrived first. Jerren, on the other hand, seemed content to take things easy.

"So what's the story with Alice's father?" he asked me. "She hasn't mentioned him once, and the man tried to strangle her."

"Did Chief tell you that?"

"No. But you just did." Jerren paused. "So who stopped him?"

"Ananias and me."

"You killed him."

"No. He fell overboard."

Kell laughed. "He *fell*? Kind of clumsy, isn't it?"

I didn't know if they were working together, but it was clear they didn't believe me. "He was surprised."

"By what?" asked Jerren. "That you wouldn't let him kill his own daughter? Or that you set fire to him?"

There was no use in pretending he was wrong. The real question was how he knew at all.

"There were burn marks on Alice's tunic," Jerren explained. "I asked her about them and she wouldn't tell me anything. This morning, she turned up in new clothes. And I got to thinking, why would Alice and Tarn keep something like that to themselves? And if you're responsible, why are they standing by you?"

It took all my concentration to stay calm. Jerren and Kell had chosen me for their boat deliberately. They had ques-

186

tions, and didn't want Alice along to answer for me. I was already trying to second-guess what she might have said.

I expected them to press me for an answer. But neither of them spoke again. It was as if I'd already told them everything they needed to know.

CHAPTER 26

W e pulled into a beachy cove, where an outcrop of rocks hid us from Sumter and protected the boats from waves. Jerren and Alice tied the catamarans to buoys instead of beaching them. "Rats'll climb on any solid surface," Jerren explained before I could ask. "Trust me, we don't want them on the boats."

We stepped into knee-deep water. Instinctively, I scanned the sandy beach, and beyond, to the trees and grass, and the fort itself. But there was nothing out there.

Not yet, anyway.

Kell removed a container from his bag. "Here," he said, "scoop this into your hand and smear it across every piece of exposed skin." He looked Alice up and down. "That'll take longer for some than for others."

Nyla went first. She used the goo sparingly. It had a pungent odor I couldn't place.

"What is this?" Rose asked.

"Chief's concoction. Some vegetables, herbs, fish oil. He

says it repels fleas. I think he's a liar, but I'd rather stink than get the Plague because one of the suckers bit me, you know?"

While I applied the stuff to my hands and lower legs, Kell went over the rules: A single shout at the first sight of rats. Another shout a moment later. Then run straight to the beach and into the water.

"Don't panic," he reminded us. "Rats aren't fast runners. But don't hesitate, either. The last group that saw rats said they're more aggressive than they used to be. Their food sources are running out, and the day'll come when they go straight for us. If today's that day, get back here. Fast." He watched us carefully, making sure we were listening. "All right. Jerren and Alice will pair. Thomas, you go with Nyla."

"Actually, I'll go with Rose," I said, joining her.

"No, you won't. You'll do what I say because I'm in charge of this gathering. Is that clear?" He didn't say it cruelly, but there was no mistaking his tone. This was another test, just like coming to Moultrie. Fail the test, and we might be looking for a new home soon.

Fort Moultrie was set back from the water, and the flat land fronting it had been thoroughly planted. Kell pointed to a series of wooden posts that divided the area into parcels, each one with a different sun-shade balance that allowed for multiple crops, vegetables, and fruits. It looked familiar from the map he'd shown us.

The plan was for each pair to gather food from one parcel. When everyone was ready, we'd enter the fort itself, where the chilly underground armories acted as storerooms for cured meats. I didn't need to ask which part of the gathering would be most dangerous. There was a reason we'd be entering the fort together.

No one moved when Kell finished explaining the situation. Being close to the boats felt safe, as hard to leave as a blanket on a cold night. I imagined tiny movements across the land even though I hadn't seen anything.

Alice was first to go. She probably did it to wipe the smug expression from Jerren's face. I followed her, and Nyla came with me. When I looked back, Rose was moving too, fear hidden behind a stoic expression.

"Kell didn't want you coming today," I remarked to Nyla.

She narrowed her eyes. "Kell thinks girls should stay inside the fort. Doesn't take years of practice to wash a shirt, though, and I'm not going to be stuck inside Sumter every day of my life. This is my chance to show what I can do. So keep your eyes open. I'll never get another chance if you catch the Plague."

"I'll do my best," I promised. "Griffin wouldn't accept anything less."

I thought she'd like hearing his name. Instead Nyla frowned and pressed ahead to our parcel.

Back across the harbor entrance, Sumter appeared tiny. Hard to believe so many people had lived there for so long, like wasps in a nest, always busy but always together.

"You keep lookout," said Nyla, kneeling beside a row of kale. Some of the leaves had been eaten. "Rabbits," she explained, without turning around. "They'll eat anything, but

Chief likes us to pick the leaves anyway. He uses them in hot infusions and ointments."

I listened without answering, split between watching for rats and keeping an eye on Rose and Kell. They were about fifty yards away. I didn't like the way he stood so close to her as she pulled roots from the ground.

"Here." Nyla handed me her bag, already full, and took mine. She wasted no time, tearing leaves recklessly, eyes flashing from left to right. She didn't trust me as her lookout.

When she'd filled my bag too, we placed them beside a nearby water barrel and switched roles. While she watched the land around us, I filled the two metal buckets that had been left out and watered the roots of the plants, exactly as I'd seen the Guardians do back at our original colony. It didn't take long, and I figured we'd be the first to finish.

We were last. We walked briskly to where the others stood waiting for us. Together again, we followed a path around the perimeter of the fort. Where earlier we'd cast shadows, now the sky was clouding over. It cooled the air and allowed me to stop squinting.

Finally we reached an arch in the western wall. Through it, a tunnel stretched ahead of us. It was maybe ten yards long, but felt more like fifty. Doorways to the side remained in shadow—a haven for anything that wanted to remain unseen.

Suddenly Rose grabbed my hand and pulled me back. "There!" she screamed. "At the end."

I stared through the darkness, trying to find the rat. "Where?"

"It . . . it's gone now." Her hand shook wildly.

Kell circled around us. "Gone, huh? Are you sure you saw something?"

Rose hesitated. "I think so."

Jerren placed a hand on Kell's arm. "Come on," he said calmly. "Whatever it was, we should keep moving."

Kell glared at Rose, and turned his attention to the rest of us. "The powder magazine is through the tunnel. We'll take a left at the end, follow the path around, and go through the gate. The entrance to the building will be right in front of us. Everyone got it?"

He didn't wait for us to nod or say yes. Whether or not Rose had really seen a rat, this needed to be a quick mission. In and out. The good news was that our destination was close to the entrance.

Our footsteps echoed against the brick walls as we crept through the tunnel. At the end was a bright yellow building— no doors or windows as far as I could tell. Kell walked around it and through a gateway. Here was another yellow building, but this one had an arched doorway and windows at the end. It wasn't very light inside, but peering through the metal bars in the door, I could just make out crates stacked against the walls.

Kell yanked the door open. "Over here," he said, pointing to the back. "Leave your bags by the door. Open each crate slowly—we don't know for sure what we'll find inside."

He and Jerren went in and we followed right behind. They

pulled the lid from the first crate and removed two small boxes before retreating to the door.

Alice made eye contact with Rose and me. "Ready?" she asked, fingers placed against the seam below the lid.

We pulled the lid off so slowly, the crate creaked. Alice leaned over and swept her hand around inside, a puzzled expression across her face. "It's empty," she said.

There was a strange sound from behind us. Alice's eyes grew wide.

We spun around together, darting for the door, but it closed before we got there. After that, there was nothing but a resounding clunk as a lock secured it.

With us inside.

CHAPTER 27

Alice threw herself against the bars. "Are you crazy, Jerren?"

He stood back to admire his handiwork. "Crazy? No, but you are."

She thrust a hand through the bars, snatching at his tunic, but she couldn't reach him. "Why are you doing this?"

"Is that a serious question?" Jerren shook his head. "You turn up out of nowhere. There's only a handful of colonies left, but no one's ever seen you before. Oh, and somehow you managed to steal Dare's ship."

I looked for a way out, but there wasn't one. The whole thing was a setup. They'd even made us leave our bags outside because they didn't want to waste the food when they left us behind.

Jerren placed his box on the ground as Kell took a step back.

"You can't do this," said Alice, still defiant and hopeful. "You haven't got it in you to watch us die."

He opened the box. "We won't be watching."

"Correction," said Kell. "*I* won't be watching. Now please get your hand away from there, Jerren."

Jerren froze. He kept his hand over the open box.

"Don't be the first victim, boy. It's not worth it." Kell stepped forward and placed the barrel of a gun against Jerren's head.

Somehow Jerren smiled. "*Boy*, huh?"

"You think I don't know that it was you on the ship the other night?"

"It was me and Rose," I said.

Kell looked up. "Yes. But who helped you get back into the fort without being seen?" He laughed in the face of my silence. "You shouldn't have hidden from us on the ship, Jerren. If you'd just stepped out, we'd have known you had nothing to hide. But then, you *did* have something to hide, didn't you? Wanted to scope it out, see if you could sail it." He *tsk*ed. "I guess your parents would've approved of that."

"Not after you killed them." Jerren gritted his teeth. "I always knew it was you. Always."

Kell raised his hand, but before he could strike Jerren, a figure leaped off the wall and landed on him. His gun bounced harmlessly away.

I'd completely forgotten Nyla had been with us. In his haste, so had Kell. Now Jerren had picked up his gun, as well as the one from his own box. He pointed them both at Kell.

Jerren's hands were shaking from anger, not fear. I could see it in his rigid shoulders and the set of his jaw. "I begged

195

our father not to come to Moultrie that day," he muttered. "I told him it was a trap, but he said I was wrong, that you'd never betray us. Said Mother needed him. And that you were his closest friend."

"Your parents stole supplies and hid them," spat Kell. "They planned to steal our ship too. Chief decided having people like that wasn't good for the long-term health of the colony."

Jerren slammed one of the guns against the bars. The ringing sound reverberated around the tunnels. "Was this where you locked her? Right here? Did she really get bitten at all?"

This time, Kell didn't answer.

"You were going to put me in there too, huh? How was I going to die? A bullet to the head? Or was it going to be slow? Starvation or Plague—a nice, painful death for a traitor."

"As you say, boy: a *traitor*."

There was a click as Jerren cocked the gun. "Where did you put my parents?"

"I don't know what you're talking about." Kell sounded bored now, but I wasn't fooled. He wiped his sleeve across his forehead to hide the perspiration. "I think it's time you gave me back my gun."

Before he could move, Jerren fired. The shot was loud; the scream that followed, deafening. Kell creased up, right hand clasped against his left biceps. Blood was already seeping through his sleeve.

"You shot me!" he yelled in disbelief. "You . . . you shot me."

Jerren lowered the other gun so that it pointed at Kell's leg.

196

"A flesh wound to the arm. Next time it'll be your leg. Now, where are my parents?"

"Let us out, Jerren," Alice implored him. "We can help—"

"Shut up! You're staying right there. You're not one of us, and you never will be." He jabbed the gun closer to Kell's right leg. "As soon as Kell tells me what I want to know, we're done here. But you won't be coming back with us."

Jerren's words must have reassured him, because Kell began talking. "They were buried in a storeroom under one of the cannons. There are dirt mounds there."

Jerren took a deep breath. The tension that had marked his features slowly disappeared. He beckoned Nyla to him and handed her one of the guns. With his free hand he removed a key from his pocket and gave her that too. "Let them out," he told her.

Kell's eyes opened wide. "But . . . you can't. They're not like us."

"*Us?*" Jerren snorted. "There's no *us*, Kell."

Nyla fumbled with the lock. As soon as the door was open, we burst through. Alice snatched the gun from Nyla and pointed it straight at Jerren.

"That's right," said Kell. "Tell him to end this, Alice."

Jerren didn't flinch or turn toward her. It was as if he'd expected nothing else. "Who do you trust right now, Alice?" he asked calmly. "After what you've just heard . . . who do you trust?"

She kept the gun on him a while longer, but then lowered it. When Jerren held out his free hand, she returned it to him.

"There's rope in my bag," he said. "Tie Kell's hands behind his back and throw him in there. Give him a taste of what it's like to be locked up."

Alice and I tied Kell's hands and legs securely and pulled him to his feet. Rose stood behind him and pushed him, shuffling, into the cell. Immediately, Nyla closed the door again and locked it.

I stepped forward to stop her and felt a click at the side of my head. "Rose stays in there too, Thomas," said Jerren. "I'm not going to risk you three turning on me."

Alice shot him a furious look. "Let her out, Jerren. This is stupid."

He kept the two guns on us. "No, it's not. She'll be fine. Something tells me your knots are as good as anyone's." He smiled. "Even Kell here will be free soon, as long as those directions work out. If we dig up those mounds and find nothing there, though . . . well, then Kell's stay here will get extended."

Kell broke eye contact.

"Want to change your mind on those directions?" Jerren taunted.

Kell spat through the bars. "Your parents are under the lookout tower. Go through the iron door and down the steps to the end of the corridor. There's a chamber on the right. It's sealed. They're inside. Can't promise what kind of state they'll be in, though."

Jerren flicked his hand, signaling for Alice and me to go.

Rose shuffled to the corner of the cell, as far from Kell as possible.

"Please, Jerren," I tried again. "Rose doesn't need to stay."

"It's all right," she called out. From the shadows, she fixed her gaze on Jerren, not me. "I want him to understand that he can trust us. And if locking me in here with his parents' murderer pleases him, then so be it."

If she was trying to make him feel guilty, it didn't seem to be working.

"Let me stay instead," I pleaded.

Rose huffed. "No, Thomas. Just hurry up so we can get back to Sumter." She watched Kell from the corner of her eye. "I don't think Kell is acting alone."

That hadn't occurred to me. I'd figured all of this was just one more twist in the secret battle between Kell and Jerren. "Did someone put you up to this?"

Kell hesitated. He knew he was supposed to keep quiet, but couldn't resist the power of his knowledge. Wanted to see its effect on us. "Chief knows everything. *Everything.* What interests me is what he has planned for your parents and siblings." He bowed his head, but kept his eyes fixed on us. "I'd say it can't be any worse than this, but history tells me that's not true."

CHAPTER 28

J erren turned and ran. Nyla was right behind him. They had the key to the cell, which meant we had no choice but to follow. I wouldn't let him leave the island until Rose had been released. And from Alice's expression, I could tell that she wouldn't either.

We crossed the undulating grounds, eyes flitting from right to left, taking in every detail of the sun-scorched grass. Rats might be big enough to see with the naked eye, but missing one could be so costly. Only Jerren seemed to be focused on what was in front of him, as if seeing his parents again could override the dangers we were facing.

Moultrie was no bigger than Sumter, but I was disoriented. Gaps appeared in man-made banks, dark tunnels leading who-knew-where? Jerren knew where he was going, though. He moved from grass to path and sprinted up a series of steps to the lookout tower. From here we had a clear view to Sumter, a mile away. Were we being watched at that very moment?

Or were Chief's men busy dealing with the remaining members of our colony?

Jerren stopped beside a green metal door. He wasn't waving the guns at us anymore—barely seemed to notice us at all—but Alice and I didn't take advantage of the situation. This was a quest to find his parents and put the past to rest.

He took a moment before opening the door. Stairs led down to a corridor that felt more like a tunnel. The light was low, the temperature strikingly cooler than outside. To either side were rooms, full of furniture encased behind glass. Parallel bars ran vertically along the entire corridor. From the way he walked slowly, I knew that this part of the fort was new to Jerren, and he was as uncomfortable to be here as we were.

Another dozen or so steps and the light grew dimmer still. Jerren nudged forward and drew alongside the next room. He glanced left and jumped back so suddenly, his back collided against the glass wall behind him.

"What is it?" shouted Alice.

He pointed into the room, eyes wide. "It's . . . a person. But not a person."

Sure enough, there was a man sitting beside a desk, pretending to write. But as realistic as he looked, he wasn't human. "What was this place?" I asked.

Jerren exhaled slowly. "A long time ago it was a fort, like Sumter. But that must have been over a hundred years ago."

"I don't like it," said Alice. She followed Jerren a little farther. "Did you know it was Dare's ship as soon as we arrived?"

He didn't answer, but Nyla did: "Yes. There aren't many ships left. They're as easy to tell apart as people."

"So why didn't someone say something?"

"Because Chief wanted to find out what was going on," replied Jerren. He flicked his head at me. "He watched you dumping that body overboard, which is suspicious enough. Next thing, the ship drops anchor and you swim ashore instead of Dare. Like you're the captain. He knew something was up."

"Who cares? It's a refugee camp. What difference does it make how we got here?"

Jerren stopped walking and faced her at last. "Exactly how many refugees have you seen on this island?"

"How would I know?"

"Put it this way: How many people look like Nyla and me?" His muscles tensed as he gripped one of the metal bars beside him. "I saw you all staring at us when you got off the ship. Point is, they stopped taking refugees after my parents died. That's how I knew they'd worked out my parents were trying to escape, because they shut the place down. Any boat that made it as far as Sumter was greeted with a long line of guns."

"So why do they keep broadcasting that message?" I asked. "The one calling refugees to Sumter?"

"Because the colony's falling apart. There's not even enough wire to mend the chicken coop. But Chief can't go after ships like Dare does. He has to lure them here instead."

"Does it work?" Alice asked.

Jerren nodded. "If the ship is well-armed, he'll try to trade instead, then send them away. But if it's weak . . ." He didn't bother to complete the thought.

I thought of the sleek ship moored just off Sumter. Was that one of Chief's spoils?

"Dare isn't the only pirate. Chief's a pirate too, and he's smart enough to get his victims to sail to *him*. That's what's happened to you, right? Chief got lucky: Dare's ship without the armed guard. See, he can live without you, but a ship that big is very valuable. And now he has it." He kept walking. "The plan was to lock you up and leave you here, the way they left my mother. Then your parents would rush over to save you, just like my father did. I suppose they'd never get to leave after that. The rats would do the rest."

"If they want to kill us, why not just shoot us? I've seen the guns."

"Because killing uses ammunition. Chief won't waste a single bullet on you when he knows the rats will do the job for him. Besides, killing's a messy business. There are children on Sumter, in case you hadn't noticed. Chief doesn't want them having nightmares just because he had to kill you."

"How thoughtful," muttered Alice. "And what about Griffin and Dennis? They're children too."

Jerren ran his hand along the wall. "They'll be spared, most likely. The colony needs some new blood. Especially kids young enough not to suspect anything. That's why they kept Nyla and me around."

"So why are you crossing them now? You have to know your chances are better with Kell than with us."

Jerren had reached the end of the corridor. The light from tiny windows near the ceiling was barely enough to see by, but our eyes were becoming accustomed to it. Still, he wouldn't look through the iron door to his right. "Chief isn't the only one who wants your ship. I swam over the other night to check it out. Everyone always said that Dare's ship was one of the best on the ocean. It is too, but I'll need a crew to escape this place. I'll need *you*."

Alice huffed. "And you think we'll trust you?"

"I think," replied Jerren, "that you won't be able to get back into Sumter without my help." He gripped the wheel in the center of the door. "And if anyone sees you getting back in, Chief won't worry about wasting ammunition anymore."

Nyla had joined her brother now. She held his free hand and tugged it gently, urging him to look through the small circular window in the door. He'd been putting it off, I realized, struck at last by the finality of what he might see through it.

As one, they turned their heads and stared inside. Neither of them said anything after that, but I knew their parents were in there. However much he'd tried to prepare himself for this moment, Jerren was overwhelmed. He fought back tears, but it was no use. Nyla, meanwhile, simply stared straight ahead, her face hardening.

Jerren spun the wheel in the door and pulled it open. He stepped inside the room and knelt on the floor.

I followed Alice to where Nyla stood just outside. I didn't

204

want to look, but did anyway out of respect for Jerren and Nyla. They shouldn't be the only ones to know what had happened, how low their colony had sunk to destroy any threat. Then I closed my eyes again to block out the image that I knew I'd never forget: two bodies, shrunken, mummified, arms wrapped around each other.

Jerren fingered the remains of his parents' tunics. They'd been white once, I was sure of it, but the fronts were rust-colored.

Blood.

Jerren poked a finger through tiny holes positioned over their chests. "Shot," he murmured. "They were shot."

"Who would've done it?" asked Alice gently.

"Kell." He wiped his sleeve across his eyes. "He loved them. Did it so they wouldn't suffer."

"What?"

"He didn't want them to starve, or get Plague. He didn't want to prolong the pain, but . . . he could've just let them *live*." He broke down in racking sobs—this strong boy, who suddenly seemed no different than the rest of us.

I placed a hand on Nyla's shoulder. "I'm sorry."

Nyla didn't pull away, but she didn't speak, either. Her shoulder felt rigid.

Jerren kissed his fingers and placed them tenderly on his parents' sleeves. "I'm not sorry," he said finally. "For years, I've known something terrible happened to them. And I've spent the whole time feeling guilty, wondering if I should've tried to rescue them. Now I know it wouldn't have made any difference. I can stop feeling like a coward . . . a failure."

With a single deep breath, Jerren stood and turned his back on the grisly scene. The lingering doubts were gone now. He'd be able to move on at last.

He wrapped an arm around Nyla and tried to ease her away too. But however cathartic the situation was for him, Nyla obviously felt differently. Maybe she'd heard her brother talk about this for years but had never really believed it. Perhaps she'd held out hope that when she came face-to-face with her parents again, they'd be alive, just hiding, waiting for their children to join them. Whatever she'd envisaged, it clearly hadn't included anything like the scene confronting her now.

"We'll bury them," Jerren told her. "Give them a proper resting place. Somewhere we choose, that we'll remember . . . no matter what." His tone was intended to be comforting, but Nyla still didn't move. She didn't even blink.

Alice cast me a nervous glance. "Jerren's right, Nyla," she said. "We'll come . . ." Her voice trailed off as her eyes drifted past my shoulder and down to the floor. Her mouth opened, but no words came out.

I spun around. Halfway along the corridor, the floor rippled with something even darker than the cold stone.

Rats were advancing on us.

CHAPTER 29

"G et off the ground," yelled Alice.

She leaped against the bars and pulled herself up so that she was half a yard off the ground. I followed her lead. Jerren launched himself at the bars on the other side of the corridor.

Nyla was still staring at her parents. She seemed locked in, and no words, however horrifying, could reach her. As the rats closed to within a couple yards, I jumped down and lifted her up so that her feet rested on the horizontal bar.

The rats were right underneath us now. Kell had warned us that they were growing desperate and aggressive, but the way they loitered just below our feet didn't feel desperate. It felt calculated, like they were conserving energy, just waiting for their prey to fall to them.

"We've got to get out of here," I said.

Alice looked along the corridor. "If we stay on the bar, we can make it to the stairs."

"And then what?" demanded Jerren.

There was no good answer to that, but staying still wasn't an option. So Alice began the slow process of shimmying along, feet sliding by tiny degrees along the horizontal bar as she moved her hands from one to another vertical bar.

I wanted us to move quickly, but Jerren and Nyla were looking back at the place that had become their parents' tomb. He'd just wanted to know the truth, to give his parents the burial they deserved, but now it would never happen. Especially not when the rats divided, some lingering around us, while others scurried into the room. A moment later, snuffling sounds were replaced by the noises of something, or someone, being consumed.

I meant to tell Nyla that she needed to keep moving, but what came out was "I'm sorry."

She seemed to look straight through me. Escaping was going to be impossible if I couldn't get through to her.

Alice climbed back to us and placed a hand on Nyla's arm. "Come," she said gently. "It's time."

Nyla didn't say anything, didn't even blink, but she followed Alice now, placing her hands and feet precisely where the older girl showed her. On the other side of the corridor, Jerren continued his progress. No one commented on the sound his breath made as it caught in his throat, or the way he sniffed back tears. Or the way his sister showed almost no emotion at all.

We kept going and the rats followed, patient and organized, flanking us on all sides. We were within three yards of the stairs when Jerren stopped suddenly. "No more bars," he said.

Sure enough, the bars on his side ended. There was no way he could get to the stairs without first dropping to the floor, which wasn't an option.

"You have to jump to this side," said Alice.

We were less than two yards away, but there was no room for error. "I don't know if I can," he admitted.

"We need you to."

Jerren took a deep breath and braced himself, lowered to a crouch and prepared to leap across. With one hand he clung to the bar behind him, while the other stretched out before him, ready to grab something on the other side.

A distant scream filtered into the corridor. It was faint, but the suddenness of it surprised us. Nyla slipped from her perch and onto the floor.

The rats, so lethargic a moment before, whipped themselves into a frenzy. She tried to pull herself back onto the bars, but before she could clear the floor, one of the rats jumped. It scrabbled at her leg, nothing but beady black eyes and sharp teeth.

There was a deafening sound and the rat exploded in a mess of blood and fur. Jerren was still stretched out across the corridor, but now there was a gun in his right hand, pointed at the carnage.

I pulled Nyla up to the bars and she gripped them tightly. She was shivering. The rats had retreated along the corridor now—not hiding, but keeping a safe distance, weighing up our ability to kill them all.

"That was Rose's voice," I said. "We need to get back."

"The rats'll chase us," replied Alice.

Jerren stared at the gun in his hand. "I don't have enough bullets to kill them all. I don't even have enough to kill more than two or three."

Another scream. It was definitely Rose, and there was only one reason for her to scream.

"We go," I yelled.

Alice stared at me then. She raised her left hand, palm out, and I understood: She wanted us to combine elements. But fire was her secondary element. Even on Hatteras she'd found it hard to conjure large flames. Who knew if she'd produce anything at all out here?

She tilted her head questioningly. It was a risky thing for us to try, but not as dangerous as doing nothing, so I nodded in response.

"Jerren, Nyla," Alice said calmly. "On the count of three, jump down and run for the stairs. Don't stop and don't look back. You hear me?"

Jerren exchanged glances with Alice and me. Then he waited for Nyla to show that she understood too. She watched him blankly.

"One," began Alice. "Two." Her eyes were on me. "Three."

Jerren jumped down and grabbed his sister roughly, dragging her along behind him. Straightaway, I leaped toward Alice. We landed awkwardly, but our hands were joined, and though I wasn't facing the oncoming rats, she was. Her teeth were gritted and her right hand was stretched out before her, fingertips pressed together.

As another scream from Rose pierced the air, I sent all my energy and anger and fear through Alice. I didn't know how much power we'd wield, but it was our only chance. With the rats almost on us, she summoned a single all-consuming flame. Fueled by our panic, it erupted before us, igniting at least half a dozen rats before it disappeared just as suddenly. By then, the other rats were scurrying away, retreating to the end of the corridor and the dead bodies of Jerren's parents.

"Go," I shouted.

Alice spun around and we ran. We didn't get far though, because Jerren and Nyla were standing halfway up the stairs, watching us.

"I said, go," I yelled, pushing them away. *"Go!"*

Hand in hand, Jerren and Nyla sprinted after Alice. I stumbled along behind, the shock of losing so much energy slowing me down, making my steps awkward. The others waited for me halfway across the fort grounds. I wanted to scream at them to keep moving, to help Rose, but I could see that Alice was scared for me — that I wouldn't make it, or that the rats would regroup and catch up with me, the easy target in our group. She held out her hand, ready to pull me along if need be. I might have taken it too, but then I saw the way Jerren was staring at it, as though another flame might arise as suddenly as the last.

He wanted to ask me about it. His expression told me he needed an explanation, but just then, there was another scream.

Now I was as fast as anyone. Pain and exhaustion were

locked away. I didn't even scan the ground for rats.

Jerren pulled up beside me as I reached Rose and Kell's prison. He pointed his gun at Kell, only a couple yards behind the bars. But Kell just laughed at him. After all, he knew Jerren would never shoot. Not while he had Rose trapped in his arms. And a knife pressed tightly against her neck.

CHAPTER 30

ecognize this, Thomas?" Kell snarled. "I think you used it to cut her hair earlier. Now look—so much more effective when you use it like this." He pulled the knife tight against Rose's neck, and turned his attention to Jerren. "Don't tell me you thought the gun was my only weapon. Not on a mission as important as this one. I reckon you knew I had a blade up my sleeve. Probably wanted to see the girl get hurt. After all, Alice is the one you like, right?"

He was trying to turn Alice and me against Jerren. I wasn't falling for it, but a part of me *did* want to hurt Jerren.

Rose was looking right at me, large eyes wild with fear. What remained of her matted hair hung across part of her face, almost obscuring a bright red mark where Kell had struck her moments earlier. I fought back the urge to thrust my arms through the bars and send a jolt of energy into him. Even if I couldn't hurt him, I might shock him enough for Rose to escape.

Or more likely, he'd kill her first.

Kell was watching me again now. "Tricky, isn't it?" he teased. "To use an element from that kind of distance. So unreliable."

I wanted to believe he'd used the word *element* by accident, but he knew what he was saying. If Jerren had harbored any doubts about what he'd seen back in the corridor, Kell had assured him that it had all been real.

"Hers is water, I'd guess," ventured Kell, giving Rose a shake. "Made me choke on my own spit. Dried my mouth so quick I'd swear I hadn't drunk in days. Stupid girl's doing it right now, actually." He tugged at the knife and Rose winced. A thin band of blood appeared from the shallow slice mark across her neck. "Ah, so *now* you stop? Guess I should've cut you up earlier."

"There's no such thing as elementals," insisted Jerren. "It's just a myth."

Kell *tsk*ed. "A myth, huh? So how did they hear our message when the radio in Dare's cabin wasn't connected to solar panels?"

"Maybe they heard it somewhere else."

"Sure." Kell made it sound like they were playing a game. "I like that you're making excuses for them, Jerren. Tells me you know I'm right." He lowered his voice, pretending to confide in us. "I must admit, I'm impressed. Chief said I wouldn't have to worry about all of you—too young to know what you're doing with your elements, he said. But I think he's wrong about that. Just as well we've got the adults under armed guard. If you can do this, who knows what *they're* capable of?"

"What do you want?" snapped Alice.

"For a start, I want Jerren to throw away his guns . . . both of them."

Jerren tossed the weapons aside.

"Now I want you to unlock that door and open it nice and slow. This girl is in a bad way, but not as bad as she will be if you try anything. Once I'm out, I'll be sailing back to Sumter. Alone."

"The rats are coming," Nyla called from around the corner.

Kell didn't flinch. "Unlock the door, boy."

Jerren did as he was told. Kell bullied Rose out of the room. Blood ran down her neck, but that wasn't all. Turning to the side, she revealed an enormous circle of blood that stained her tunic just below her armpit.

Nyla sprinted around the corner, her footsteps distracting us all. Rose dug her elbow into Kell's chest and threw herself onto the ground. I grabbed her hand and pulled her away as Kell swung his blade. It sliced through the air and connected with her upper leg. Blood blossomed on her pants. He raised his hand again, but didn't get in another swing before a shot rang out.

Kell stumbled back against the bars of the prison, left hand clasped against his leg. The wound wasn't as bloody as Rose's, but the bullet had done plenty of damage. Jerren stood to my right, holding the gun.

The older man grimaced. "Do you really think you'll be able to escape on that ship, Jerren? You know what Dare told us. You can't ignore it. This is our destiny."

"Not mine, it isn't," replied Jerren.

I knelt beside Rose and tore my tunic into strips, as the name Dare ran through my mind. I pressed the strips against her wounds to stop the bleeding. She swallowed hard and smiled through her tears. I was sure I was losing her.

"When did you see Dare?" Alice demanded. "*When?*"

Kell ran a hand up the bars, pulling himself to a stand. "About a month ago. Said he'd deliver you to us. Why do you think you're here right now? Why do you think Chief made sure you each had a sibling stay behind on Sumter? They're our insurance. Anything happens to me, Chief'll make sure they suffer for it."

"What does he mean, *deliver* us to you?" Alice asked Jerren.

Jerren shook his head, confused. "It's just what Dare said: That he'd return with something important. Something that would change the world."

Alice looked at me suddenly. "That's why he tore the pages out of his log. He didn't want us to know he'd been here."

"What kind of *something*, Jerren?" I asked.

Realizing we were all distracted, Kell lurched at Jerren. But when he placed his weight on his bad leg, he crumpled to the ground. Jerren towered over him, gun aimed at the man's head.

"What kind of something?" I asked again.

"I don't know," Jerren snapped. "Dare just called it the solution."

Alice froze. So did I. I'd been worried about getting us thrown out of Sumter. Instead, Chief had simply been plotting how to lose us while keeping Griffin.

"What's the solution?" I asked, playing innocent.

Kell laughed, which made him wince. "Nice try, Thomas. Actually, Chief thought it was *you* at first. But then a friend put us on the right track again. It was simple math, really."

"Who told you? Was it Marin?"

"Help me get back to Sumter and I'll tell you."

"Rats are getting closer," yelled Nyla.

I wrapped an arm around Rose and tried to drag her away. She couldn't take her own weight.

Alice crouched beside me. "We'll carry her together," she said.

"No. I've got her. Just help her up, all right?"

Rose groaned as Alice lifted her onto my back. She seemed unable to wrap her arms around my neck, let alone hold on tightly. I placed my hands under her and twined my fingers. Her shallow breaths warmed my neck as her head sank against my shoulder.

Nyla sprinted around the corner. "The rats are splitting into groups. It's like they're trying to trap us here."

"You'll never make it out alive, Thomas." Kell swallowed hard. "Some people say rats can smell weakness. Right now, I'd say it's your girlfriend they're smelling."

When no one said anything, Kell seemed emboldened. He pulled himself up again and stared at Jerren, almost daring the boy to shoot. Jerren retreated, and Kell hobbled after him. "Last chance, Jerren," he rasped. "Take me back and we'll forget everything."

Jerren kept the guns trained on him as we backed toward

the fort entrance. Nyla shadowed his every move. But Kell matched them step for step, his right leg dragging across the ground.

"Stay back," growled Jerren.

"Or what? You'll shoot me again?" Kell's teeth chattered. "You chose the wrong side, boy. We had a visitor during the night, see? An old friend, you might say."

I flashed Alice a look, but she shook her head. "Dare's dead, Thom. Kell's just trying to rattle us." Her hands were shaking, though.

As we reached the tunnel that led out of the fort, Kell lurched forward, a grotesque smile stretching his sunburned skin. Jerren pointed one of the guns at Kell's head. Still the man didn't stop smiling. He simply eased forward until the barrel was pressed against his forehead. "Really think you've got it in you, Jerren? Really think you can be a killer too?"

Rose was heavy against me as I stepped backward from the scene, but I continued to watch. Somehow I knew that Jerren wouldn't kill his mentor.

"We need to run," murmured Alice.

Before she'd finished speaking, Kell opened his mouth and bit on the barrel. He brought his hands around and placed them on the barrel too, so that when Jerren tried to pull away, he couldn't. He'd be disarmed at any moment, I was sure of it.

Jerren seemed petrified. Again he tried to pull away, but it was no use. He was crying too. After everything, this is how it would end for him. At the same place as his parents.

Nyla reached around her brother and wrapped her hands

over his. I figured she was trying to pull the weapon away too, but when she stood on tiptoe and kissed her brother on the cheek, something in the air shifted. And I knew.

I tried to shout *no,* but the word wouldn't come out. It wouldn't have mattered anyway, because at that moment she pulled the trigger.

CHAPTER 31

I couldn't move. Couldn't breathe. I'd seen Kyte shot right in front of me, but I hadn't realized what was happening back then. Plus, the Guardian's wound had been so small. But there was no way to ignore Kell's blood spattered against the ground, or the remains of his head, sliced open like one of Rose's fish—gutted, discarded. It was gruesome.

I had to look away, which is how I saw the rats were converging on our path. Even the sound of gunfire wasn't enough to deter them anymore.

"Run!" I yelled.

Alice took Jerren's arm and pulled him from the carnage. When he dropped the guns in disgust, Nyla calmly picked them up again. As the rats closed in on her, she adjusted the bags on her shoulder like there was no hurry at all.

I looked her in the eye and she returned my gaze. As much as I hated Jerren for putting Rose in the cell with Kell, he'd never frightened me the way that Nyla did in that moment. As she left the bloody scene, she swung her arms loosely, a gun in each hand.

I staggered backward through the tunnel, unable to take my eyes off the rats. They were completely still, just watching us.

"They remember your flame," said Nyla.

When I was halfway down the tunnel they swarmed Kell's body like flies on a horse. There were sounds of clawing and tearing. When one by one the rats turned away, they carried a souvenir with them: a piece of Kell's flesh. Each one ate greedily. Then, sensing that they wouldn't be able to fight the tide and return for more, they pursued us.

I turned around and ran, pounding out one footstep after another as Rose bounced against my back, a dead weight.

Nyla quickly passed me. She followed the others out of the tunnel and along a path. When it forked left, they followed it toward the beach. I could see the water sparkling just ahead of us.

Jerren took another left turn and suddenly they were running parallel to the coast, hidden behind a row of trees and bushes. Sweat poured down my forehead. Rose moaned with every bump.

"Go this way," I yelled, veering straight toward the water.

About thirty yards ahead of me, Alice spun around. "No! Someone'll be watching from Sumter. We need to stay hidden." Her face darkened then, and it wasn't hard to imagine what she saw so close behind me.

Jerren stopped too. "Fire a shot, Nyla. It'll frighten them away."

"They might hear it on Sumter," yelled Alice.

Jerren raised his hands. "They won't."

Nyla pointed the gun at the ground and a shot rang out. For a moment, Alice seemed to relax. But only for a moment.

"Come on," Alice shouted. "It's less than fifty yards to the cove."

We were running across grass now. The footing was uneven and I stumbled but didn't fall. My head throbbed with the sound of my breathing.

From the corner of my eye I saw a rat just behind me. Then two. Then several more on the other side. They were flanking me, grouping in preparation for an attack. I had no idea what the attack would be like, only that it was inevitable.

Alice waited for me at the tree line. Seeing the rats, she threw a stick. It landed beside me, knocking a few of them aside. But others took their place. They filed between my legs so that I almost stepped on them.

Nyla turned to fire, but the gun just clicked. Empty. She tossed it at them instead.

She and Alice sprinted through the trees and I followed right behind them. The change of direction caught the rats off-guard. The water was only a few yards away.

"Thom, jump!" screamed Alice.

I leaped forward and crashed into water only a few inches deep, Rose on top of me. My face was driven into the water and against the sand. My mouth filled with both.

Someone pulled Rose off me and I pushed myself up to

the surface, gasping for air. When I looked back up to the beach, the rats had formed a line along the water's edge.

I stayed crouched down in the water so that I could hold Rose. She was breathing, but her eyes were half-closed. The blood that had soaked into her tunic made the water around her cloudy.

"Remove her clothes," said Jerren flatly. "The salt water will clean the wounds."

He was right, but it was his fault Rose was in this state at all. None of this would've happened if he'd listened to us. The contrast between him and Rose made me sick—he hadn't paid at all for his stupidity. Suddenly I couldn't see anything but Kell standing behind Rose, the knife against her neck.

"Here, I'll do it," he said when I didn't move.

"Get away from her." I slammed my hand into his chest, knocking him backward.

He bounced back up but I was ready for him, fists raised.

"No way," said Alice, stepping between us.

"So you're taking his side," I snapped. "What a surprise."

She gritted her teeth. "Not even close."

She swung her fist around, catching Jerren square in the gut and sending him to his knees. "You knew this was going to happen, and you let us walk into it."

"I saved you," Jerren moaned. "If I'd told you what Kell planned, you never would've come along."

"Exactly."

"And Chief would've had you shot. He thinks your parents are the dangerous ones—never would've sent me and Kell

223

alone to deal with you if he'd known the truth." He rubbed his stomach. "He's scared of you all, especially your parents. And when Chief is scared, he doesn't take any chances. Coming today kept you alive. Now you can help the rest of your families."

Alice joined me and together we lifted Rose out of the shallow water and onto the catamaran. We cleaned her wounds and used what was left of my tunic to bandage her neck. "We need to get back to Sumter," I said.

"Not in daylight," said Jerren. "The guards will be expecting only one boat. And I'm guessing they're only expecting one person too."

A rat ventured into the water then. Another too. Alice grasped my hand and we combined to make a flame. It was smaller than before, but enough to deter them for a while longer.

There were still a few strikes until nightfall. What was happening to our parents right now? How long before the rats attacked again?

Alice looked right past me to the shore. The rats formed a line at the water's edge, waiting for us to return. "It's not possible," she murmured. "The way the rats work together . . . I've never seen anything like it."

"That's why we call these trips suicide squads," said Jerren. "The rats here work together. No one knows how, but they've had years to learn. Chief says they're adapting to the new world, and they're doing it better than us."

Alice reached into her bag and removed the fresh-picked

greens. "We should eat this. It won't keep now it's wet. And who knows when we'll get something else."

She passed around handfuls of leaves. I didn't even look at them, just shoveled them into my mouth and chewed over and over until I could finally swallow. I checked on Rose to see if she was awake enough to eat. She shook her head.

Nyla barely ate at all. She sat in the water, watching Alice and me. Her expression was neutral, alarmingly cool.

"So Alice's element is fire," she said finally. "But what's yours?"

I stopped chewing. Alice didn't look at me, but I could tell that she was focused on me, waiting for my answer. My instinct was to play ignorant, but it was too late for that.

"We're not sure," I said. "Until a week ago, I didn't know I had an element at all. The Guardians have kept it a secret all my life. I think I can channel energy, but that's about all . . . for now."

Jerren narrowed his eyes. "What do you mean: for now?"

"The elements don't work as well here. I don't know why," I added hurriedly. "Anyway, what do you know about elementals?"

Nyla toyed with her food, but she still didn't eat. "There have always been rumors. Even at Fort Dauphin, people said they saw things."

I mulled this over. I didn't know exactly where Fort Dauphin was, but I was sure it was even farther from Roanoke Island than Fort Sumter. In which case, how had people's elements worked at all? Were there more of us elsewhere?

"So when we reach Sumter," said Alice, "will our families be alive?"

Jerren nodded. "I told you: Chief won't waste ammunition, and he's protective of the children. Doesn't want them seeing anything bad."

The water was warm, but we were cooling down from our run now. The sun was obscured by dark clouds gathering to the southwest. We climbed onto the catamarans and lay across the canvas sheets.

I beckoned Alice over to me. "What Kell was saying—"

"No." She huffed. "I know what you're thinking, and Dare's dead, all right? You saw him drown."

"I saw him go underwater and not resurface."

"Kell was just trying to scare us. Make us think we needed to keep him with us." She waved a hand in the direction of Sumter. "Did you see another ship arrive during the night? If so, where's it hidden now?"

"Dare could've anchored it behind one of the islands," suggested Jerren.

"We'd see the mast. Unless you think he made the voyage in a cutter." She gave a disdainful look. "Listen, this is exactly what I'm talking about. Kell wanted to get inside our heads, and distract us. It's working too." She turned to me. "You know as well as I do, there were no other ships back on Roanoke Island, right? And no boats big enough to make a voyage like ours, either."

226

"No, there weren't," I agreed, but my pulse continued to race.

From the corner of my eye I noticed Nyla watching me. She opened her mouth, but it was a while before she spoke. "Does Griffin . . . *see* things?" she asked.

Her question put me on my guard. There was no way she should have known about Griffin's element unless he had told her, and he'd never do that. "What do you mean?"

"Something happened before we left. Something . . . weird." She clicked her tongue. "Chief came for him this morning before we left, and Griffin went crazy."

I froze. "Crazy, how?"

Nyla seemed to be regretting the conversation now, but kept going. "He was holding my hand. It was the first time. Felt nice. Then Chief came over and patted him on the back. After that, his grip got real painful. I tried to pull away, but I couldn't. It was like . . . he wasn't even himself anymore."

So that's why they'd kept Griffin away from me. He'd had a seizure, a vision of something terrible that was about to occur. I hated knowing that I hadn't been there for him. Or that Nyla sounded so calm about it.

"When we were in the fort," I asked her, "did one of the rats bite you?"

She didn't answer at first. Then, slowly, she lifted the fabric of her pants. Though the water had rinsed the blood away, the wound remained visible: a bite mark just above her ankle.

Alice dropped her food and began to clean it right away. Jerren tore his tunic so that he could bandage it. "It's just one bite," he said. "I've heard of people who survive."

Through it all, Nyla remained completely still, just watching me. So that's why she'd been able to pull the trigger when her brother couldn't. Once she'd been bitten, she must've guessed what Griffin's seizure had meant.

Strange to think that with Rose so hurt and broken, it was Nyla, still perfectly healthy, who was as good as dead.

CHAPTER 32

I t was evening. The clouds had darkened throughout the afternoon as a storm rolled toward us. Occasionally we'd peer over the rocks at the edge of the cove and spy on Fort Sumter. It didn't look any different. Whatever horrifying things were going on were hidden behind those thick, forbidding walls.

Alice and I had repelled the rats twice more, but after each time, I'd needed to rest. No one disturbed me either. They knew that without me, Alice's element wouldn't stop anything.

Rose drifted in and out of sleep. When she was awake, I fed her morsels of food and held her head as she washed them down with sips of water. One time, she ran her hand around her neck and discovered that her pendant had gone, the cord no doubt severed by Kell's knife. Such a small thing really, but it caused a round of silent tears. She gave up eating and remained perfectly still as I brushed her hair from her face and wrapped my arms around her. A moment later, she'd drifted back to sleep.

Alice joined me. She held my hand, just as she had done back on Roanoke Island, but it felt different now. Same hand, same skin, same pressure as her fingers twined with mine, but this touch was all about reassurance and friendship. It was about letting me know she was on my side. Rose's side too.

I wanted to ask her about Eleanor, but not with Jerren and Nyla around. Besides, we'd seen enough death for one day. There was no need to revisit past horrors.

"You should give her mine," said Alice, running her pendant along the cord. "It would mean more to her, I think."

There was a deeper meaning to those words, and we both knew it. "Are you sure?"

"Yes." She loosed my hand and turned away so that I could reach the knot. "It's a sheet bend knot though, right?"

"How do you know that?"

"I could tell by your movements when you put it on me back at Roanoke. I was kind of pleased actually—it's such a *permanent* knot—but now I think you were just nervous."

I didn't reply. There was no need to confirm what she already knew to be true.

Jerren wasn't watching us, but he could hear every word. I wondered if Alice wanted him to know that something had happened between us, so he'd be jealous. But as I removed the cord and tied it gently around Rose's neck instead, I realized that wasn't it at all. She wanted him to know that she was letting go of whatever we had shared. Jerren would know the boundaries of our friendship now.

"We should go," announced Nyla. She hadn't spoken since

she'd shown us the rat bite, and hearing her voice startled me.

Jerren stared at the sky. "Thunderstorm's coming."

"It's not here yet." She tilted her head toward Alice and me. "And they won't be able to stop the rats forever."

Jerren untied the first catamaran. "All right, then. Let's go."

The breeze was strong and when we took off, we made good headway across the harbor mouth. The clouds mostly obscured the moon, but Jerren kept right behind us so that anyone watching from Sumter would only see one boat. At the sight of two sails, someone would raise the alarm for sure.

It took us only a quarter-strike to cross the water, and I held tight to Rose the whole way. Alice headed for our ship, still anchored a hundred yards from the shore. She let out the sail as we drew close, and we came to rest a few yards away. Here, no one would be able to see the catamarans at all.

Alice stared at the ship. "We need to get on board."

"You could swim around and take the rope ladder."

"No. I might show up against the dark of the ship. But if I can bring the rope ladder over this side, the rest of you can climb."

I took in the sheer wooden hull. It looked gigantic. "How are you going to get up there?"

"Skill and strength." She handed me the mainsheet. "So get us right next to the ship and let me work."

I pulled on the mainsheet. There were only a few yards still to go, but progress was slow because the ship blocked the wind. Meanwhile, Alice removed her shoes and shimmied barefoot up the catamaran mast.

"This mast isn't as high as the ship's deck," I reminded her.

"Doesn't need to be," she called back. "I just need to get past the curved part of the hull."

Sure enough, as the catamaran bumped gently against the ship, Alice leaned away from the mast and grabbed the ship's side. Her legs slipped from under her and so did her left hand, and for a moment I was sure she was about to fall, but instead she just dangled in the air. That's when I realized her right hand was clamped against the wooden ledge around a porthole. She eased her left hand up, and ran her toes across the boards until she found something that offered resistance. Then she took a moment to gather herself.

"There's only a few yards to go," I said.

She peered down. "That's very helpful. Now if you could find me a ladder, that'd be even better."

Slowly, painstakingly, Alice crept up the ship, finger by finger, toe by toe. When she finally reached the rail, I exhaled, unaware that I'd even been holding my breath.

She pulled herself onto the deck. A short while later, she reappeared with the rope ladder, which she tied to the rail and dropped over the side. I tethered our boat to the ladder and peered down at Rose. That's when I realized we had another problem.

She was still asleep. Even awake, she wasn't up to climbing the ladder. Which meant there was only one thing to do. I nudged her until she came to, and knelt down with my back to her. She understood well enough what I needed her to do, but it wasn't until Jerren had tied his boat to ours and Nyla had joined us that they were able to help her climb onto my back. She wrapped her arms around my neck and held on loosely. I hoped that she wouldn't let go.

Step by step I forced us up the ladder. The wind was stronger now, but our weight kept us in place. When we reached the rail, Alice helped Rose over. She collapsed onto the deck.

"Let's get her below deck," said Alice. "She's going to have to stay on the ship."

Nyla climbed over the rail. "I'll stay with her."

We carried Rose to the nearest cabin and laid her on a pile of blankets.

"I can't see anything," said Nyla, taking a seat beside her.

"My lantern's in the fort," said Jerren.

I remembered the candles that Griffin had been using in Dare's cabin. "There might be another way. Follow me."

Alice and Jerren came with me to Dare's cabin. The door was unlocked. I went straight to the desk and ran my hands blindly across it until I found the candle. I placed it in front of Alice and took her hand in mine. Combining our elements, she created a small flame. Jerren seemed fascinated rather than afraid.

I kept my hand around the flame, and my body between the candle and the windows. The stern windows shouldn't have been visible from Sumter, but I wasn't taking any chances.

In the light we saw other candles, which we lit from the first. Once we each had one, I figured we'd hurry to Nyla and on to the fort, but Jerren stared at the maps on the wall, transfixed. "This is Dare's cabin, isn't it?"

I nodded.

"Look at the detail on this map," he continued. "Chief has maps like this, but he keeps them hidden. My father used to say that information is power. Chief keeps the power for himself." He tapped the map. "Why do you think he marked this route?"

Alice looked closer. "He didn't. That was Griffin. He was tracing the route that Dare took to get to us. If the pages hadn't been ripped out of Dare's log, we'd have known he'd been here." As she spoke, she grew quieter.

"What is it, Alice?" I asked.

She shook her head. "It doesn't make sense. Dare wouldn't have removed the pages unless he knew we were planning to steal his ship. But if he wanted that to happen, why did he attack us in the middle of a hurricane?"

"And why didn't he foresee his own death?" I added. "His element should've been working better on Roanoke than anywhere else. He's a seer. He must've known what would happen."

Alice was perfectly still now. "Dare said he'd *deliver* us to you, right?" she asked Jerren. "Those were his exact words."

"Yeah. Why?"

Alice turned to me but didn't speak. I knew what she was thinking, though. "You just said it was impossible for him to be here," I reminded her. "You can't believe he's alive."

"Why not? You do. Why else are you whispering?"

Jerren raised his candle. "I'm giving this to Nyla now. I don't need to hear about any more ghosts."

He left the room, but Alice and I stayed. She perched on the corner of the desk. "What if Dare came on *this* ship?"

"Impossible. We would've seen him. Or heard him."

A moment's silence, and then her eyes shot back to the map. She ran her finger along Griffin's route. "Oh, no. How did we miss it?"

"Miss *what*?"

Alice circled the room, dragging items of furniture away from the walls.

"What are you doing, Alice?"

She moved shelves, a table, and finally, the desk. It didn't scrape across the floor as it came away because the legs weren't actually touching the ground. The whole thing pivoted, attached to the wall with hidden hinges.

Now a part of the wall was missing entirely. Behind it was empty space.

Alice crouched down and I handed her the candle. When she'd taken a look, she moved out of the way so that I could see too.

It was a passageway. The candlelight shone several yards until it was swallowed in darkness.

"I think it goes right around the ship," said Alice. "It's how Dare spied on his men. That's how he knew about the plot to kill him, even though they were hundreds of miles from Roanoke Island. His element doesn't work any better than anyone else's. He doesn't need it to. He just eavesdrops on his men instead."

I moved the candle around and caught a glimpse of something on the floor a couple yards away. I crawled in and retrieved it.

It was the missing journal from Kyte's dune box—the one Rose had left on the beach at Hatteras, back when everything had started.

I flicked through it. It didn't look the same as the others. Griffin had said that it probably worked in parallel with them, in which case he'd finally be able to complete the story that presently made so little sense. But where he'd feel the relief of having solved a mystery, I felt only panic.

Dare hadn't delivered us at all. We'd delivered him.

CHAPTER 33

"How did Dare survive?" muttered Alice. "It was a hurricane. We were lucky the ship didn't capsize. Lucky we didn't all drown."

"What about the sailboats we tethered to the ship. They *did* capsize, remember? And I'm guessing he tied himself to one of them and rode out the storm that way."

I replayed the night we'd endured the hurricane. How Dare had chosen to attack us during the eye of the storm. Why hadn't it occurred to me that he never would've had time to capture us all, lock us up, and still return to Roanoke Island? Which meant he either knew we'd all survive the night, or he was willing to risk everything in order to keep us on board his ship. I'd assumed his main concern was to colonize Roanoke, but what if that was for his men's benefit, not his own?

I gripped the desk. "The night that Kell came aboard, he wasn't looking for signs of the Plague. He was looking for Dare."

"Do you think he found him?"

237

"I don't think so. Otherwise, Dare would've come ashore before last night."

Alice stared at the journal. "So why *did* he stay on board?"

"I have no idea. But I'm sure there's a reason. Seems like nothing Dare does is an accident."

"This makes no sense." She narrowed her eyes. "Your father said being a solution just means that you're the first to show a new element. But elements don't work as well here as they do on Roanoke Island. Dare would know that."

"They still work a little, though. And I'm guessing there's something in Sumter that Dare doesn't have. Something that makes it worth taking the risk."

There was a creak above us. We ran along the corridor, covering the candles to hide the flames. Nyla and Rose were still inside the cabin, but Jerren wasn't there. He was walking down the stairs.

"Was that you up there?" snapped Alice.

"Yes," he said. "I was preparing the ship."

"We need to get to our families, not ready the ship."

"Your families won't be able to escape unless this ship is ready to sail. You think Chief is going to wait for us to get everything ready? No, he'll come after us, and for once he won't be afraid to waste bullets."

While Jerren returned to the deck, Alice and I went into the cabin and inspected Nyla's ankle. The bite mark was an angry red color. She winced as I touched the skin around it.

"I'm so sorry, Nyla," I said. "When we come back, we'll look at it again."

She wouldn't meet my eyes. "*If* you come back."

I handed the candles to her. "Just remember, you have to stay on this side of the ship so that people on shore can't see the light through the porthole."

"I don't think I'll be going anywhere." She frowned. "Please watch out for Jerren."

"I will."

I still had the journal in my left hand, so I placed it beside Rose. I hoped Griffin got the chance to read it one day.

Up on deck, the thunderstorm was almost upon us. Drops of rain spattered on the planks and lightning flashed faster and closer than before. In the glow of their torches, I saw a group of guards waiting at the entrance to the fort. I even detected the outline of other men on the battlements. So many men. They weren't waiting for Kell anymore, that was certain.

Once we'd prepared the ship, we climbed down the rope ladder and onto one of the catamarans.

"We can't sail over," said Alice. "They'll see us for sure, even if we head for the back of the island."

"Then let's swim around," said Jerren. "We can hide behind the animal enclosures and see if that side has fewer guards."

Without another word we dove off the boat and into the water. The swell was building, waves propelled by the stiffening wind. I counted every stroke, wondering if I was really getting closer or if we were caught in a tide that would keep us at arm's length from the island.

Alice pulled away from Jerren and me with every stroke.

239

Finally, she treaded water and waited for us. "We can't make it all the way around," she said, facing away from the fort so that her voice wouldn't carry across the water. "It'll take forever at this rate."

Jerren stared at the battlements. His breathing was labored. "Maybe we can climb along the rocks at the bottom of the perimeter wall. It'll be difficult for the guards to see straight down from the esplanade. We'll be hidden."

We headed straight for shore, pausing every dozen or so strokes because of movement on the battlements. Figures wandered back and forth along the top of the walls, but they seemed distracted, as if something far more important was going on elsewhere in the fort. I was certain it involved Griffin.

When we were less than twenty yards from the rocks that ran along the base of the wall, a couple of men took up positions directly in front of us. They were talking, words I couldn't make out, and there was no way we could continue until they had passed. We treaded water again, waiting, while the rain that had fallen softly before finally came down in sheets. The initial burst of warmth I'd felt when I'd begun swimming was over, and as my muscles grew tired, a numb exhaustion took over instead.

Alice tapped me on the shoulder, startling me. "We have to move on."

We continued swimming around the island. We were closer now than before and made faster progress, but there was also more risk of us being seen. I imagined there were dozens of armed men watching from the battlements, not a couple of men distracted by their own conversation.

Finally I made out the animal enclosures. Men were leaning against the coop, guns slung over their shoulders.

Alice and Jerren stopped swimming. "What now?" she asked.

Jerren shook his head. "They must realize this is where I got into the fort the other night."

"So they know about the route up the wall?"

"Everyone knows about the route up the wall. They just don't use it because it's dangerous. One slip and you'll break a leg. Or worse."

"We need to get in," pressed Alice. "Is there any other way?"

Jerren looked around him and his expression changed. He swam back a little ways and stopped. A moment later, he waved once and stood. Somehow he was only waist-deep in the water.

I felt something round, hard, and smooth knock against my legs as I joined him.

"The wastewater pipe," he explained. "It leads into the fort's sewer system."

"How far does it run underwater?" I asked.

"I don't know. I've been in the sewer before, but never down as far as the water line. The pipe slopes slightly, but it could be completely underwater for several yards. Maybe twenty yards because of the tide."

It was the only way into the fort. But what if the pipe was underwater for more than twenty yards? What if it was thirty?

Or forty? What if we didn't make it out the other end before our breath gave out?

"Is there another way?" asked Alice.

Jerren looked around him as though he might find an answer in the darkness. "No, there isn't."

I was frustrated and tired. But at the back of my mind was Rose, wounded by Kell, and Griffin, prisoner of Chief and possibly Dare too. I'd promised them safety, but I'd delivered them into a situation as horrifying as the one we'd fought to escape.

I walked down the pipe until I slipped off the edge and into deeper water.

"What are you doing, Thom?" whispered Alice.

"Wait for me," I said.

I took a deep breath and ducked below the surface, heading into the blind enclosed space of the pipe.

CHAPTER 34

The pipe's smooth stone grazed my elbow. Heart pounding, I focused only on pushing forward, one stroke after another. Waste brushed up against me and ran past me—debris and dirt and human filth. I swam faster and faster, desperately searching out the end of the tunnel.

I collided with an object—a metal pole, most likely. It scraped my arm. There'd be blood, I was sure. A part of me knew there was time to turn around and get out the way I'd come in, but I swam onward. My strokes grew inefficient because I was half-focused on shielding myself from anything that might hit me. The darkness wasn't just around me but inside me. As much as I tried to block it out, I couldn't shake the feeling that I might die.

I kicked for Rose and Griffin, for Ananias and my father, and for Alice. My heart and lungs screamed. My chest felt like it would implode.

My hand broke the surface suddenly. I pushed my legs against the bottom of the pipe and launched my entire body into the air, gasping, retching. It was stale air too, rancid and gassy, and seared my lungs as I inhaled. There was no way I could fill my lungs with this air and hope to make it back. I was light-headed from breathing it.

But if I didn't go back, what about Alice and Jerren? Would they surrender? Risk their lives to find another way in? I stood in the darkness, swaying from side to side as I choked on the air.

There was no other choice. I had to keep going.

I stumbled along the pipe, bent double. When I coughed, the sound echoed, so I fought to stay silent. My hands dragged through the waist-deep water, human waste sliding through my fingers; I felt the texture of it, and gagged.

Finally the water level fell to my knees, and then my ankles. A shaft rose vertically above me, and the air from above was fresher. I breathed deeply as voices from the fort carried down, the words indistinct.

I ran my hand around the shaft and found a ladder. There wasn't much room, but I kept my body pressed against it and climbed until I reached a metal grate. The voices weren't loud—I hoped it was because they were well away from me— but I'd have to be careful not to make a sound.

I kept my feet on the ladder, pressed my back against the opposite side of the shaft, and positioned both hands on the center of the circular grate. I lifted it slowly and slid it to one side. It made a noise, but not enough to draw attention. Not with all the other activity going on inside the fort.

I emerged from the shaft to a different fort than I'd seen

before. I was next to the barracks, but instead of silence and darkness, men and women strode back and forth carrying torches. The place was bustling. No one was looking in my direction at all.

I stepped onto the dirt and savored the feel of hard ground. I wanted to find somewhere to hide for a moment, but I had to replace the grate first—nothing would give me away faster than an open shaft. So I knelt beside it and lifted, eased it across and let it slide into place.

I should have realized it would make a sound. The low clang rang out across the grounds.

"Is someone there?" A man's voice carried down from the battlements. He held his torch out in front of him to get a better look.

I took two quick steps and slithered over the nearby wall, landing in a heap in the space where Rose and I had passed our first night together. By then, someone else was coming over to investigate. The glow from a torch drifted over the wall. Footsteps splashed through puddles. The men on the battlement above me edged closer.

Their torches revealed a shadowy space in one corner. It was a hollow in the wall. I crept over and slid inside. I barely fit, but as the footsteps shuffled above me, I knew I was hidden. Well, as long as no one smelled me.

"Did you see something?" someone asked the first guard.

"No. Heard something, though. It was over here, near the sewer."

More guards joined them. "Sewer grate is on fine," said one.

"Yeah," admitted the first guard. "But actually—"

Whatever he was going to say was drowned out by the sound of shouting. I recognized Ananias's voice.

I worked my way through the maze-like ruins of the barracks following my brother's shouts. The noise of the rain covered the sound of my footsteps, and no one on the battlements looked down. Finally, I peered around a corner and saw that he was being held prisoner in one of the casemates. A row of iron bars ran across the entrance, and two men stood guard. In the light of their torches I could see them talking animatedly, though I couldn't make out their words. Ananias shouted again, but neither man replied.

I followed the glow back through the room. My father was there, propped up against a wall. Tarn too. But there was no sign of Griffin, or Marin and Dennis.

Other guards were descending on the prison now, drawn by Ananias's shouting. I wanted him to stop—there was no way I could take on several men—but I couldn't communicate with him. Instead I picked up a stone from the ground and threw it toward him. There was a loud bang as it hit one of the metal bars.

Immediately, the guards turned toward Ananias, their weapons raised. But Ananias wasn't watching them. He was squinting into the darkness. He scanned the area, and when his eyes fell on me, hidden in an archway, he gave a slight nod.

"Griffin's going to escape from the gunroom," he told the men. "You won't be able to hold him."

This seemed to amuse the guards. "You can stop talking now," one of them said.

"You're all going to die—"

"I said, shut up!" He slammed his gun against the bars.

Even though I knew Griffin's location, I still had no idea how to cross the fort without being captured. And the guards were growing restless.

"You're scared," Ananias taunted.

The guard raised his gun and pointed it at my brother.

"You're still shaking."

"Stop it, Ananias," Tarn warned him.

Ananias wouldn't take his eyes off the guard. "No. I'm only just getting started, see?"

The words were barely out of his mouth when he flung himself at the bars and grabbed the gun barrel. The guard lost his balance and slipped to the ground. He was mumbling something, fighting to regain control when the gun fired. It seemed accidental. But the result was the same.

Ananias collapsed to the floor, holding his shoulder. Father dropped to his knees beside his son, and Tarn rushed to his side. Footsteps pounded toward the casemate from around the fort. Ananias grimaced, but his eyes were fixed on me again.

It was my chance.

All the torches in one place left much of the fort in darkness, so I sprinted back through the barracks and used the ruins to climb up onto the battlements. No one was there anymore. I kept low and ran along it, heading for the battery. I had no idea how I'd be able to help Griffin when I got to the gunroom. I just knew I had to try.

Three yards later, someone tackled me.

CHAPTER 35

tried to roll out from under my attacker, but our legs got tangled. I couldn't see to punch, and I didn't want to make a sound in case other guards came over.

"Thom?"

"Alice? Why did you attack me?"

"I didn't even see you," she whispered. "Although I probably should've been able to smell you." She leaned away. "All the guards left the peninsula when you created that diversion. So we climbed the wall and jumped over."

"Where's Jerren?"

Someone else landed beside us. "Good work," said Jerren. "How did you do it?"

"I didn't. Ananias did."

"How?"

"By getting himself shot. Don't worry, he'll live," I added. "But he won't be pleased if we waste this chance, so we need to think. Griffin wasn't with him. Neither was Dennis or Marin. Ananias shouted that Griffin's in the gunroom."

Alice sighed. "And I suppose you know a way for us to get in."

Jerren ran a hand through his wet hair. "I do."

Near the main gate, guards were drifting away from the scene of the shooting. No one had died and Ananias had worked alone, so there was nothing more they could do. They returned to their stations, torches giving out a steady light as the rain eased off.

We sank to all fours and crawled along the battlements, keeping to the shadows. After ten yards we reached the sheer wall of the battery.

"There's a fence at the top," said Jerren. "Watch tower's a few yards behind it. Get on my shoulders and I'll lift you up."

He tried to get Alice up first, but she hesitated. "What'll *you* do?" she asked.

"I'll be taking the route around the outside. Lethal if you don't know what you're doing."

"And you do know, right?"

He snorted. "Are you worried about me, Alice?"

"Fine," she snapped. "Fall to your death for all I care."

"That's more like it."

He lifted her onto his shoulders. She grabbed the metal fence and pulled herself up. With another breath, he readied for me.

"Are you sure you can lift me, Jerren?"

"Stop talking and climb."

I stood on his shoulders and joined Alice on the battery roof. She was lying on her side, face turned away from the men and women carrying torches less than twenty yards away.

I was certain they would see us, but the torchlight must have blinded them.

Jerren seemed to take forever to arrive, but I couldn't blame him for that. It was a miracle he'd been able to climb the wall at all. We hustled into the empty watch tower so he could catch his breath.

"Lucky we decided to come at night," he said. "This would've been occupied all day."

"We did something right, then," replied Alice. "Now all we need is for everyone to surrender and let us leave on our ship. What are the chances of that?"

"Unless we get some help, pretty slim."

"Thought so."

We left the tower and crossed the battery roof, keeping low and pausing behind walls whenever someone drew near. Finally we reached the top of the stairs above the gunroom. Two armed guards stood sentry at the door, talking in hushed tones, unaware of how close we were.

"What now?" I whispered.

"Follow me," replied Jerren.

He ran over the roof to the far end. Dangling his legs over the side, he slid onto a fence below. From there he swung onto the walkway that led to our room. Alice and I followed, our descent slow and awkward. At least there was no one around this part of the fort to hear us as we landed.

When Jerren entered the corridor that led to our room, I grew suspicious. By the time he entered our room, I wasn't the only one. Alice had stopped walking too.

"You're going to have to trust me," he called out from the darkness.

Alice didn't move. "Why?"

"Because you weren't the first people to be put in this room." He pried open the door. "It's where they put Nyla and me after our parents died. They didn't want us around everyone else until they were sure we could be controlled."

"How do you know that?"

"Because I heard them say so. There's a vent at the top of the wall. Behind that, ductwork runs along the ceiling. It would've provided hot and cold air back in the old days. Doesn't work now, but it connects with the gunroom next door. I used to stand by the vent cover and listen to the voices. They were faint, but I knew what was going on. Knew what was at stake. That's how I was sure they'd killed my parents."

Jerren moved through the pitch-dark room confidently, having memorized every part of it. There was the faint sound of something scraping across the floor, and then he called us toward him. "Help me with the bunk. We need to take the mattress off and lean it against the wall. We can climb up the slats like a ladder."

We wrestled the bunk into place. Jerren climbed up first and pulled the metal screen away. He handed it to me and I placed it against the wall. By the time I reached up to check that he was all right, he had gone.

"You go next," said Alice.

I climbed the slats and slid into the crawlspace. Jerren was just inside too, so we moved to either side to make room for Alice. I figured she'd find it harder to pull herself in, as she was shorter than us. But when I offered her my hand she batted it away. She vaulted up and in, taking her place between us.

Now that we were still, sounds drifted along the metal duct: voices, and a low, faint hum. The voices, I'd expected, but the hum was unlike any sound I'd heard before, completely unchanging in tone and pitch.

"You'll have to lead, Thomas," Jerren whispered. "No room to change places."

I shuffled along on all fours, trying to glide instead of lifting my limbs so that we'd keep the noise down. Alice and Jerren were behind me, but I couldn't hear anything except their breathing. The duct occasionally bowed under our combined weight. Ahead of me, the hum grew louder.

I concentrated on the men's voices, which is why I didn't feel the metal edge. Or the gap. My hand slid into the room below. Though I tried to rein it in, I gasped.

The men in the gunroom stopped talking. The hum was the only sound, resonating along the metal duct.

Gradually the voices returned. Still, I waited for clues: occasional pauses in the conversation, something that suggested they were suspicious. But the exchanges were rapid and the voices were raised. Whatever was happening was reaching a climax.

I reached into the gap but couldn't feel the bottom. It was at least half a yard across and there wasn't much room to move about. So I flattened myself and stretched both hands across the gap, waited until my arms were safely on the other side, and pushed off with both feet against the edge. My knees rubbed against the duct, but the noise was drowned out by sounds from the room.

Alice and Jerren followed behind me, each wrestling with the gap. The duct was wider here, but after a few yards, it split left and right. In either direction, the new ducts were much smaller.

The voices were coming from the right, so I chose that way. But I'd only gone a yard when I felt the metal shifting beneath me. With three of us, it would be impossible to stay quiet. More likely, the whole duct would give out and send us crashing to the floor.

"You'll have to wait here," I whispered over my shoulder: "It's not strong enough for all of us."

Alice huffed. "Then what'll we do?"

"There's vent covers in every room," offered Jerren. "This duct must lead to one. Tell us what you see through it."

I slunk forward. The voices felt so close. One of them was Chief's. He was usually so calm, but now he spoke quickly. "He'll be back soon, so let's get moving."

Another flurry of activity, but no more talking.

I pushed on a couple more yards. The hum was loud, but I still held my breath, desperate to stay quiet. Just ahead of me, light filtered through the vertical spaces in the duct vent. I pulled alongside it and rested on my elbow so that I could see down into the room.

It was the largest room in the fort. The walls were black,

lined with flameless lanterns. The solar generators must have been powering them. They cast overlapping circles of light on the dark floor, and on the group of four men who stood together. But the strangest sight was the space beneath the lanterns, where several guns were propped against the wall in orderly rows, just as Dennis had told us.

The hum seemed to come from a large machine to one side of the room. There was a table beside it, with an assortment of old-looking knives and other ominous metal objects arranged neatly on a white cloth. And a chair, with crisscrossing leather straps.

"Is the generator charged?" demanded Chief.

A man beside the machine nodded. "It's ready."

"Let's start."

I shifted position so that I could watch Chief as he moved creakily toward a rail. Below him was a giant glass cube, showered in even brighter light than the rest of the room. Two men stood beside the cube, dressed in bright white clothing that covered every part of their bodies. There was someone inside too.

Griffin.

He leaned against one of the walls. On the other side of the cube, separated by a glass divider, the floor was black.

Suddenly a door burst open. Out of my line of sight, someone strode across the floor. "What's going on, Chief?" the new arrival demanded, silky smooth voice tinged with venom.

I couldn't see him, but I didn't need to. I'd have recognized Dare's voice anywhere.

CHAPTER 36

A ll's well with the natives, I assume." Chief addressed Dare without looking at him. "Or are they getting restless?"

"One of your trigger-happy men just shot Ananias," replied Dare.

"Such a waste. We'll never get that bullet back." Chief gave an exaggerated sigh. "All the same, it hardly concerns you. You said yourself that you have no connection to those people. Although," he added, watching Dare from the corner of his eye, "from the way you just burst in here, I'm wondering if maybe that's not the case."

Dare's expression didn't change at all. "Where are the children, Chief?"

The old man *tsk*ed. "Why? Are you getting sentimental in your old age?"

"I told you to imprison *all* of them."

"Yes. But you didn't tell me *where*." He adjusted the sleeves of his tunic. "The children are on Moultrie. Behind bars, exactly as you requested."

"There are rats on Moultrie. You're giving them the Plague."

"Indeed, I am. Think of them as my security. Just to make sure everything goes to plan."

"Why wouldn't it?" Dare's eyes did a measured sweep of the room. He had the look of a man on edge. "I don't like to see children suffer, Chief."

Chief stifled a laugh. "You might have wanted to think about that before you handed me Griffin."

Dare stepped forward. In response, the guards raised their guns. "Your men seem anxious."

"As do you." Chief sighed deeply. "I'd given you up for dead until last night, Dare. But your arrival doesn't change anything. You're our *guest*, and we have plans for young Griffin."

Dare continued past the older man and surveyed the room with the glass cube. "What's going on here? Our agreement last month was for an injection."

"I told you that could never work. Anyway, what does it matter? He's the solution." Chief stepped beside a large machine. He ran a hand across it gently, as if he were reacquainting with an old friend. When he turned a dial, the hum became a high-pitched whine. "Anyone might survive a small dose of Plague. But there's only one person who could survive a massive dose, and we both know it's that boy in there."

"You may as well torture him. This is inhumane."

Chief spun around. "When was this ever *humane*? Is that what you thought all those years ago, when we stood in this very room? Did you convince yourself that an injection of the

Plague bacterium was somehow more humane than direct contact with the rats themselves?"

"Of course it's different."

"Let me remind you that you claimed to have delivered the solution to me. You promised me the Plague years were over, and I threw all our resources into making it so. But she wasn't the solution, was she? And in the end, the only reason that woman survived is because *I* gave her the therapy," Chief roared. "You offered her up for slaughter, and *I* cured her. Not you. Don't ever forget that."

Chief strode toward the rail. He regarded the glass cube proudly.

Griffin didn't look up. All his attention was fixed on the other side of the divider, where the black floor began to shift. Only, it wasn't a floor at all. The floor wouldn't move, wouldn't ripple like that. The floor wouldn't make a sound.

It was rats, and they were desperate to get to Griffin.

I couldn't take my eyes away. On Hatteras, the Guardians had told us to keep our distance from rats, and to warn someone if we came across a dead one. They were easy instructions to follow because the rats were shy creatures, more frightened of us than we were of them. But these rats were like the ones on Moultrie — violent and hostile.

"Alice," I whispered loudly, but there was no response.

"You don't get it, do you," said Chief, voice calmer again. "Twenty rats won't just prove that Griffin is resistant. Such a large dose of Plague will boost his antibody titers. It'll help *him* in the long run." He opened his arms wide. It was a ges-

257

ture I'd seen more than once, and which I'd trusted to be genuine. He pointed to the machine as if coaxing Dare to join him over there. "The plasmapheresis unit still works. My technician has been testing it on himself. In a matter of days, we'll be able to extract antibodies. Because Griffin's titers will be so high, we'll need less of his blood to treat everyone. Think about it, Dare: For the first time in a generation, we can passively immunize people."

"Your people."

"No, Dare. *Our* people." Chief wore the expression of a disappointed parent. "I know those colonists are related to you. Same birthplace. Same ability to survive against all odds. I saw them all for elementals the moment they arrived. That's why the adults are imprisoned in Sumter, where we can keep an eye on them. Someone saw Marin catching a fish, you see. Lured it toward her and caught it barehanded. There's no way I'm taking any chances against an element as strong as that."

A strange transformation overtook Dare then. "Tell me, Chief. Exactly whom did you send to lock up the children? Was it Kell?"

"The fate of the children on Moultrie rests in our hands now," replied Chief, ignoring him. "Griffin's blood *will* save them."

"Kell hasn't returned. Has he?"

"Enough!" Chief rapped his knuckles against the machine impatiently. "You don't have your cronies around you anymore, Dare, and I've tolerated your questions long enough."

He raised a hand and gave a signal to the man across the room. "Raise the divider."

Dare strode toward Chief until a guard stepped in his way. "You thought it was adults you needed to worry about, didn't you? But elements peak in late adolescence. Kell wouldn't have stood a chance."

Chief spat on the ground. For a moment, I saw his fear. Even in a heavily guarded fort, he was scared of the one thing he couldn't control. "I said, raise the divider!" he yelled.

I scanned the room, searching for weakness. The guns against the wall were well out of reach, and Chief had the advantage of numbers. I tried to get Alice's attention again, but there was no response.

One of the men beside the cube flicked a lever. The machine's whine grew louder. There was another sound too: the grinding of a pulley coming to life, a wheel turning slowly, and the divider inching upward, pulled by a series of thin, strong cords.

I could barely breathe in the confines of the ductwork. I needed to stop this, but three guards carried guns and I didn't doubt they'd be willing to use them. Griffin was so near to me, but he may as well have been on another island.

The men in full-body outfits slunk away from the cube, terror written in their jerky movements and rapidly exchanged glances. They exited the area and sealed the door behind them.

Rats snuffled at the gap appearing beneath the divider, and

pawed at it furiously. Maybe they'd been starved to make them more desperate. Or maybe this is what they'd been driven to become.

Then they were through.

It happened so quickly. They scattered across the floor, sliding toward Griffin. He tried to move away, but it was futile. His hands and feet were bound, and there was nowhere for him to hide. In a heartbeat, they smothered him, biting and clawing, and now there was a new sound: Griffin screaming so loudly, the noise of the machine seemed to fade away completely.

Blind fury overtook me. I pressed my back against the rounded side of the duct and my legs against the vent cover. Then I kicked off.

The cover flew out, hitting one of the armed guards. As another looked up, I launched myself from the duct and stretched my arms out to make sure I took him down with me. We collapsed onto the ground together. With the wind knocked out of me, I couldn't move at first, but I caught a glimpse of Dare disarming the third guard. He sent the man to the floor with a single swing of the gun. Chief responded by kicking the gun from Dare's hands. It landed right next to me.

I grabbed it and stood.

The scene grew still. I pointed the barrel at Dare, then at Chief. When a guard approached the gun rack against the wall, I swung around to face him. My hands were shaking. Griffin's cries still filled the air.

"Good boy, Thomas," said Chief, edging toward me. "I can take that from you now."

I jabbed the barrel at him, making him flinch. "Stay back."

"What do you think you're going to do?" he chided. "Kill us all? Escape?" He wiped his sleeve across his mouth and smiled triumphantly. "Tell him, Dare. Tell him how close we are. How we've waited years for this. There's a new world coming, Thomas."

I just wanted to stop Griffin's screams, but lowering the divider wouldn't achieve anything now that the rats were all over him. "Let my brother go."

Chief shook his head. "I can't do that. This isn't about Griffin anymore. It's humankind's last chance at survival."

He moved closer. So did Dare. As I retreated to the railing, the guard edged toward the gun rack again. My legs bumped against the railing. I spun around and fired at the cube's glass panels. Griffin's cries were drowned out by the sound of shattering glass. Dare and Chief sprinted toward me as the rats scattered.

I braced for the attack. Instead, the duct rattled above us and Alice jumped out. She landed on Dare and both went sprawling onto the ground. The suddenness of it made Chief hesitate.

Behind him, another guard was arming himself. He ran toward me too, but Jerren launched himself from the duct just in time. He landed on the guard, crushing him.

Chief turned to face me again, fists balled at his sides and

261

jaw twitching. "Shouldn't have done that, Thomas," he said. "This has nothing to do with you."

"It has *everything* to do with me. He's not a solution. He's my brother."

I swung the gun at him, but Chief leaned back. Before I could bring the weapon around again, he lunged at me. He wrapped me up from behind, one arm squeezed against my neck.

On the far side of the room, something banged against the door. I flashed a quick look. Someone was attempting to force it open. More than one person, most likely.

"My reinforcements," Chief muttered.

He had me in a chokehold. I couldn't breathe. I flailed my arms behind me, trying to land an elbow, but it was pointless.

Below us, Griffin shuffled away from the broken remains of the cube. The rats scurried around the perimeter of the room, searching for a way out. It gave me an idea.

With my last breath, I placed one hand on the rail and the other behind me, pulling Chief tight against me. He was so hell bent on strangling me, he didn't resist.

I swung my right leg over the rail. With our combined momentum, it wasn't difficult to swing the other leg over too. Before Chief could react, we were over the edge and falling toward the glass.

CHAPTER 37

C hief hit the ground first and cushioned my fall. I landed flat against him. The air was knocked out of me so completely that I couldn't produce a sound when I opened my mouth to scream.

I stared directly upward, but I couldn't see Alice and Jerren at all. Griffin slithered toward me, a mess of ripped clothes and bloody bite marks. The rats still circled the room, snuffling at every gap.

Griffin got close to me. I knew from his expression that he wanted me to do something, but I was dazed. When he didn't sign, I remembered that he was bound.

I couldn't reach the rope around his wrist, so I rolled off Chief, who moaned in response. The knots were secure, but simple. I removed them and Griffin reached down to untie his ankles.

Chief was quiet now, motionless except for his left hand, which he pressed tightly against his neck to staunch the flow of blood. Blood seeped out anyway.

With his right hand, he pulled a key from his pocket. He held it out to me. "Open the door, Thomas. W-we can still get out."

I stared at the key. "What about the rats? What about your colony?"

Chief knew that he was beaten. He dropped the key onto the ground and eased his hand away from his neck. Blood ran across his tunic in a torrent. A moment later, his head drooped to the side and though his eyes were still open, I knew that he was dead.

One of the rats had found a space in the far corner of the wall. The others were sliding through it too. They disappeared like water into a drain. From there, they could reach the rest of the fort, I was certain. Sumter, Plague-free for eighteen years, was about to become infested.

Griffin was free now, but he was surrounded by broken glass and didn't know which way to turn. When he pulled to a stand, he smeared blood on everything he touched.

There were sounds of fighting from above. Where were Alice and Jerren?

I stepped over Chief's body and reached for a metal ladder built into one of the walls. My back and neck were throbbing, but I began to climb anyway. After a couple rungs, Alice and Jerren appeared above me.

"Get back," she screamed.

I dropped to the floor and grabbed the key beside Chief. I didn't understand how they'd escaped from Dare, but there wasn't time to ask. Especially not when a loud bang came from above.

Chief's reinforcements had broken through at last. They were too late to save him, but that wouldn't stop them from coming after us.

I tossed Chief's key to Alice. She jammed the key into the lock and forced the door open. The men in the full-body outfits had left. Alice and Jerren passed through. Griffin and I held on to each other and lurched after them.

I looked over my shoulder as we left the room. Dare had climbed down too, and was rifling through Chief's pockets. When he pulled out a folded piece of paper, he froze. Something about the suddenness of it made me pause too. Griffin was trying to pull me out of the room after him, but I couldn't look away as Dare unfolded the paper. On it was a picture, drawn in Griffin's unmistakable style. It was of Chief, his eyes wide open but somehow glassy, as though the old man were looking straight through us.

As the guards appeared above him, Dare's mouth twisted into a smile. And then he laughed.

I was as desperate as Griffin to leave now. We followed a narrow corridor that led outside to the parade grounds. Alice and Jerren sprinted ahead, taking everything in, while I struggled to keep Griffin moving at all. I had my arm tight around him, but the blood made everything feel slick. Every breath he took sounded agonizing.

It was raining again and visibility was poor, but people hurried by, alerted to the new danger. They pounded across the hard ground and splashed through puddles, heading everywhere and nowhere. A siren started slowly and built to a deafening whine.

Guards appeared only ten yards away, but they either didn't see us or weren't looking. They ran among the crowd yelling, "Assemble! Assemble!" Everyone responded by hurrying up the nearest steps to the esplanade. Some tripped and fell, but the stream of people kept flowing from the living quarters below. A couple struggled to light extra torches in the rain.

Panic hung in the air. Everyone seemed to have prepared for this moment without ever believing it could really happen. They clearly had an assembly protocol, but in all their rehearsals, they'd surely never had to deal with darkness and rain and screaming children.

Griffin slumped to the ground beside me, so I helped him back up again. His clothes were sticky with blood. The feel of it on my fingers made me flinch.

He looked right into my eyes. *Me. Solution*, he signed. It almost choked me up that he could be so certain. But as he continued to watch me, I realized it wasn't a statement at all. It was a question.

I wanted so much to be strong for him, but I wouldn't lie to him again. He'd see through it at once. So I just pulled him closer and kept moving.

As people streamed upward, the grounds began to clear. Others emerged from various parts of the fort, torches in hand. They walked a few yards apart and kept their lights close to the ground, eyes scanning for rats. It helped us that they were distracted.

We kept to the perimeter as we approached the casemate where my father and Ananias and Tarn were being held captive. It was far away enough from everyone that we couldn't see the Sumter families congregating. We could hear them, though. The sound of children's crying grew louder.

Jerren led the way now, jogging toward the casemate, gun raised. Neither guard heard him until he was beside them, with the barrel pointed at one guard's head. The man obediently dropped his gun, and as the other guard recognized Jerren, he did too.

Alice joined Jerren and retrieved the men's guns. Once I'd helped Griffin to sit against a wall, I searched the guards' pockets. I found a ring of keys and began trying them one by one in the lock, which clicked on the fourth try.

I'd just got the heavy door open when the guards dropped their torches. The light was extinguished, and in the confusion, the second guard bolted into the darkness. Jerren turned momentarily, giving the first just enough time to retrieve his weapon. Unable to see his target clearly, Jerren threw himself at the man, pinning him against the bars just beside me. Tarn reached through the bars and wrapped her hands around the guard's neck.

He struggled for a moment, but he was being suffocated. With no other choice, he dropped his weapon.

Jerren shoved him away from us. He fell to the ground. Once he'd caught his breath, he jumped up and ran into the darkness.

With the door open, everyone staggered out. Ananias and my father leaned against each other for support. When they saw Griffin they hugged him. It was lucky they couldn't see the extent of his wounds, or they'd have panicked for sure.

"We have to hurry," said Jerren. "There'll be reinforcements soon."

While he led everyone toward the main gate, I looked around for Dennis and his mother. I'd hoped they were at the back of the casemate, hidden from view, but they weren't.

I caught up to my father and brothers. "Where's Dennis?"

"No one knows," Ananias muttered. "They weren't with us when the guards rounded us up, and they haven't come since." He grimaced. "What happened to Griffin?"

"They set rats on him."

Father inhaled sharply, but he and Ananias kept moving.

We continued through the main gate and along the jetty. Nobody had taken the cutter yet, so I helped everyone climb in. They pressed against the sides to make room for me, but I untethered the rope and kicked the boat away from the jetty.

"Thom?" cried Alice. "What are you doing?"

"We can't leave without Marin and Dennis."

"We *have* to."

"No. If I leave them here, I'll never be able to face Rose again."

Alice stood suddenly, ready to join me, but Jerren pushed her back down. He leaped onto the jetty beside me. "I'm the one who knows this place," he said. "Alice, get one of the catamarans and come back for us."

Alice seemed caught between anger and concern. "All right," she said, grabbing one of the oars. "Be quick."

Tarn took the other oar, and what remained of our colony

began the short but arduous journey to the ship. Behind us, the noise grew louder as reinforcements arrived. Fighting back was no longer an option.

We should've run away right then. Neither of us moved, though, because we were too busy staring at the ship. When we'd left it, it had been anchored a hundred yards to the northwest. Now it was almost due north of us. And it looked as if it was drifting away.

CHAPTER 38

There wasn't time to go back through the main gate. The guards were approaching, and the glow from their torches rose above the fort walls in a hazy arc. Even if we made it back inside, they'd see us.

"This way," said Jerren, breathless.

He ran toward the enclosures. I was fairly sure I knew what he had in mind, but I hoped I was wrong. He'd said it was impossible to climb the perimeter wall unless you knew where to put your hands and feet. What would make him think any differently now?

Sure enough, he stopped at the low point of the wall. "Climb on my shoulders," he said.

"Again?"

"It's how Alice and I got up earlier."

"I'm heavier than Alice."

"Just do it!"

I placed my feet on his shoulders and rested my hands against the wall. With an enormous effort he pushed upward.

"Above you and to the right, there's a gap in the brick. Reach for it," he instructed me.

I ran my hand across the bricks, floundering for the hole. "Got it," I said, jamming my right hand into the space.

"Good. I'll get your right foot to the next hole." He shifted slightly to the right and pushed my foot up a little, finding the space. I was sure he was going to drop me, or I'd fall, so I tightened my grip and attempted to take more of my weight. A moment later, I felt my foot slide into another gap. "Now push up and feel around. Above the bricks are rows of planks, with studs sticking out. They're there, trust me."

I did trust him, but I was distracted. The guards' footsteps drummed on the jetty, which meant they'd be launching a second cutter to go after the first. Those who couldn't fit inside would be circling around the perimeter walls, searching for anyone left behind.

Jerren had already caught up to me. "Right hand up a little," he whispered. "Left foot too."

When I pulled up now, I could just get the fingertips of my left hand over the edge. One more foot adjustment and I heaved myself over the wall. Jerren followed right behind me, but not before a series of shouts from below made it clear that he'd been spotted.

"This way," he said, pointing toward the battery. "We'll take the same route as earlier."

"Wait!" There was something on the battlement just in front of us. It was so dark that I could barely make it out.

Then it squeaked. Straightaway, there was an answering squeak from another rat. I didn't stop to see how many of them there were coming toward us, I just ran back in the other direction.

"Keep low," said Jerren. "Stop when we're directly over the main gate."

I did as he said. When we reached the main gate, guards were filing out of the fort directly below us. They stayed in pairs, one with a gun and the other with a torch. Every single pair headed toward the battlements where we'd climbed the wall only moments before.

"Just keep going north," whispered Jerren. "They're all looking at the south wall. It's our only chance."

Again, we kept low and sprinted. My entire body ached, but I kept going until we were circling around to the esplanade. There we paused in the shadow of the bank where Rose and I had hid that same morning.

The armed guards who weren't searching for us had formed a tight perimeter around the other Sumter colonists. Men, women, and children sat huddled beside the monument, large eyes peering out into the darkness, fearing the worst. Rain drummed against the ground as the siren split the air.

Dennis and his mother were in the crowd too. While everyone else kept their focus on the familiar sight of the fort grounds, Dennis stared in our direction. I hoped he had seen us, but there wasn't even a flicker of recognition.

"Why don't they make a run for it?" Jerren asked. "Everyone's too busy to notice."

I glanced over my shoulder. In the distance, the ship had

moved farther still to the east. The foresail had been lowered. Had everyone from the cutter made it on board? If not, who was sailing it?

Tentatively I raised my hand, hoping to get Dennis's attention. His eyes shifted toward me and he blinked. Slowly, he raised a hand in response. Then he tilted his head toward his mother and shook his head from left to right.

"I don't get it," said Jerren. "What's he saying?"

I felt my entire body deflate. "She doesn't want to come," I mumbled.

"What?"

"She told us this morning that she was with this colony now, not us." I punched the ground. "Chief didn't separate her from the others . . . she *chose* to stay."

Just then, Dennis's mother turned her head and noticed the ship sailing away. I held my breath as she narrowed her eyes, deep in thought. Maybe she would change her mind. There was still time.

Instead she looked away again. She'd made a decision and she would stick by it.

Only, I couldn't let her do that. Not for Rose's sake. Or for Dennis's.

"We have to do something," I said. "The ship is leaving."

Jerren bowed his head and said nothing.

"Did you hear me?"

"What do you want me to say? It'll be suicide to rescue them."

"It was almost murder to leave Rose with Kell, but that didn't stop you."

"Hey, I'm here with you now." He clenched his fists and stared ahead. He was breathing fast. "Look, I'm sorry for that. I was wrong. And whatever happens from now on, I want you to forgive me."

I met his eyes. There was fear in them. "Forgive you for what?"

"Just . . . *please*." He grabbed my hand and pulled me out into the open to get the attention of the guards.

He was double-crossing me. I couldn't believe it. Not after everything we'd been through.

As the guards reached for their guns, he pulled me down so that we were kneeling. Then he raised his free hand and turned it around like he was sculpting the air. I wanted to run away, but his grip on me was painfully tight.

There was something else too: a strange feeling, as if he was trying to feel my power. Or wanted me to channel energy *through* him.

I was so shocked, I couldn't react. But then calmness swept over me and I knew what to do. I focused all my energy on his hand twisting above us. I studied the way his fingers moved so deliberately. Then came the sound of the siren—piercing, deafening—as if he'd collected its energy and focused it just on us.

As suddenly as it had started, it was over. The sound that had been inside my head and pulsating through my body disappeared so completely that the silence that replaced it felt unreal. Not total silence, though. It was like we were caught in a bubble, where the ocean could be heard again, and even the cries of the men from below. Everything except the siren.

Now something was happening to the men advancing on us. They dropped their weapons and pressed their hands against their ears, lips pulled back, teeth gritted. And when that wasn't enough, they staggered backward, tripping in their haste to escape. Children were screaming at the intensity of the sound—the siren, I guessed. Nothing would make it stop.

I was already growing weak. Surely Jerren wouldn't be able to keep it going much longer. I looked over my shoulder, hoping against hope that there was somewhere left to run, but we'd trapped ourselves on the esplanade.

Marin and Dennis still wouldn't leave the group, but they were on the edge of it now. The group was leaving them.

Jerren moved his hand again and something shifted. It was like he was diverting the sound away from Marin and Dennis. While everyone else cried out from the noise, they clearly weren't affected. They may have considered themselves part of this new colony, but now they stood out entirely.

The Sumter colonists were retreating. One lunged at Dennis, probably hoping to hold him hostage until Jerren stopped. But Dennis wormed free, and the man jammed his hands against his ears again. A couple tried to edge toward Marin, but one look at their furious expressions and she stepped away. And with that small gesture, her new life on Sumter was over. At best, she and Dennis would be shunned; at worse, killed.

Marin grasped Dennis's hand and strode toward us. She wouldn't look at me, but I didn't care. We weren't doing this for her.

275

Jerren was shaking from the stress. His control was weakening—I could see it in the way that the men on the perimeter of the group were able to break free, tearing their hands away from their ears. They looked at the guns lying a few yards away.

The wind was strong and seemed to be nudging us toward the edge of the esplanade. I didn't want to be forced that way, but there was nowhere else to go. Below us, the harbor churned, throwing waves against the boulders at the base of the wall. Even worse, the ship was to the northeast now. It was sailing away from us. Stranding us.

But then I spied another boat—a catamaran. I didn't need to see Alice to know that she was sailing it. She was almost flying, and when she turned about, the sail dipped so low, I was sure she'd capsize. Instead she threw her weight backward, stabilizing the craft.

"Can't . . . hold," muttered Jerren, panting.

Could Alice see this from the boat? Did she have any idea that Jerren was an elemental too?

As Marin and Dennis reached us, I struggled to take stock of the situation. My mind was as sluggish as my body. I remembered that the pipe I'd swum through had been fully submerged, so it must have been high tide. That meant we'd have deeper water to jump into, as long as we cleared the rocks.

"Step back," I said, tugging Jerren until we toed the edge of the wall.

"If we jump, we'll hit the rocks," shouted Dennis.

"Or get shot here."

Dennis looked at his mother and then at me. Finally, as the guards lunged for their guns, he pulled me away from Jerren. I was too tired to resist. "Give me your element," he said, voice low.

I stared blankly ahead. "Can't—"

"Give it to me!"

Energy trickled through me as Dennis stared at the sky. In what felt like a full strike but must have been only a moment, he turned the wind directly on the approaching guards. Hit by a wall of air and horizontal rain, they collapsed as one.

Before they could get up, Dennis yelled, "Turn around."

Alice was maybe thirty yards away. She was sailing close to the rocks—too close really—and moving fast. I fought to stay awake, stay conscious.

"Now!" yelled Dennis.

He flicked his wrist again, turning the wind onto us. It hit me from behind with the force of a blast, toppling us all and sending us out into space. I was laid out horizontally as I landed with a crash.

CHAPTER 39

I hit water but smashed onto the rocks that lay just below the surface. The pain shocked me awake again. I couldn't tell if I'd broken a rib, or sliced up my stomach — I just knew that I was in agony. Heat radiated from the wound, burning me up from the inside.

I surfaced after the others. Alice was only a few yards away. She'd let out the sail to slow the boat, but I couldn't reach the rope she tossed out to us. If I missed that rope, it was all over. She'd never be able to turn around before the guards regrouped.

Dennis and his mother lunged for the rope and caught it. Jerren did too. But the boat was drifting past me. I wasn't going to reach it.

Jerren loosened his grip so that his left hand slid along the rope. He clasped the very end and swung his right arm out toward me, catching a flap of my tunic. I shut out the pain in my chest and raised my right hand so that I was holding his arm too.

Something whipped into the water beside me. I wasn't sure what it was until someone fired the gun again. Bullets dashed against the surface of the water.

So much for not wasting ammunition.

Alice pulled on the mainsheet, but the boat responded sluggishly. The catamaran was a light craft, not made for five people, and I was acting like an anchor. Jerren eyed the side of the boat. It was so close, but without the use of his right arm, he was stuck. Bullets rained down.

"Jibe," I said as loudly as I could.

"Don't be crazy," shouted Alice.

"Do it!"

As water crashed against me, Alice yanked the tiller toward her. The boat began to turn, the rope drew closer to the side, and I was able to grab the back. I released Jerren's arm and he pulled himself to the boat and on board. "Abort the jibe," I croaked.

Spurred on by the sound of a bullet cracking against the hull, Alice did exactly as I said for once. We'd lost almost all our momentum, but now the catamaran responded to her movements. Jerren slid to the back and helped me aboard too. I was almost onto the canvas deck when he cried out.

"What is it?" cried Alice.

I slithered beside him as he clasped his left forearm. "What happened?" I asked him.

He spat onto the deck. "My arm."

Blood was trickling out, but it was impossible to know

exactly where he'd been hit or how severe the wound was. "We'll get you to the ship. Look at it there."

Jerren nodded. He knew there was nothing else we could do for him.

Alice tried to maintain balance and keep the sails full. The ship was a few hundred yards away, nothing but a shadowy outline in the darkness. It was so much farther away than the last time we'd seen it.

"Are we going to make it?" asked Dennis.

Alice didn't answer.

He tilted his head toward me. "Is Griffin alive? I saw that room. The rats. I wanted to tell you—"

"He's alive," I said. I didn't add: *for now*.

I stole a glance behind us. Sumter was already fading into the darkness. The black reminded me of rats. Would the colonists get them under control again? For the children's sake, I hoped so.

I ran a finger across my chest wound and felt a loose flap of skin. The pain was excruciating, but I was almost relieved. A broken bone would take longer to heal.

Alice kept her eyes fixed on the ship. She didn't take the direct line, but moved quickly over the ship's wake and onto the calmer water it was leaving behind. Good thing too, because we'd be leaving the harbor soon and heading out onto the ocean, where the waves were bigger. By contrast, our water was smooth.

Little by little, we drew closer. When we were a hundred yards away, Alice began to veer right.

"Rope ladder's on the other side," I wheezed.

"Forget the rope ladder. If we sail to port side, we'll be in the ship's wind shadow. We'll lose control of the sails. Stop dead in the water."

Someone on board must have realized the same thing. As we crossed their wake and entered turbulent water again, the ladder was unfurled on our side. It touched the water and was dragged backward.

The waves must have been at least three feet high, too much for the catamaran. The ship's bow carved a channel through the ocean, creating wake that threatened to overturn us. Only Alice remained seated now. Even Dennis and his mother were lying down, gripping the frame tightly.

Alice eased us alongside the ship, but she was struggling to maintain control.

"Dennis, go!" she yelled.

Kneeling on the canvas, one hand around the metal frame, Dennis reached out and grabbed the ladder. Once he had a good grip, he looked back to check that Marin was following. Only then did he place his other hand on the ladder and begin to climb.

Marin went next. We'd saved her life, but she wouldn't even look at us. When she was halfway up, Jerren grunted. "We risked our lives for *her*?"

"Not for her," I told him. "For Dennis."

He peered at his injured arm and winced. "Your turn now."

"Uh-uh. Not before you."

I wrapped an arm around him and pushed him across the

slick canvas. Once he had a grip on the ladder, I helped him get his footing. He climbed slowly, his left arm only good for draping over the rungs.

"Go, Thom," Alice shouted.

I was about to reach for the rung, but stopped myself. "Wait. You can't reach the ladder and hold the boat steady."

"Don't worry about me. Just go."

My mind flashed back to Eleanor lying broken on the deck. I still didn't understand why she'd chosen to die, but there was no way I was going to let Alice follow her.

Once Jerren had boarded the ship, I pulled the rope ladder toward us. I grabbed the highest rung I could reach and shouted for Alice to place a hand on the lowest.

She transferred the mainsheet to her left hand. It was a risky move—now she was unable to control the tiller and sail independently—but it freed up her right to take the ladder. With a single defiant nod, she drove the tiller away. The catamaran whipped to the right and the wet canvas deck slid from right under us. I was left dangling as Alice plummeted into the water.

Her body banged against the side of the ship. She still had hold of the rung, but the fast-moving water dragged her under.

I coiled my right arm around a rung and reached down with my free hand. I couldn't get to her, so I grabbed one of the lower rungs and heaved that upward instead. Alice resurfaced. Gasping for breath, she slapped at the next rung. Then the next. A moment later, she swung a leg up and got a foothold.

Just as well, because I lost my grip on the lower rung. Alice crashed back into the ocean.

This time only her legs went under. Her head and torso stayed above water, and she continued her climb. With Jerren shouting encouragement from above, she followed me to the top, where someone dragged me over the side. I leaned against the rail and stared back at Sumter. There were tiny dots of light from the torches, and the faint echoes of the siren. But a mile separated us, and no one was following.

We'd escaped. Not without casualties, but still, we were free again. There wasn't room in my mind for anything but that thought.

I flopped onto the deck and lay there, not thinking, not even aware if I was breathing anymore. As I tilted my head, I caught sight of Ananias limping toward me, supported by our father. They knelt on either side of me, and hugged me so tightly that I wasn't sure which of us was crying.

CHAPTER 40

woke up in a cabin, woozy and disoriented, stealing shallow breaths so that my chest wouldn't hurt so badly. I wanted to sleep longer, but every part of me ached. Outside, the sky was the deep, dark blue that preceded sunrise.

Rose was beside me, one thick bandage tied around her neck and another across her chest and around her torso. Her face was bruised.

She saw me watching her and frowned. "That bad, huh?"

I leaned over and kissed her gently on the cheek. "You're alive. That's what matters." My mind flashed back to the night's events. In the almost silence, it was difficult to imagine everything that had happened to us. "Where's Griffin?"

Rose tilted her head away from me. "They put him in a cabin with Nyla."

"They're in quarantine—"

"No. Ananias says it's just so they can observe them more easily. The incubation period is three days."

Three days until we'd know whether they were going to

live or die. Less, really, because they'd both been bitten the day before.

"If he's the solution . . ." Rose began, but she didn't finish the thought. Until we knew for sure, there was always the other possibility. And what about Nyla?

"I have to go see him," I told her.

"I know."

She reached up and placed her hand on my cheek. I leaned in and kissed her, first on the cheek, then on the lips. She swallowed hard, and as our lips came together again, she opened her mouth. I opened mine too, and for a precious moment there was no ship, and no Plague, and no enemies or pain or death. It was just the two of us.

I left the cabin and staggered along the corridor. I knew where we'd taken Nyla the night before, but when I opened the door, Griffin was alone, sleeping. Apart from the blanket covering his chest and upper legs, he was naked. Every exposed piece of skin was covered in scratches and bite marks. It took me back to the room with the glass cube, and the sight of the rats crawling all over him.

Were we measuring his life in hours or days?

I'd promised to keep Griffin safe. We'd left Roanoke so that he might live normally, away from the pirates who'd risked everything to capture him. In the end I'd sacrificed him to Chief instead. Everyone else might have believed in a solution, but all I could see was a boy in pain, flesh scarred, body infected with the Plague.

"I'll look after him," said Nyla.

I hadn't heard her enter. She looked so well, it was impossible to believe she might be sick too. "How do you feel?" I asked her.

"Scared." She padded across the floor and knelt beside Griffin, watching him. Looking back, it was impossible not to wonder if she'd used their friendship as a way to learn about us, to find our weaknesses. But the way she gazed at him now was genuinely caring. She was as scared for him as for herself.

"I'm so sorry, Nyla. I wish there was something we could do."

"You rescued us from Sumter. That's enough."

I touched the wound on my stomach. Another scar to add to the collection. "So I found out about Jerren's element. What's yours?"

She didn't look up. "I don't think I have one. Jerren started twisting sound when he was young. Mom and Dad warned him to keep it a secret, so he did it in private. Then one day, he saw a bunch of guys hurting Mom. He didn't even think about what he was doing. He just turned sound on them until they knew something was wrong. It distracted them long enough for Mom to escape, but when they worked out it was Jerren doing that, they went after him. Dad threw some stuff on a sailboat and we all took off. He said it was better to die together than to sacrifice a child."

"Did a clan ship really rescue you?"

"Yeah. It's incredible, but true. After that, Mom was convinced that we were destined to go to Sumter. That it was meant to be."

The door creaked open and Jerren joined us. "I heard

voices," he said. Leaning closer to me, he added, "You look terrible."

"Unlike you," I replied, admiring his sling.

"Flesh wound, fortunately."

"We'll both have scars."

He shrugged. "Alice likes them, right? Could work in my favor." He glanced at his sister, and peered around the door to make sure that we weren't being overheard. "Is Griffin really the solution?" he whispered. "Back in that room, they were ready to risk everything on him surviving the Plague."

I had no answer for that.

"I mean, I hated Chief for what he did to my family, but he was still the smartest man I ever met. The most cautious too. I can't believe he'd have risked everything unless he *knew* somehow."

"I hope you're right."

Jerren closed the door and sat with his back to it, blocking anyone from joining us. "Look, there's something I need to tell you. Alice says . . . you need to know." He gave a frustrated sigh. "You know that Dare came here about a month ago. Not a surprise, really—he stopped off every year to trade food and materials and news. But this time was different."

"How?"

"Well, we've always known the pirates had an island base in the Atlantic Ocean. Kell reckons some of them are married. But this was the first time Dare brought a woman with him. Just one. And she was . . . *strange*." He clasped his hands together. "The men all stayed away from her, like they were frightened. At first, I figured she must be Dare's wife because she was about the same age. But the way they acted around each other . . . no way they're married."

"But you don't know for sure."

Still seated, Jerren shuffled forward. "One night, she came to see Nyla and me. It wasn't an accident, either. She wanted us to be alone. She started asking us questions: Where were we from? How did we get to Sumter? What were our elements?"

My pulse quickened. "You must have done something."

"No way. Nothing. She just . . . *knew*. And so we told her everything. We didn't even care if she passed it on to Chief, because we'd given up ever escaping. But when we were finished, she told us to be ready, that help was coming. She told us we weren't alone." He took a deep breath. "After Dare left, everyone was talking about the woman. Kell told me he'd seen her before, years ago. Back then, Dare had called her the solution."

I struggled to keep my voice even. "How long ago did Kell see her?"

"About thirteen years, he said."

"Did the woman touch you?"

He nodded. "She held our hands almost the whole time. It was weird at first, but also kind of nice. Our mother used to do it. Maybe that's why we let her. She stared at us too, like she was looking right inside us. And even though I'd given up hope, I knew everything she said was the truth." He shrugged. "It was a miracle. I really believe that."

Yes, it was a miracle. A seer around Dare's age, mistaken for the solution and brought to Sumter thirteen years ago. What had Kell told us? It was simple math to work out that Griffin was the solution.

The woman had to be my mother. But she'd died the morning after Griffin was born. Murdered by her own brother, Dare.

That's what my father had told us, anyway.

Another memory returned then: of standing on a water tower on Roanoke Island, watching the pirates disembark in groups. I'd hoped that they would lead our families off the ship too, but Dare had kept them locked up on board. There hadn't been any women among the crew, I was sure of that. I'd have noticed straightaway.

Or would I?

The pirates had lowered a large wooden box into a cutter that day. They'd done it gently too, reverently, as if there were something or someone important inside.

Someone like Dare's sister.

"Are you all right, Thomas?" Nyla's voice was full of concern.

No, I wasn't all right. The day I'd seen the wooden box, I'd described it to Tessa. Had she foreseen who was inside? Is that why she chose to stay on Roanoke Island?

My head spun. I was so tired, and the hope I'd felt at hearing Jerren's words already felt like old news. The only thing

I knew for certain was that I'd had a chance to kill Dare, and I'd left him behind instead.

I made a vow then: No matter what happened in the future, if Dare was alive, I would find him. And I'd make him pay for everything he'd done.

EPILOGUE

Alice brought a couple water canisters for us to share. Jerren took a sip from the first and tried to hand it to Nyla, but she wouldn't take it. "You should share with Thomas," she said.

"I'm not going to get Plague from a water bottle, Nyla." As soon as he'd said it, Jerren frowned. He passed the canister to me without another word.

Alice remained standing beside the door. "I've been thinking about Dare. All that time on this ship, and he never showed himself."

"Are you afraid he's on this ship right now?" I asked.

She snorted. "Not a chance. I've checked every part of that secret compartment. He's not on board. But still—"

She broke off as footsteps pounded along the corridor. Ananias pushed the door open, hitting her. "You should come upstairs," he said.

Alice rubbed her back. "Now?"

"Yes."

I pulled myself up and followed Ananias. Cloaked in darkness, the corridor still felt horribly familiar. Even *smelled* familiar. I was relieved to climb the steps and emerge into a fresh breeze and the first faint glow of dawn.

Tarn stood at the wheel. She stared straight ahead, so focused that I assumed she hadn't seen us. The massive sails had been lowered and the ship sliced a clear path through calm sea.

My father was on deck too. Even Dennis and his mother. But they weren't moving at all. They stood at the stern rail, staring at the ship's wake.

Or rather, the ocean behind it.

I sloped across the deck toward them, drawn there by the vessel trailing us by a mile. It was the ship from Sumter, its massive sails unfurled to take advantage of every breath of wind.

Ananias followed me. "It's smaller than this ship," he said. "Sleeker. Faster."

When I reached my father, I half expected him to hug me again. Instead he handed me a pair of binoculars.

I didn't raise them to my eyes at first. I was still struggling to make sense of everything that had happened. I wanted just one morning when we could all talk, open up, become a colony again.

It would have to wait.

I adjusted the focus on the binoculars and studied the ship. A group of five men stood at the bow. Each man held a gun.

"Looks like they've found something worthy of their

292

ammunition after all," Alice said. "And this time there's no Chief to tell them to save their bullets."

Beside me, Ananias huffed. "We can beat them. You said it: There's no Chief anymore. No Kell, either. That's a reconnaissance ship. Limited range. They can't track us forever. They probably don't even know these waters."

There was a murmur of agreement from the others. It was the closest we'd come to sounding like a team in days.

But they weren't seeing what I was seeing.

A taller man stepped through the line of guns and took up position at the tip of the bow. He didn't have a telescope anymore, so there was no way he could have known I was watching him. But he seemed to be watching *me* all the same.

Dare raised one colored arm and gave a defiant wave.

ACKNOWLEDGMENTS:

Sincere thanks to:

The entire Dial team: my brilliant and inspiring editor, Liz Waniewski; also Regina Castillo, Jasmin Rubero, Heather Alexander, Lauri Hornik, Kathy Dawson, and Scottie Bowditch.

The park rangers at Fort Sumter—Nate Johnson, Michelle Welker, Olivia Williams, Tommie Williams—for granting me an extended stay, and answering hundreds of the most bizarre questions any visitor has asked. Also the rangers at Fort Moultrie, who were subjected to similar interrogation, and never blinked.

My father- and mother-in-law, Charles and Sandy Odom, who hosted me while I conducted research in South Carolina. And my Charleston insiders, Peggy Mitchem and Mark Hales, who guided me through the city's lesser-known military installations and explained harbor fishing.

St. Louis Public Library and St. Louis County Library, especially the teen librarians. Also the booksellers, teachers, bloggers, and readers who got behind *Elemental* and gave it so much love.

My trusted beta readers: Audrey, Clare, and Christina Ahn Hickey.

Tony Sahara, for the awe-inspiring cover. And Steve Stankie-wicz, for the beautiful map.

And my agent, Ted Malawer, a constant source of support and encouragement.

ABOUT THE AUTHOR

Antony John (www.antonyjohn.net) is the award-winning author of *Five Flavors of Dumb* and *Thou Shalt Not Road Trip*. In this sequel to *Elemental*, the action moves to South Carolina, where he briefly lived. During one memorable trip he visited Charleston Harbor and historical Fort Sumter, the site of the first battle of the Civil War. Fort Sumter is an eerie and awe-inspiring place, isolated and impenetrable, designed to be self-sufficient even during a siege. He couldn't help wondering: What if the attackers weren't humans, but rats? Antony now lives with his family in St. Louis, Missouri.